# DELPHINE

## the CAJUN SERIES

# CHERIE
AWARD-WINNING AUTHOR
# CLAIRE

DELPHINE
The Cajun Series Book Four
© 2016 Cheré Dastugue Coen

First printing and copyright in 2002 as The Acadians: Delphine by
Cherie Claire by Kensington Publishing Corp.

For more information, visit www.cherieclaire.net

Printed in the USA.

Cover Design and Interior Format

*This project is supported in part by ArtSpark, an Individual Artist stipend
supported by the Lafayette Economic Development Authority and adminis-
tered by the Acadiana Center for the Arts, Lafayette, Louisiana.*

*Merci beaucoup to the many people who have helped me: Professor Ben Martin at LSU for his amazing information; Michele Sorrentino for the help on the other side of the Atlantic; the two-thirds of the Three Muskateers, Glynnis Campbell and Lori Royal-Gordon, for keeping me sane; Carol Carter and Lizzy Benway for their endless encouragement; the wonderful people of the Louisiana library system who make authors feel like celebrities, Mimi Foster, Sally Braud, Clara Maynard, Judy Smith and Debbie Penny; to Janet, Gerard and Christine Martin and their wonderful children, Ariane, Chloé, Julien, Antoine and Camille, for the unforgettable evening on the Vermilion River and swamp; and the wonderful members of the Heart of Louisiana chapter of RWA, who constantly send love via email. Finally, to Delphine Brezina Perez Dastugue, a courageous woman who came before, who will live on through me and never be forgotten.*

# PROLOGUE

*New Orleans, Louisiana Territory,*
*January 6, 1778*

GAIETY KNEW NO BOUNDS IN the portside city of New Orleans. Surrounded by dangerous swamps, sometimes hostile natives and the ever-encroaching British, the French and Spanish residents took every opportunity to satisfy their *joie de vivre*. Rich Creoles born in the colony of French and Spanish parentage offset their daily toil with nights of lavish parties. French and American sailors and privateers spent their profits on gambling and loose women inhabiting dens along the riverfront, while Spanish military men fresh from Havana joined them despite the language barrier.

Some called it decadence. Pious religious leaders pointed fingers, denouncing the relaxed morals of the New World citizens. To Philibert Bertrand, it was a natural defense. Every summer disease overtook the town, decimating the population. Storms raged in from the Gulf of Mexico with enough fury to destroy homes and flood fields. One heavy spring rain could ruin a crop. A harsh winter upriver could cause the Mississippi to flood New Orleans.

Jubilant times was the musket New Orleanians held high against the ongoing assault of tragedy. Celebrate now, the citizens seemed to say, for tomorrow you may be lying in the cemetery tombs at the back of town.

Today marked the Epiphany, otherwise known as Twelfth Night and the beginning of Carnival, the highest season of revelry in New Orleans. From now until Mardi Gras, the day before Ash Wednesday, the Catholic citizens would eat and drink to their heart's content before the long stretch of Lent and sacrifice. From now until Mardi Gras, New Orleans residents would relish every moment.

Today also marked Gabrielle Bouclaire's birthday, the Acadian wife of Phil's partner, Jean Bouclaire. He had promised to attend the party of his best friend and business associate as soon as he unloaded his cargo and registered the profits in the ship's log. But that was before the parchment arrived. Now, Phil had to return upriver.

Despite the laughter and shouting emanating from the docks, Phil heard the unmistakable sound of petticoats on the ladderway. It could be only one person. Only one woman dared to risk gossip by visiting *La Belle Amie* at the onset of dusk. And no doubt she was alone.

"What are you doing here, Phiney?"

He didn't have to look up from his work to know that Delphine Delaronde stood on the threshold to his cabin. Having watched his partner's daughter grow from a child, Phil could sense Delphine's presence anywhere.

"You promised to come to the party."

Phil removed his reading spectacles and glanced up at the woman now almost as tall as her privateering father. Even in the darkness of the oncoming twilight, Delphine's beauty was astonishing. Her brown curls lightened by days at sea were tied elegantly atop her head, cascading down upon her shoulders in streams of soft rivulets. Yards of bright yellow silk billowed from her hip, while a snug bodice accented her abundant curves and a long, graceful neck. Had it not been for the tanned hue of her skin and the sweet dimple gracing one cheek, Delphine Delaronde could have easily passed as one of society's best. One glance at her tonight and no one would be the wiser that those long, slender legs braced a deck like a seasoned sailor or that her aim was as keen as a pirate's.

"You look beautiful," Phil said, leaning back in his chair to get a better view. The comment was grossly understating.

Delphine turned around to give him the full benefit of her new gown, bought, no doubt, for the occasion.

"Do you like it? The seamstress said that a woman of my color shouldn't wear yellow, but I think the brightness works well with my dark features, don't you?"

Fishing for compliments. She was doing that a lot lately. But then Delphine was just shy of twenty, more than likely anxious to test the marriage waters and wanting his approval. Phil pushed the uncomfortable thought aside. He couldn't imagine another man touching his Phiney. "You look lovely. The color suits you."

Her smile remained, but a look of apprehension glistened in her eyes. "I am wearing it for someone special, someone I was hoping would ask me to dance tonight."

A spark of jealousy ignited in his belly, burning up his spine like a fuse on a cannon. He had to get used to the idea that she was no longer a child, but Phil had seen too much of the world, knew too well the evils of men. His own past was proof of the deadly passions men carried. Despite his better judgment and his efforts to remain calm when talk turned to Delphine's prospects of marriage, Phil wanted to pummel every man who dared kiss her hand.

"Who is this man?" He tried to keep his voice level, but his emotions betrayed him. 'Twas a good thing he had no sisters.

Delphine's long fingers, rough from her work aboard ship, rearranged the objects on his desk while she stared at the parchment. "Is this what kept you from the party?"

Phil took the paper and stuffed it into his inner waistcoat pocket. "I must go back upriver, pet. I'm afraid it's important business I cannot deny."

"From the governor?"

The woman was too keen for her own good, another reason Phil remained too protective of his partner's hard-headed daughter. She craved excitement, loved a dare, adored the thrill of a fight, and the glory of victory. She needed a man to watch over her, not so much to defend herself against an enemy — she was quite capable with a knife and gun — but to protect her from her over-inquis-itive nature.

"It's none of your concern," Phil said, rising and putting on his coat. "This is a trip that I cannot speak of."

"Does my father know?"

"Yes, your father knows."

"Then, why can't I...?"

Phil placed his hands on her arms, amazed that they stood almost eye to eye. New Orleans residents loved to point fingers at *La Belle Amie* and joke that seawater and salt air caused residents of the New World to grow taller. Little did it matter that Jean and Phil had both been born in France, sons of equally tall men.

But Delphine. Phil wondered what world she would eventually fit into. She adored the sea, but would she find a man capable of satisfying her seafaring appetite? She would be safer on shore, securing a profitable marriage with one of the noble families of New Orleans, but would she be content to attend the endless streams of societal functions? Would a woman too tall and too tanned for proper eti-quette be welcomed into society's fold?

For an instant, before he pushed the dangerous thought away, Phil wanted to stick her in his pocket with the parch-ment and carry her away with him.

"It's a dangerous mission. I cannot speak of it. But when I return, I'll explain everything."

What apprehension lurked before disappeared and she warmed to his touch. "Promise?"

Phil smiled, encouraged by the dimple. "Promise."

Delphine lowered her eyes and lightly touched the brass button gracing his waistcoat. The gesture was too intimate for friends and Phil felt his breath shorten. They were too close for polite company — he could smell the lilac water used in her bath — but damned if he could move away.

"I shouldn't believe you. After all, you promised me a dance."

For an instant, he imagined she had bought that dress for him. But that was ridiculous. He was ten years her senior.

"Who is this man you were waiting for, this man blind to the most interesting girl in New Orleans?" he asked with a smile.

Delphine glanced up, bending forward at the waist, her lips a breath away from his. She flattened her palm against his chest and Phil grabbed it, more to halt her advances than to feel its warmth, he told himself. They were dangerously close.

"Don't you know?" Delphine whispered. "I was waiting for you."

So many times Phil had dreamed of kissing those lips, chastising himself for the impure thoughts of the girl he had vowed to protect. So many times he had wished she desired him as well. Dear God, she was but a child and the daughter of his partner. He had no business thinking...

He wasn't sure who had moved first, but suddenly his lips met hers and the hand held so delicately in his own slipped away, circling his neck and drawing them closer. He moved his hands to her waist and pulled her gently against his chest, savoring the feeling of her long, silky back. They felt so right together, like pieces of a puzzle finally united. All logic disappeared and all Phil could fathom was the delicious lips he savored and his darling in his arms.

Someone moaned in pleasure — it must have been him for her fingers laced through his hair and tightened and her chest rose and fell seductively against his. Her tall form

filled his embrace, her generous curves so warm and welcomed beneath his touch. Phil pulled away briefly to savor
the feel of her cheek against his lips, the delicious scent
below her earlobe.

"Oh Phiney," Phil whispered as he tilted his head,
returned to her lips and deepened the kiss. Passion roared
between them and the world and all its complications vanished.

When they finally came up for air, Delphine whispered,
"Take me with you."

So many times they shared voyages together, traveling to
the Caribbean and upriver to the English outposts. This
time, they would share a bed.

Awareness shot through Phil like a lightning bolt. He
pulled away abruptly, causing Delphine to lose her balance.
He grabbed her shoulders to steady her, but held her at an
arm's distance.

"What just happened?"

Delphine gazed at him in shock, his lips swollen from
his heated kisses, her dress wrinkled from his rough touch.
Guilt raked his being.

"Dear God, Delphine, I never meant to..."

She slipped from his grip, then moved closer. "Please
Phil, don't."

Phil pressed his hand against his mouth and tried to
resume a steady breath. God in heaven, he had just rav-
ished his partner's daughter!

"Don't regret this," Delphine pleaded, touching his arm.
"If you must blame someone, blame me."

Gazing into her enormous black eyes, Phil knew the
blame was his to bear. Standing there in her cloud of yellow, he wanted nothing but to kiss her again. "I should
never have touched you like that."

A tear slid down one cheek but Delphine let it go. "I
love you," she whispered. "I always have."

Phil shook his head. When had this youthful crush

begun? "I'm twice your age."

Delphine straightened and wiped the tear away. "You're thirty to my twenty, hardly twice my age."

"I'm still too old for you."

"Says who?" Delphine pulled a handkerchief from her sleeve. "I have lots of acquaintances who have married men your age. It's done all the time."

Marriage? She expected marriage? Phil moved to the porthole and leaned an arm against the wall. Marriage was for people who lived on land, who farmed or owned shops and had bedrooms for children, people who lived in houses that didn't rock from leeward to starboard.

And love? He had loved once. Swore to never love again. That very love affair would tarnish the name of Bertrand forever.

There were so many other reasons.

"I'm a commoner," he said, stating the most obvious.

Phil turned and found her sitting in his chair, wiping the remaining tears from her eyes. "What does that matter?"

He kneeled before her and took her hands in his. "Your father is a nobleman."

Delphine rolled her eyes, reminding him of her younger days. "My father married a commoner."

"Your father doesn't have a scandal on his head."

She stared at him with a woman's eyes, her fingers gently stroking his cheek. "I love you. I don't care what you have done."

Phil took those fingers and kissed them, but he returned them to her lap. "You are young, Delphine. You have yet to see the world. It's understandable that you would fall in love with me, considering the voyages we have spent together. But in time, you may realize your mistake. In time, you may see this as nothing more than a youthful passion."

Her eyes darkened. "Have you?"

He knew she spoke of Marie and the passion of his own

youth, and the memory of that love still burned his heart as if the duel was yesterday.

Tears gathered in Delphine's eyes and she looked away, biting her lower lip. "That's it, isn't it? You're still in love with her."

Did he still love Marie, after twelve years? Was that why he never accepted the affections of women or kept a mistress? He honestly didn't know. But for Delphine's sake, it gave him an exit.

"Yes, Delphine," he lied. "I'm still in love with her."

She closed her eyes as if the action helped brace her against the painful words. Then her lids parted, tears lingering on the lashes, and she attempted a feeble smile. "Well, that's that then."

Phil couldn't bear looking at her, couldn't bear thinking he had crushed the one person he had pledged to defend, the one person he adored more than life itself. He took her hand again. "Delphine..."

She quickly withdrew her fingers and rose, reaching the doorway before he could follow. "I should return to the party. My father will worry."

Her father will murder him, he thought. "Does he know you're here?"

"Yes, but my instructions were to retrieve you."

"Please give Gabrielle my regrets, let your father know our request from the governor has arrived."

She turned at the news, for a moment appearing as if nothing had transpired between them, as if she might start an inquiry, but the moment instantly vanished and the sadness returned.

"You said in time I might regret my mistake, might see you as a youthful passion." She paused and straightened her skirt. All traces of sadness disappeared and a proud, determined woman stood before him. "I will always love you, Phil. Always. Nothing will change that."

Her declaration sliced his heart like a knife, making him

regret every word he had spoken that had caused her pain. Before logic could intercede, he started to retract his love for Marie, but in a breath, Delphine was gone. Phil rushed up the ladderway in time to help her across the gangplank, but, as was so typical of Delphine, she brushed his assistance away.

"Let me see you home," he insisted.

As soon as her feet touched mud, she turned and shook her head. "I have my carriage. You have work to do."

Standing at the ship's railing, watching Delphine enter the carriage, chin held high, Phil felt the wind leave his sails. As the carriage headed back toward town, Phil witnessed the rudder of his life's voyage roll out of sight.

An intense pain splintered his heart, an anguish he knew only too well. He knew his life would never be the same again.

# CHAPTER ONE

"LET ME GET THIS STRAIGHT," Phil asked Bernardo de Galvez, the newly installed Spanish governor of Louisiana. "You are bringing in residents from the Canary Islands to form militias upriver?"

"The English have fortresses at Manchac and Baton Rouge," the young leader said. "I intend to populate the frontier opposite these posts with Spanish and French citizens to keep the English from migrating into Louisiana."

The Spaniard paused, sending Phil a steady gaze, one that made Phil realize he was dealing with a formidable man. "I don't trust the English. I will be more confident when the territory is filled with Catholic citizens sympathetic to our countries. But this is nothing new to you, no? Have not you and your partner done the same?"

Phil grinned, staring down into the wine the Spaniard had graciously offered. Galvez had spent little time gathering information on their smuggling enterprise.

"My partner, Jean Bouclaire, is married to an Acadian woman whose family was splintered when the English exiled them from Nova Scotia in 1755," Phil explained. "Since these French neutrals were scattered throughout the American colonies, the Caribbean and France, he has made it his mission in life to help bring them to Louisiana and recreate their Acadia, their homeland here."

"Precisely," Galvez replied, leaning forward in his chair,

eyes blazing. "And we have welcomed them into this colony, given them land grants and tools to start anew."

"Which we have been thankful for, your excellency."

"But you will not help me in this endeavor?"

Phil tossed back the remnants of the fine Spanish wine. "Sir, there is no money to be made in bringing exiles into this territory. I am of one mind with my partner, but I am the money-making arm of our operation. Which hasn't been easy since the Spanish forbade trade with other nations when they took over Louisiana from the French a few years ago."

"I have changed positions on that point," the governor quickly stated. "We have opened trade with France, Cuba and the Yucatan."

"Yes, sir, and we are grateful for it. Now, we are in a position to lessen the impact of English smuggling and make a nice profit for ourselves."

"Precisely the reason I reversed our stand," the governor said with a nod. "I will not have the citizens of this territory filling the English purses with coin to satisfy their appetite for European goods."

Phil leaned back in his chair, allowing the governor's servant to refill his glass. "I am more than happy to satisfy their appetites through trade with France and Spain, filling our own country's purses..."

"And your own," the governor added with a knowing smile.

"And my own," Phil acknowledged. "But there is the problem of duties."

Galvez grinned and waved the servant away. "You match your reputation, Monsieur Bertrand."

Phil bowed slightly and mirrored his smile. "A man must survive in the frontier, your excellency. Knowing how to bargain well may mean the difference between a hungry winter and a comfortable one."

The governor rose and moved toward his desk, then hastily put pen to paper. "This should take care of the duties," he said, but he didn't hand Phil the parchment. "Now, will you help us?"

The request didn't ring true to Phil; something larger was at stake here. "You want me to transport the Canary Islanders upriver? As I informed you, sir, I'm not the exile hero. You should be speaking to my partner."

Galvez dropped wax from his desk's candle on to the parchment, then sealed it with the insignia of his ring. "I have spoken to your partner and he's willing to transport them."

Phil frowned. "Then what do you wish of me?"

Galvez resumed his seat before Phil, the parchment worth hundreds of *piastres* still clutched between his fingers. "The Islenos are one piece of a very large puzzle used to keep the English at bay. You, Monsieur Bertrand, I wish to be another."

Phil couldn't help smirking. "I'm a smuggler intent on keeping my belly full. Nothing more. If you're speaking of the Americans and their fruitless attempt at sovereignty, I have no use for causes."

Galvez leaned forward, his arms upon his knees and his dark eyes sparkling in the candlelight. "The English have increased their numbers at Pensacola. They are patrolling the lake behind this city in a ship called the West Florida. At Baton Rouge, their numbers increase inside a fort that could cut this territory in two should they decide to blockade the Mississippi."

"Over my dead body." Phil couldn't help himself. He wasn't a patriot, but he'd die first before relinquishing control of his river.

The edges of the governor's lips turned upward in a grim smile, but Phil knew he wasn't convinced. "I believe they are planning an attack on New Orleans."

If Galvez wanted to incite Phil into action, his last sentence hit its target. "How? When?"

"When the time is right. They know we are unprepared for an assault, that Spain is neutral in the war between the English and the Americans. They know we will not attack them first. At present, they respect our boundaries and we theirs. However, if France allies with the Americans, Spain is likely to follow, and then we will be at war as well. We are at the mercy of our English neighbors should they happen to attack and lay claim to this territory."

Phil thought of the consequences of such an action. The hundreds of Acadian refugees in Louisiana, forced from their homes in Nova Scotia years before by a merciless English governor, would now be at the benevolence of their former tormentors. The Spanish would lose the Mississippi and trade with the Illinois territory and New France. The American colonists would have their enemy firmly planted at their backs. They had enough to worry about with the English arriving in droves upon their shores.

But Delphine's image was the first to come to mind.

Phil rose and stared out the window on to the peaceful streets of New Orleans. The city had been a precarious spot for a settlement, strategically placed in the bend of the mighty river but well upriver from the Gulf and almost completely surrounded by water with a massive lake at its back and swamps all around. Unless the Spanish proposed beefing up its fortifications at New Orleans and the surrounding areas, the English could easily capture the city. Placing the Canary Islanders upriver and arming the Acadian settlements was a good plan. But would it hold off the world's greatest army?

Would it keep his Phiney safe?

Thoughts of her defeated and crushed in his cabin returned and Phil closed his eyes to the pain pressing at his heart. Three weeks had not lessened the fact that he had destroyed the one person he had sworn to defend.

A young girl skipped by on the street below, curls teeming beneath a wide bonnet, oblivious to the politics at hand. She so reminded Phil of their first meeting when Delphine was just a child, when her sweet voice was the only thing Phil could adequately decipher as she stood on the same threshold she had graced three weeks before.

"What's the matter with him," Phil remembered Delphine asking her father, as she gazed into his cabin. "Why is he so bruised?"

"Some mean men hurt him," Jean had whispered back. "They threw him in the harbor at St. Malo and left him for dead but I fished him out and brought him here."

"Oh Papa," Delphine exclaimed, the tears evident in her voice. "He will live, won't he?"

"I don't know," Jean replied. "He has been scarcely holding on to life during the voyage across the Atlantic."

Phil recalled those words as if they were spoken yesterday, remembering how little he cared for living at that moment. He had prayed for death, prayed for the end of his suffering, but then a tiny angel had placed a cool palm against his forehead.

"Don't die," Delphine whispered to him that morning. "I will take care of you. I will nurse you back to health. Please don't die."

A tear had fallen upon his cheek and Phil attempted to open his eyes. Through the darkness of the cabin, he made out the outline of a soft head of curls. When the tiny fingers stroked his cheek, he realized God had given him a second chance, that forgiveness was at hand for the sins he had foolishly committed.

As Delphine gently brushed his hair from the cuts on his face, applying fresh water in its place, he swore at that moment he would forever protect his angel.

"Monsieur Bertrand?"

Phil wiped back around, wondering how long he had been lost in memories. He wondered, too, when he had forgotten his promises. He sat back down in front of the Spanish governor, the soldier who had made his name against the Sioux in Texas, a nobleman willing to risk his life in the name of the Spanish king and to protect the city composed mostly of French citizens.

Phil toasted Galvez in a salute.

"What do you wish for me to do?"


"Havana?" Jean stared at his partner in disbelief. Phil wasn't one for causes. "You're running guns and money from Havana to the American colonists?"

Phil paced the parlor of Jean's home, wondering why the house appeared so empty. Where was Delphine?

"Phil?"

It was one thing having to explain his reversal regarding politics, quite another asking his partner for his daughter's hand. When he looked into Jean's eyes, his courage faltered. Would there be words between them, accusations regarding his intentions. Had Delphine confessed all when she returned to the party that night?

It didn't matter. Phil was determined to do the right thing, to dedicate his life to making Delphine happy, to keeping her safe. Marriage wasn't something he had anticipated, but he owed her as much after his disgraceful actions on the ship that night. He had to admit, marrying Delphine wasn't a disagreeable notion. If only he could see her first, talk to her.

"Phil?" Jean placed a steadying hand on his shoulder. "Stop your pacing and tell me what happened."

Phil sighed and fell into a nearby chair, his long legs stretched before him, savoring the warmth emanating from the blazing fire. He longed for summer, longed for the warm Gulf winds to carry him away from this cold, damp climate. This time he would take Delphine with him to the Caribbean. This time, with Jean's blessing, they would share a cabin. No, marriage wasn't a disagreeable notion at all.

"I must speak with you," Phil finally said.

To his surprise, Jean laughed, then poured him a drink. "Of course, you must. You have to explain what the devil got into you to accept such a mission from the governor."

Phil emptied his glass, the dark rum burning a trail down his throat. Between the Spanish wine and the rum, he should have been relaxed, but his muscles tensed as if preparing for battle and his head remained clear. "He believes the English are planning an attack on New Orleans."

Jean nodded. "The Spanish have been wary ever since the English took over Spanish West Florida. This is nothing new."

"But it will be if France allies with the Americans."

Jean sat down with his own drink and rubbed his chin. "I had heard of this. Since France and Spain have a 'family compact,' Spain will follow France into the American's war." Turning to Phil, his skeptical gaze returned. "But what has this to do with you? The man who always said, 'Profits first, country second?' "

Phil wanted to smile at the comment, but his vow to protect Delphine preceded his selfishness now. Still, he offered Jean what Galvez had offered him. "I'm allowed to transport any goods into Havana and return with what I please, duty free. A third of the hold will be reserved for the ammunition, carefully concealed with whatever merchandise I bring back. In fact, my goods will be a decoy."

"And the money from Havana?"

This time, Phil did smile. *La Belle Amie* offered many secret compartments. Despite Louisiana's past embargo against trade with any nation but Spain, Jean and Phil had managed to smuggle many French items into the territory. "Hidden in its usual places."

Jean still wasn't convinced. "A third of the hole will eat into our profits, even minus the duty charge. It's not like you to give up cash for the sake of a cause, especially one with such an unlikely outcome."

Phil had many reasons for helping the Spanish, Delphine at the top of the list, but somewhere in his long conversation with Galvez he had changed his opinion about the Americans.

"I'm not so sure the Americans are doomed to failure." Phil pulled his toes from before the fire now that they were quite toasty. He leaned forward to share his views with Jean, as they had for years as partners and the best of friends. For a moment, all memory of him ruining his daughter disappeared. "If France allies with the Americans, and Galvez helps fund the American efforts from the western frontier, the colonists stand a good chance. If Spain joins France in the war, the Americans will have two nations behind them."

"Against the world's finest army," Jean reminded him. "And only years after England defeated both the French and the Spanish in a lengthy war. Louisiana stands as an example of that defeat. France ceded this territory to Spain to compensate for Spain's loss of West Florida in that war."

Both men paused, then laughed. "Poor Spain," Jean finally said. "If only they knew what a bankrupt, wild colony they would inherit. Not much of a trade."

Jean poured them both another round and Phil began to feel at ease, grateful that their camaraderie was still intact.

"There is an American upriver who is using his own fortune to run guns into Illinois," Phil continued.

"Oliver Pollock."

When Phil sent Jean a questioning look, the same dimple that graced Delphine's cheek emerged. "I met with our astute governor this morning."

"Then you know that between Galvez and Pollock, the Americans are gaining quite an ally at New Orleans. And that Galvez has spies at Pensacola so he has the English at a disadvantage on the Gulf."

The dimple grew deeper. "He really convinced you, didn't he?"

Reminded again of Delphine and why he had come, Phil stood and began pacing again. Where was she? "Why is the house so quiet?" he asked.

Jean's face turned solemn or maybe it was Phil's fears getting the best of him. "It's past ten, Phil, the children are asleep. Gabrielle is finishing the wash."

Phil swallowed, realizing it was now or never. "And Delphine?"

A darkness clouded Jean's features and Phil knew Delphine had explained everything that had transpired between them.

"Jean," Phil said softly, "I can explain."

Jean appeared not to hear him. Instead, he gazed up at Phil and smiled grimly. "Delphine has sailed for France."

Nothing prepared Phil for the blow those words caused. "France?"

His partner studied him hard at the outburst, but continued. "Her grandmother is ill. She has sent for her."

"I thought your parents were deceased."

"They are," Jean replied. "I am speaking of the Comte Delaronde's mother."

If news of her departure weren't startling enough, the fact that Jean sent his daughter into the Delaronde household nearly undid him. "You did what?" he practically yelled.

Jean's countenance hardened. "She is my daughter, Phil, but she is legally bound to that family."

"Hardly. What has the Delaronde family ever done for her."

Now it was Jean's turn to pace, and it was then Phil realized how upsetting Delphine's departure had been for him. Jean poured himself another drink and leaned an elbow on the mantle, staring down into the dying embers. Phil immediately regretted his outburst.

Delphine was Jean's daughter by birthright, but she was bound by legalities to the Delarondes and the King. She had been the product of a wild garden party, when Jean and Louise Herpin imbued too much wine and sought the comfort of each other's arms. When Jean learned Louise was with child, he offered marriage, but Louise refused since Jean was a second son with little inheritance and forced to smuggling for his livelihood. Instead, Louise trapped the rich and influential Comte Delaronde into her bed, posing their child as his.

Only the blind and the feeble-minded would not have recognized Delphine as Jean's child. Sporting dark curly hair as a babe and the trademark Bouclaire dimple, the Count quickly realized he had been duped. He collected Louise's dowry and returned to France, never to speak to Delphine or Louise again. Even when Jean traveled to St. Malo in the hopes of securing a French education for Delphine, the Count had refused him admittance into the Delaronde castle.

In all that time, Jean supported the two women in New Orleans, sneaking in back doors to visit his daughter without placing scandal on her head. Ironically, it was her mother who caused the most gossip, traipsing with rich men to feed her appetite for fine gowns and social functions. When she died eight years before, Delphine came to live with Jean and Gabrielle. She was only too happy to oblige. The two adored one another, were inseparable. The Atlantic ocean was too large for the likes of father and daughter.

"It will be good for her to see France," Jean finally said. "She needs to know what the world has to offer."

Phil poured himself a drink and drank it all down. His Phiney was heading for St. Malo, the city that had taught him a cruel lesson or two. "The world can be a horrid place. She needs to be here, safe with us."

Jean turned and studied Phil again. For the second time that night, Phil wondered if he knew of their indiscretion. "The Delarondes are an influential family. They possess an enormous fortune."

Was he hinting at something, Phil wondered. He couldn't possibly mean what he thought Jean meant.

"She is the last descendant," Jean continued. "Now that her father is gone, she will be next in line to inherit everything."

Phil slammed his glass on to the table. "You can't be serious. You're insinuating that Delphine denounce the name of Bouclaire for the sake of a fortune?"

"I'm saying nothing of the sort."

"She's happy here. With us."

Was it his voice that had been raised in anger? Dear God, what was happening to him? Phil closed his eyes and took a deep breath, trying to tame his wildly beating heart. He couldn't fathom that his Phiney was halfway across the Atlantic.

"I never asked her to change her name," Jean said in a steadier voice. "She is a Delaronde by legal birth and by baptism. Unless the grandmother wishes to denounce her, she will inherit the fortune and land and become the next Countess Delaronde by order of the king."

The knowledge of that title hit Phil with hurricane force. He fell into the chair, the rum now beating furiously at his temples. It was one thing that she was the daughter of Jean, a nobleman, but to possess a title? To be an heiress to an estate?

"She must marry a nobleman now," Phil said softly. "If she marries a commoner, she will lose her land and title."

He felt Jean's hand on his shoulder, but he refused to meet his eyes. He didn't know whom he ached for more, Delphine and the aristocrat she must now marry or his own pitiful heart. For a blessed afternoon, Phil had felt hope. And it had been snatched from his grip as fast as he had envisioned it.

Phil heard the door to the study open and Gabrielle's welcoming words. He felt her gentle hand on his arm, but he hadn't the strength for conversation. Instead, he bid them both *adieu*, retrieved his hat and headed for the comfort of a bottle of rum. And the air of the open sea.

Jean watched his young partner, shoulders slumped and hat askew, disappear into the fog enveloping Saint Anne Street. Fighting back a shiver, he wrapped a loving arm about his wife. Never before had he seen two people more in pain.

"I won, didn't I?" Gabrielle asked. "I won the bet."

Jean pulled a gold coin from his pocket and handed it to his wife, but Gabrielle was not gloating over her winnings as was usual. She, too, felt the anguish of unrequited love and snuggled deeper into Jean's embrace for comfort.

"I must say, I had no idea of his feelings until tonight," Jean said.

Gabrielle leaned her head against his shoulder and sighed. "I don't think he realized his feelings either."

"He was very sad to hear Delphine had gone."

"Maybe we shouldn't have let her go."

Jean would have fought a nation to have kept Delphine at home close to his side, but she had insisted. Once Delphine made up her mind, there was no moving her. The dimple wasn't the only thing she had inherited from him.

"Perhaps it's for the best," Gabrielle added. "The separation might do them good, make their reunion all the more special. Then, in a few month's time, they can resolve whatever spat they had and we can prepare a big wedding."

Jean turned to his beloved wife and kissed her soundly. Things like matters of the heart were so simple to Gabrielle, which was what he adored about her. It was also what he cherished about the Acadians. Braving a winter, celebrating the birth of a healthy pig, these were the things that mattered to a people who carved a wilderness out of Nova Scotia. Not the title that followed a person's name.

But now, that title would matter to his daughter. And

very likely it would prevent her happiness.

"They can't marry," he said softly. "She will be a titled noblewoman soon."

Gabrielle most have understood for she said nothing and in that silence a sadness passed between them more powerful than the agony they had witnessed on Phil and Delphine's faces.

Yet, all was not lost.

"There is a way," Jean said.

# CHAPTER TWO

THE WALLED CITY OF ST. Malo slowly came into view as the sailors labored the dingy closer to the ramparts. With the massive tides out and the pink rocks of the rugged promontory exposed, it had been a long row to shore.

The sky turned gray before landfall, mirroring the dark stones of the town's buildings and massive fortifications. Delphine gazed up at the imposing city, a town within a fortress, wishing for not the first time since leaving New Orleans that she was back in her native colony.

The dingy landed upon the beach and two men offered Delphine their hands. Charles Armand stepped in between and gently took Delphine's elbow and the satchel clutched in her frigid fingers. "Thank you, gentlemen, but I'll see Mademoiselle Delaronde to her home."

The New Orleans landowner had been a blessing on the torturous voyage, forever providing Delphine with humorous stories and tales of his adventures between the colony and France. As much as Delphine wanted to retreat to her cabin and wallow in her misery, Charles consistently knocked on her door, drawing her out to deck. If her instincts served her well, the man was in love with her. But then, she was about to become one of the most eligible women in France, with a title and a hefty inheritance to offer a nobleman. Perhaps it was the money he coveted.

Delphine followed Charles along the beach to the long stairs leading up the ramparts, while above she heard carts moving down cobblestone streets and the lone cries of a cathedral bell. The smell of baking bread and rotting meat floated down to welcome them.

She remembered her father's description of European cities: crowded, smelly and filthy. Watch your personal possessions and never walk the streets alone, he had warned her. New Orleans was hardly an improvement to this picture, but still the image of St. Malo with its hoards of people and winding streets with granite houses pressed together convinced Delphine that Jean was right.

Charles hailed a carriage and Delphine preferred watching the impressive city from the inside of a safe cabriolet. Other smells of decay assaulted her nose so she drew away from the carriage window, leaning back into the leather interior that, too, smelled musty and old.

"You will love France," Charles said, taking her hand. "When the sun emerges, you will see that Brittany is the most beautiful place on earth."

Delphine wanted to say that the most beautiful place on earth was full sails above the West Indies, when the sunsets cast fairies upon the water, their feet lightly dancing upon the waves. But she held her tongue. Only two men and Gabrielle understood her love for the sea and the beauty that it entailed.

"I hope you like it here," Charles said, rubbing his thumb across her fingers.

So, it was money after all, Delphine thought. Of course, he would want her to remain in France, so they would live on the massive Delaronde estate. Regardless of what she may inherit, Delphine had no intention of staying in France. Or marrying Charles Armand for that matter. She had no intention of marrying anyone or becoming the next Countess Delaronde. She withdrew her fingers and gazed out the window.

The carriage halted suddenly, only a few moments from the water's edge.

"Is this the house?" Delphine asked, amazed at the large structure before her.

"This is just the family townhouse," Charles explained. "The *malouinière*, the estate, is many miles from here. If your grandmother is not present, the servants here will take care of you until a journey is arranged to Chateau de la Ronde."

Delphine swallowed, wondering how large the Delaronde estate was compared to this monstrosity. When she descended the carriage and entered the mansion's foyer, her astonishment doubled. Standing in a long line were servants in various states of dress. When Charles announced Delphine, the long line curtsied and bowed.

"Welcome home, mademoiselle," the formal servant to her right said. "Your grandmother anxiously awaits you in her bedchamber."

Charles turned and kissed her hand, sending her an encouraging wink before leaving her alone with the army of attendants. A man to her left retrieved her satchel while the formal servant barked instructions for the rest of her things. An elderly lady with a Romanesque nose began to remove her wrap, but Delphine clutched the familiar material to her breast.

"If you please, mademoiselle," the woman said, attempting the action again, "you are damp from the journey."

Delphine clung to the cotonnade shawl Gabrielle's mother had lovingly woven and Gabrielle had sewn. It was her cherished reminder of home and she would not relinquish it, especially since the house appeared damper than her cloth. "If it's all the same to you, madame, I'd prefer to keep it about me."

Something she said sent the woman aback and several servants whispered and giggled. Delphine wondered if she had insulted the matriarch of the house. "I beg your pardon, madame, I did not mean to..."

The woman huffed, took her elbow and led her toward the stairs. "You are a Delaronde," she whispered for Delphine's ears alone. "You must not consider my feelings."

Delphine was thoroughly confused but she let the Romanesque woman lead her up the massive stairtower with walls lined with family portraits. So many men in different styles of dress. She wondered if the Count and his disapproving stare looked down upon her now.

It seemed an eternity before they reached her grandmother's threshold, crossing three flights of stairs and two dark, cold hallways. The thick stone walls appeared as damp as the light rain outside, the air as humid as the swamps back home. Delphine pulled her shawl tighter and bit down on her lower lip to keep from shaking.

When she entered her grandmother's bedroom, a lone candle illuminated her relative's face and nothing else. Despite the darkness, Delphine could tell by the shadows against the drawn curtains that the ceiling reached high above her head.

"Come here, child," her grandmother instructed.

Delphine approached the bed and gazed down into a face that held no resemblance to her own, the mother of the man who had deserted his family, left Delphine and mother destitute for not Jean's financial assistance. She owed this woman nothing, but something in her eyes stirred Delphine's heart.

"You are so tall," the old woman managed. "Is this a trait of residents of the New World?"

The comment unnerved Delphine. Surely, this woman knew of her parentage. It most certainly wasn't Delaronde.

"I know who you are, child," the woman said, as if reading her thoughts. "Come here and let me get a good look at you."

Delphine crept closer to the bed, studying her legal grandmother in the process. Madame Sandrine Magon,

Countess Delaronde, matriarch of the proud Delaronde family and heiress to a fortune, stared back with eyes the color of the Caribbean sea. Ignoring her deathly pale face and stern countenance, Delphine found herself enchanted by those eyes, drawn into their depths as if they called to her like a sea siren.

To her surprise, her grandmother laughed. "No, you are most definitely not blood related to me."

Turning to the servant, she barked orders to be left alone. When the woman bowed and left the room, her grandmother patted the bed beside her and Delphine sat down. "We will not speak of your Louisiana father. Your lineage remains between us, *comprends-tu?*"

Delphine bolted upright. "I will not denounce my father's name nor will I be ashamed to be the result of an illicit affair. I realize my mother tricked your son into marriage, but the Count deserted us while my father put food on our table and saw to my education. Despite the scandal surrounding my entrance into this world, I am proud of who I am and were it not for legalities, I would carry the Bouclaire name."

Her grandmother blanched and stared, saying nothing, and Delphine immediately regretted her outburst. She would not retract her words, but she reprimanded herself for being rude to her elders, particularly her estranged grandmother who had paid handsomely for her to visit France.

"Forgive me," Delphine said, hanging her head. "I am tired from the journey. I do not mean to..."

"You meant every word," her grandmother insisted.

Delphine met that aquamarine stare and recognized a sparkle — pride perhaps? She also realized there was no lying to this woman — not that she had any intention — that her grandmother would not mince words nor want to be humored because of her ill health and age.

"Yes, madame," Delphine said softly. "I meant every

word."

Her grandmother patted the bed again and Delphine sat back down. "And I meant no disrespect child. But if you are to inherit the Delaronde fortune, you must keep your parentage a secret, at least while in France. Understood?"

Delphine pulled her shawl tighter. She prayed she would stop shivering. "Grandmama, I don't wish to sound ungrateful, but I don't want to inherit the title or the fortune. Surely, you must have another relative..."

At this news, her grandmother pushed herself up in bed, her pale face turning crimson at the exertion. "Don't wish to inherit? What nonsense is this?"

Delphine took a deep breath. She hadn't figured on having this discussion so soon upon meeting, but perhaps it was well and good they cleared the air. "I'm happy living the life I lead. I don't wish for more."

"Don't wish for more?" the old woman belted out. "You will be the envy of all young women in St. Malo. You will be the most sought-after bride in Brittany? Do you have any idea how much money I possess? Not only am I a Delaronde, child, but I come from the Magon family, merchants of the *Ancien Régime*. This house was my father's."

If anything, the news only confirmed Delphine's position. "I wouldn't know what to do with all this," she said, glancing around the room her New Orleans home would fit into. "I have never had use for fine clothes or estates. I may be a nobleman's daughter, but he's a privateer and a smuggler. I grew up sailing the backwoods of Louisiana and down into the West Indies, a life I've enjoyed. I repeat, Grandmama, I do not wish for more."

The old woman eyed her suspiciously. "Alligators, swamps and corsairs? This is what you want?"

Delphine thought of her life aboard *La Belle Amie*, of the endless adventures and the exhilarating feel of sea breezes and salt air upon her cheek. Yes, it was what she wanted. More than anything. But the picture wasn't complete without one man. And he had made it all too clear he loved another.

She had accepted this trip to France — for what? Curiosity? A chance to see the town of Phil's birth, where the Count had lived his last years while his legal wife perished in New Orleans? Or was it simply a chance to place an ocean in the chasm she had created between she and Phil, anything to ease the pain gripping her heart?

"You're not telling me all," her grandmother said, breaking the silence.

Delphine tugged at her cotonnade, then stood and began pacing. "It's dreadfully cold in here, Grandmama. You should warm this room. No wonder you are feeling ill."

"I am dying, child. And I am used to the cold."

Delphine turned back toward the bed and found a distinct sadness in those stern, wise eyes. Without thinking, Delphine took her grandmother's hand, sat back upon the bed and raised her fingers to her chest where she held them tight. She couldn't explain the feeling, but she liked this woman. And she didn't want her to die.

"I have some training in herbs," Delphine told her. "My father's wife in Louisiana is Acadian and she has taught me many things. Perhaps there is something I can give you."

The sadness disappeared and the Countess smiled. "I have seen the best of doctors and my time is near. I face my end proudly." She reached up with her other hand and touched Delphine's cheek. "But you dear, are you that scared of becoming the next Countess?"

"Terrified. But I must admit, now that I have met you..."

She didn't know what had come over her, but tears burned Delphine's eyes. She didn't know this woman; they had only met. Perhaps she had come to St. Malo for answers, to find reason for the heartache that was consuming her. Something in her grandmother's eyes spoke of solutions. Something familiar lingered between them.

"What are you not telling me?" her grandmother

repeated.

The tears poured forth and Delphine let them fall. She was tired of being brave, tired of smiling at Charles' jokes upon ship, tired of pretending to Gabrielle and Jean that she hadn't thrown herself at Phil and ruined the finest friendship she had ever known. Tired of pushing the painful memory aside.

"I'm in love with a man. And he loves another."

Her grandmother squeezed Delphine's hand. "We will talk of inheritance tomorrow." She then removed her fingers from her grasp and opened her arms, inviting Delphine into her embrace. "Come now," the Countess whispered as Delphine laid her head upon her grandmother's chest. "Tell me all about him."


Elise, the servant assigned to Delphine, tugged at the strings on her corset. It had taken a week of the Countess insisting, but Delphine had finally agreed to sit for a tailor.

"Nothing fancy, I fear," Delphine said, pulling on her robe. "I've heard women in France these days are wearing wigs as high as the ceiling."

The Countess huffed. "You will be fitted with the best fashions there are to find in St. Malo, but nothing extravagant. Delarondes are not known for their extravagance."

Delphine peered back at her grandmother, seated royally in her high-backed, embroidered chair. The stately woman's color had returned and her stamina much improved. If the doctor hadn't insisted otherwise, Delphine imagined the Countess headed toward recovery.

"Her happiness has a lot to do with it," the doctor had informed Delphine. "Keep her spirits up and her life will be prolonged."

That prescription was the very reason she was agreeing to the fitting. In the past week, Delphine had grown accustomed to her grandmother, amazed at the similarities in their lives. Born into a family of seafaring merchants, the Countess preferred stealing aboard her father's ships than dancing at balls and attending teas, but she acquiesced when le Comte Delaronde proposed marriage. Since the death of her husband many years before, she had retreated from society, happy to linger at home with her books.

This, too, the women had in common. After discovering the house's enormous library, Delphine had spent hours with her grandmother discussing books, the Countess recommending titles Delphine consumed immediately.

Delphine would have been happy reading and talking with her grandmother, never setting foot outside the house, but the Countess insisted she be introduced into St. Malo society. "It will ease your suffering," the Countess had said. "If nothing else, you will have a chance to see what other men are like, what other men have to offer. And they will offer you plenty, considering the size of your inheritance."

Delphine said nothing, knowing her heart belonged to one man who could offer her very little.

Except happiness.

"Send the tailor in, Elise." The Countess attempted to sit straight in her chair, but Delphine knew the proud gesture was exhausting her energy. She quickly placed a pillow at her grandmother's back, who thanked her with a kiss on her cheek.

"Don't worry," the Countess whispered in her ear. "Nothing too fancy for my beautiful pirate granddaughter."

Delphine answered with a smile, then met the dandy who appeared like a vision, volumes of lace at his neck and wrists, every piece of his being perfectly creased and ironed. "Monsieur Bonnair, at your service, mademoiselle." Turning to the Countess, he bowed deeply. "I am humbled, Countess."

Her grandmother waved away his ministrations. "My granddaughter needs a wardrobe. Something elegant, sophisticated."

"And practical," Delphine added, which caused Monsieur Bonnair's eyebrows to rise. She had refused numerous invitations to social events, begging her grandmother to remain at home, which the Countess did not approve of. Delphine hoped her wardrobe would be more suitable to everyday life than aristocratic balls, giving her another excuse to spend more time in the library and at her grandmother's side.

"For walks and riding," the Countess interjected. "The child will need everything, but mainly ball gowns. Spare no expense."

This last piece of information illuminated the man's face. He happily circled Delphine and examined her from head to toe, while Delphine frowned under the scrutiny. "In all due respect, Countess, she is hardly a child."

The Countess puffed out her chest. "I have eyes, monsieur. But she is a child to my advanced age. Now, what can you do for her?"

Monsieur Bonnair snapped his fingers and two female servants approached and began measuring Delphine's arms, waist and length of her legs. When one assistant lifted a leg to study the size for her shoes and stockings, the assistant gasped and fell back on her rear.

"What on earth?" the Countess bellowed.

Delphine stifled a smile, then raised her petticoats. Strapped to her lower leg by a garter was a long, slender knife accented by a red handle. "Pirate's Rule Number Two," she recited. "Always be prepared."

Monsieur Bonnair paled, one servant covered her mouth to keep from smiling and the other lying on the floor stared in horror. Delphine glanced at her grandmother, wondering if she would be censored, but the Countess offered a quick smile before returning to her usual haughty self. "My granddaughter, monsieur, lives in the wilds of Louisiana. This must be the norm for young ladies there."

The dandy placed an effeminate hand on his chest, staring at the knife with disgust. "You use this thing, mademoiselle?"

"I'm sure she must defend herself against alligators and natives," her grandmother interjected with a wink to Delphine.

"Actually, Grandmama, it was given to me by a friend to protect myself against dangers worse than alligators and natives." Delphine tossed her head back with a grin. "Those predators who walk on two legs."

Again, the dandy's eyes widened and the girl to her left let a giggle escape. The Countess waved a hand to set them back into motion, but her grandmother's curiosity was piqued. For the past week, almost every conversation had reverted to Delphine's escapades at sea and her life in the sultry colony.

"This friend you keep referring to, does he not have a name?"

Delphine sighed, feeling the familiar grief grip her heart. Three months and still it stabbed her as painfully as the day it happened.

"I see. It's that dreadful man, isn't it?" Her grandmother frowned. After explaining how she had thrown herself at Phil and his reaction to her kiss, her grandmother had been sympathetic but furious at Phil's refusal. But when she had learned Phil was a commoner, her grandmother had worked relentlessly to bar him from Delphine's thoughts.

"I told you Grandmama, I practically grew up with him aboard my father's ship. He taught me many things, including the rules of the sea."

Delphine noticed how Monsieur Bonnair and the servants were leaning close, listening to every word. Surely, having lived in St. Malo, the City of the Corsairs where fortunes were made by pirates, they had heard these stories before?

"You never speak his name," her grandmother continued. "It's not as if I would know the man. Has he not a name?"

Delphine froze, half for not wishing to hear his name upon her lips for fear it might unravel her and half was not wishing those around her to know of her association with one of the town's most scandalous episodes.

Her grandmother sensed her feelings and, once the assistants had taken the measurements, sent everyone from the room, demanding that Monsieur Bonnair bring in his samples of fabric as an excuse. When the two women were alone, Delphine sat at her grandmother's knee, allowing the older woman to lean comfortably back in her chair.

"I'm hesitant because you might know him," Delphine said.

The Countess smiled doubtfully and touched Delphine's cheek. "How is that possible, dear?"

"He is from St. Malo."

Her countenance didn't falter. "Many men, especially corsairs and West Indies merchants, sailed from St. Malo. Jacques Cartier, explorer of Canada, had been a native son." Her grandmother paused, catching her breath. Delphine knew the tailor visit was wearing on her. "If he is a commoner, I doubt..."

"He is a commoner," Delphine continued, "but you may know of him. When I was but ten and obstinate about attending school in New Orleans, my father traveled to St. Malo to try and convince the Count to educate me in France."

"I never heard of this," the Countess said.

"The Count refused to see him."

Again, the old woman's back straightened. "I would have reacted differently, for what it's worth. You would have prospered under my tutelage."

Delphine took the woman's hand and warmed it at her cheek. "I'm thankful you didn't, Grandmama. If you had, I would have missed the things I so dearly love, including the last years of my mother's life."

Delphine paused, thinking about her mother who would have swam to France to be standing in Delphine's shoes, a beautiful noblewoman who desired society so fiercely.

"But what has this to do with that dreadful man?"

Philibert. The image of him lying half-dead in her father's first mate's cabin was as familiar to Delphine as that fateful day.

"On the way out of the harbor, my father pulled a man from the sea, a man who had been beaten and left to die. He nursed him through the voyage back to Louisiana. The man survived and has been my father's best friend and partner ever since."

The Countess leaned forward, a frown playing her forehead. Delphine wondered if she had heard of Phil's scandal. "Who was this man?"

"As a young man, he was in love with a woman of nobility, but she was promised to wed another," Delphine continued. "He was going to sail for the Indies with the French navy, try to erase her from his mind, but received a letter from this woman asking to see him before he left. When he arrived at her house that night, he stumbled upon her wedding. He was called out by the woman's husband and they dueled in the garden. He won the duel, although he only wounded the husband, but other men of the nobility beat him senseless, then threw his body into the harbor. And that was how my father found him."

The Countess leaned back in her chair, her eyes reflecting a deep sadness. "Philibert Bertrand."

If the memory of Phil and her embarrassing spectacle hadn't caused enough pain, his name spoken aloud nearly undid her. Tears flooded her eyes, but now a mixture of anger, pride and betrayal caused them. "*Oui*," Delphine said, wondering what her grandmother knew of this scandal.

"I was at that wedding," her grandmother whispered.

"We all were. We were going in to dinner when he came bursting into the house. The men later boasted how they had murdered that poor boy, how arrogant he had been to approach Marie on her wedding day. But I saw his eyes that night. So full of longing, so full of pain. It almost seemed as if..."

Tears rolled down Delphine's cheek, more for Phil's pain now than her own. "As if what, Grandmama?"

The Countess grew solemn. "As if he were betrayed."

The door swung open as Monsieur Bonnair entered with bolts of fabric, followed by his two servants, their arms stretched with materials. The intrusion startled both women, who jumped at the noise, Delphine quickly wiping the tears from her face.

"Take care, man." The Countess stomped her cane against the floor.

The dandy bowed gallantly, then placed the fabric in front of the Delaronde women and began chatting endlessly about the quality of silk and the proper colors for what society expected of Delphine. She heard little, haunted by her grandmother's words.

"Is she really that beautiful?"

All talking ceased and Monsieur Bonnair gazed from one woman to another, confused. "Pardon, mademoiselle?"

The Countess ignored him. To her grandaughter she offered a sympathetic smile. "Yes, Delphine, Marie Labarthe, Countess de la Candelier, is the most beautiful woman in St. Malo."

For the first time, Delphine considered that the ravishing woman Phil adored, the noblewoman Phil risked his life for, still lived and walked the streets of St. Malo. She visited the same social circles that Delphine was now admitted to, was part of the same social class. So many ideas passed through Delphine's head.

"You'd like to meet her, *non*?"

Again, the room became eerily quiet and Delphine

wondered if Monsieur Bonnair and his servants would tell others of the mysterious knife-toting Delaronde grand-daughter. She had to be careful, for her grandmother's sake as well as her own. If she was to meet Marie, she didn't want the woman knowing of Phil's whereabouts. At least, not until she got what she wanted from the notorious woman.

"Pirate's Rule Number Four," Phil used to instruct her. "Know thy enemy."

"Yes," Delphine whispered to her grandmother, her heart beating wildly at the prospect of meeting her nemesis. "I wish to meet her."

The Countess gathered her remaining energy and leaned forward, gazing at Delphine sternly. "I will do this for you, my child, but you must promise me two things."

Delphine nodded, although she dreaded hearing what those two items would be.

"You must promise to enter society, meet other men, learn how to act like a Delaronde."

All the things she feared most, but Delphine nodded again.

Leaning close, her grandmother imparted her second condition for Delphine's ears only. "And more than anything, you must never, ever become a woman like Marie Labarthe."

# CHAPTER THREE

CHARLES ARMAND HAD TOLD DELPHINE that Brittany boasted a temperate climate, but the sky had drizzled consistently since their arrival. That morning a chilling fog had rolled in, obstructing her view of the front courtyard.

"Come away from that window," her grandmother admonished. "A lady doesn't spy on her guests."

This wasn't any guest, Delphine thought. This was Marie Labarthe, the woman who had stolen the heart of the man she loved. If she had a flintlock handy, she would have found a strategic spot and waited.

"What are you thinking, child?"

Delphine moved away from the window and began pacing the room. Heavens, what was she imagining? "I'm thinking that if these clothes were any tighter, I would die from suffocation."

"Sit down by me." Her grandmother patted the settee.

Delphine stared at the comfortable seat and sighed. Breathing was labored standing, how would she manage it sitting down? "I can't, Grandmama. My corset strings are too tight."

"That's not all that's too tight," the Countess said with a laugh. "Relax."

"How can I relax when the bane of my existence is expected?"

Delphine felt her grandmother's weathered hand cover hers. "Marie can't hold a candle to you, child." Staring down into sincere eyes beneath her maiden's laced cap, Delphine wished with all her soul that her grandmother was right.

"Besides," the Countess said with a wink, "you're ten years younger. There's a lot to be said for youth."

Remembering Phil's remarks about the differences in their ages, she doubted being one and twenty was an attribute, especially when it came to "the most beautiful woman in St. Malo."

Delphine resumed pacing, pausing short of the window and resisting the urge to check for Marie's arrival. "Grandmama, you won't mention Philibert, will you?"

The Countess straightened her skirts and soothed the fabric. "I agreed to this meeting on the promise that you would not emulate that woman, Delphine, and I expect you to hold to that. I will keep Philibert's fate to myself as long as you don't start imitating Marie. If this commoner doesn't have the sense to love you over Marie Labarthe, then you are wasting your time on a fool."

Delphine smiled, warmed that her grandmother had taken a likening to her. The feeling was definitely mutual. But her words puzzled her. "You don't like Marie, do you?"

The Countess didn't hesitate. "No, I do not."

"Why?"

"I can't tell you exactly." The Countess shifted nervously. "It's a gut feeling I have that something about that woman isn't quite right. Perhaps it's her condescending manner with insubordinates. It's one thing to be a member of the aristocracy, born to privilege and education, and quite another to believe you're inherently better than others."

Delphine locked her hands behind her and rocked back on her new high heels, shoes she had no business wearing. "You're quite the revolutionary, aren't you Grandmama?"

The Countess responded with her usual huff. "Nonsense. Everyone has their place, aristocracy included. But we as nobility must show compassion and charity to those beneath us."

"You can't fool me." Delphine moved to the rows of books above her grandmother's head and touched her fingers to several titles. "Voltaire, Rousseau." Her eyebrows raised. "Ninon de Lanclos. Looking through your library, I might assume you agree with those radical Americans."

"Let's not forget Thomas Paine and *The Rights of Man.*" Her grandmother sent her a sly smile. "I acquired that controversial book from a visiting American. But my copy is in English. I don't suppose you read or speak that horrid language?"

Delphine had managed to learn a few words of English on her trips upriver to Baton Rouge, when she and Phil had sold rum to the soldiers there. She mostly wanted to know what choice words they had shouted at her, but Phil had refused to translate.

"No, I don't speak English," Delphine answered.

"Marie does."

Delphine cringed. "Is there anything this woman doesn't do?"

"Might be why I distrust her so."

Delphine gazed back at her grandmother and was about to inquire further when carriage wheels on cobblestones sounded, followed by Etienne the butler heading through the hallway to the front door. "She wouldn't understand Paine, let alone agree with him," the Countess did offer. "Stop comparing yourself. Stop it now before that woman arrives."

If only it were that easy. Delphine was the daughter of a smuggler, a man taken to privateering for the Spanish governor and transporting Acadian refugees into Louisiana. She had been raised aboard a schooner, more accustomed to facing squalls than gorgeous women who caused men to duel. Her finest gown, the yellow one made for Gabrielle's party, had been labeled a disgrace by Monsieur Bonnair and her mannerisms declared unfit for society by the Countess. How could she possibly match "that woman," the famous Marie Labarthe?

Etienne opened the parlor doors and announced the Countess de la Candelier. Nothing prepared Delphine for the image that delicately cascaded over the threshold. Marie wore a sky-blue gown of the finest Oriental silk, billowing fabric at both hips from a bodice that hugged her slim waist. Lace accented her modest but ample bosom and a strand of perfectly matched pearls adorned an elegant, ivory neck. Her hair resembled auburn silk, flowing down upon her shoulders beneath a wide hat that sheltered both shoulders and was topped by a majestic ostrich plume. When she bowed before her grandmother, Delphine caught the outline of her perfect face: long, luscious eyelashes, a small but flawless nose, high aristocratic cheekbones and pert lips any man would desire.

She was, in essence, stunning.

"Countess Delaronde, how good of you to call for me. Since we have not seen you at this season's functions, we have all been worried about our favorite matriarch."

"Thank you, Marie. I have not been well."

"Nothing serious, I fear."

"Nothing to worry yourself over."

All the time the two women spoke, Marie never glanced in Delphine's direction. Delphine would have thought herself invisible had it not been for her height and the reams of fabric puffing out at her generous hips in the latest Paris style. Funny, she felt like a spectacle when she first donned the gown. Now, in the presence of this goddess, Delphine became a wallflower.

"Marie," her grandmother said, breaking conversation. "I'd like you to meet my granddaughter, Delphine Delaronde, newly arrived from the colony of Louisiana."

The envy of St. Malo and the heartthrob of Philibert

Bertrand turned her eyes upon Delphine. Again, the elegance and beauty of the woman took Delphine's breath away. When Marie offered her hands, Delphine accepted them mutely.

"Your granddaughter," Marie exclaimed. "How wonderful. It is such a pleasure to meet you. The resemblance is astonishing."

Delphine had rehearsed a thousand retorts but could remember none of them now, especially faced with such a blatant lie. She swallowed, praying for the words but none came.

"My granddaughter is more comfortable meeting alligators than addressing members of her own class," she heard her grandmother say. "Perhaps you can help me train her to be a proper lady, a woman capable of becoming the next Countess."

A sly sparkle appeared in those doe-brown eyes. "It would be my honor, Countess." Still holding on to Delphine's hands, she studied her beneath seductive lashes. "I have heard such wonderful tales of the brave colonist who wears a dagger upon her body."

Delphine carefully avoided glancing at her grandmother, knowing well the elderly woman was frowning at the gossip now spreading among the streets of St. Malo. "Exactly why you are needed here, Marie. My granddaughter could use instruction in the finer aspects of life."

Marie met Delphine's eyes, boring into her soul. Delphine shivered, wondering if the goddess knew of her true plans. She finally dropped Delphine's hands, but the examination continued. "Perhaps we can make a pact?"

The Countess leaned forward on the settee. "A pact, Marie?"

"I will be more than happy to impart my wisdom on this lovely girl if she will provide me with stories of Louisiana."

Finally, Delphine found her voice. "You wish to hear of my life back home?"

"Ah, she speaks." The Countess rose from the settee, leaning on her cane for support. "I trust you two can make arrangements?"

Delphine rushed to her grandmother's side, but as usual, she pushed her assistance away. "I am in need of rest, child. I will see to tea. Meanwhile, you two acquaint yourselves."

Delphine followed her grandmother to the door, holding her elbow despite her objections. When the butler met them at the foyer, the Countess ordered the doors closed, leaving Delphine alone with Marie.

"Come sit by me and tell me all about that fascinating colony of yours."

When Delphine turned around, Marie had taken her grandmother's place, removing her hat and shawl and relaxing among the pillows. Even in her current state of undress, she was the picture of perfection.

"There is so much to tell." Delphine sat next to Marie, but could not recline with the corset bones pinching her side. "Why does Louisiana interest you?"

"I've always wanted to visit the New World," Marie said dreamily. "Does that sound unusual?"

"Coming from a distinguished lady such as yourself, yes it does."

Marie pouted her lips and blushed ever so slightly. She was a master of seduction, Delphine was sure of it. "You are a lady, too, Delphine. You are a Delaronde and a Magon, a member of two of France's finest families. Surely, you live a comparable life in Louisiana."

Yes, there were balls and parties by Creole nobility, those French aristocrats born in the colony, but nothing to match Marie's society. And most of the balls and parties of New Orleans Delphine scorned, preferring the open sea next to Phil and her father. "I'm afraid I'm not much for Creole society, madame."

Marie appeared genuinely surprised. "Then how do you spend your time?"

"My fath..." Delphine instantly remembered her promise to her grandmother, to keep her parentage a secret. "I have family who are in the merchant marine business. I have been allowed to accompany them on their trips to the West Indies."

To her surprise, Marie appeared more curious than ever. "How utterly fascinating. I must hear all about it."

Marie appeared sincere, but Delphine was on a mission and thoughts of the West Indies were as far from her mind as they were in leagues. "Regarding our pact, madame, you will teach me everything you know?"

Marie laughed. "Everything I know? That may take a good while."

Ignoring the thought that Marie might be self-absorbed, Delphine pressed the issue. "I will be forever grateful, madame, if you will take me under your tutelage. I long to be able to carry myself as you do so elegantly."

Marie smiled that dreamy smile, one that said she welcomed complements, and straightened her hair that held not a pin out of place. "First you must call me Marie."

Delphine smiled, eager to learn the secrets this woman owned. Anything to win Phil from Marie's heart. "Agreed."

"We shall meet in the afternoons. A lesson in social graces first, then a story of the mysterious land across the ocean."

Delphine extended her hand and, after the initial shock of the gesture wore off, Marie accepted it and shook. For the life of her, Delphine couldn't imagine what could be so fascinating to this goddess about the swamplands she called home, but none of that mattered. She had met the enemy, and per Phil's instructions, she would learn her mind.

Delphine had traveled too far this time, agreeing to her grandmother's wishes while ignoring her intuition. The ball, given by a prominent St. Malo family in honor of Charles Armand's recent visit, was held on the opposite side of the city. Now, Delphine had to endure a long carriage ride home.

"Can't you go any faster?" she yelled to the driver through the window.

"We're going as fast as allowed through the city streets, mademoiselle," the driver answered back.

Leaning back in her seat, Delphine watched the townhouses of *Le Rue Chat Qui Danse* pass by in a haze, wondering why residents named the street for a dancing cat. The next street, *Rue du Gros Mollet*, or fat calf, made more sense, but certainly children of the Enlightenment could choose better names for their streets?

Delphine rubbed the bridge of her nose. Why hadn't she listened to her heart and remained home that evening? Like numerous times in the past year she had let her grandmother's rationale sway her, allowed the Countess to talk her into yet another societal event. Dressing up in her finest gown, preparing her dark locks high above her head with pads and pomade and donning her grandmother's family jewels continually delighted the elderly woman. But she had gone too far this night.

She knew what her grandmother wanted, a Countess to carry on the family title and estate, a woman capable of such an honor. Determined to please her grandmother in her final year of life, Delphine mastered the art of society, learning through Marie's tutelage the proper bows, retorts, mannerisms and dances. Marie insisted that only noble blood could succeed at such niceties, but Delphine knew her talent for imitation was more important than her bloodline, which held none of France's two finest families.

At her first function, Delphine was pleased to find St. Malo society eager to make the acquaintance of "the daggered woman," the daughter of the wilds of Louisiana. Like Marie, society's best was enthralled by the tales of natives, alligators and mosquitoes the size of a person's thumb. Delphine related stories of her escapades at sea, careful not to be too brazen in her descriptions, and every dazzling head leaned forward in rapture. She explained how during the spring months, the river sometimes rose higher than the rooftops of New Orleans, that only a small levee protected the town. She talked about the English at Baton Rouge and the Spanish government and its varied relationship with the French residents, a topic Marie found captivating.

Despite her lack of proper upbringing, Delphine's bow into St. Malo society was an immediate success. And her popularity continued throughout the year as members of St. Malo's best invited her to a host of functions.

Delphine partly enjoyed herself; she loved bragging of her homeland to residents of the Mother Country. But she longed to remain at her grandmother's side, especially when her health deteriorated during the spring months. She would have stayed home that evening had not the Countess insisted otherwise, practically ordering the servants to haul Delphine into Charles's carriage. Besides becoming the next Countess, her grandmother wished for a prosperous marriage contract too.

Finally, the carriage arrived and Delphine bolted out the door before the footman had a chance to reach its side. "Please tell Charles thanks for the use of his carriage," she shouted as she ran toward the front door.

A distraught Etienne met her at the foyer and quickly took her wrap. "She told me not to contact you, mademoiselle, but I feared the worse."

"You did the right thing, Etienne." Delphine touched his arm and the gesture brought tears to the man's eyes. Suddenly, a fear she had not experienced since the death of her mother gripped her heart. Delphine raised her skirts high above her ankles and rushed up the stairway, taking two steps at a time.

For more than a year Delphine had lived in France and she knew any day might be the last for her grandmother. But nothing prepared her for the pale image of her beloved friend lying still upon her bed, surrounded by weeping servants. Delphine slowly made her way to her side, kneeling at her grandmother's head.

"Grandmama." Delphine uttered her name more as a command, hoping the word would bring her grandmother back, keep her safe on the earth, out of God's reach.

The Countess opened her eyes but the effort consumed her. Delphine took her hand lying across her chest, held it tightly, then raised it to her lips.

"Knowing you has been my life's greatest pleasure," the Countess whispered.

Tears poured down Delphine's cheeks. "Don't leave me," she pleaded.

The Countess attempted a smile. "I thought my pirate was afraid of nothing."

Delphine shook her head. She was scared to death. "I love you. I don't want you to go."

The Countess closed her eyes briefly, her breathing labored. When she opened them again, shivers passed across Delphine's arms. "Do not fear your future, child. It holds wonderful possibilities."

Marriage to a nobleman she could not love, an estate she did not wish to manage, her home thousands of leagues away. For her grandmother's sake, Delphine nodded. "I will do you proud."

Her grandmother's eyes sparkled in the candlelight. "Do something more for me."

Delphine leaned forward to hear her grandmother's soft message. "Yes, Grandmama. Anything."

"Be happy."

And with those final words, Madame Sandrine Magon, Countess Delaronde, was gone.

The harbor at night was no place for a lady, let alone the next Countess Delaronde, but Delphine had to view the vibrant sea pulsating with life, breathe the fresh salt air into her lungs. She wore her dark cloak over the dress she had worn on arrival to St. Malo, the hood concealing her face. If someone were to spot her, she would call herself another name.

At the moment, she didn't care who recognized her. Grief and an acute sense of isolation pressed at her heart.

She felt her father's letter in her cloak pocket and took comfort in that, wishing with all her heart it was his ship resting in the harbor that night. She would write immediately and request that he come for her. In the time he would sail for France, Delphine would settle the estate and arrange for a land manager to run the country chateau. She would ask Charles for more time to consider his proposal, time to return home and consider her "possibilities."

Time to see Phil again.

Where once thoughts of Phil caused her pain, anger now took its place. He had never written in the past year nor sent his regards in Gabrielle and Jean's letters. They had mentioned his numerous voyages to the Caribbean, that he was seldom seen at New Orleans, but nothing excused him from his blatant disregard.

She had been dismissed by her best friend and confidant.

Tears of grief burned in her eyes. Delphine still loved him, of that she was certain. But she would never forgive him.

A carriage turned the corner of *Rue De La Clouterie* and Delphine ducked into the shadows of the ramparts.

"Excuse me, mademoiselle, but this spot is taken."

Delphine gasped and moved away from the deep, male voice. When the man's face appeared in the glow of a nearby lamplight, Delphine feared for her sanity. Standing before her was the mirror image of Phil, but dressed in Acadian costume.

"Didn't mean to shock you," the imitation said with a seductive grin. "But you did step on my toes."

Mouth dropped to her chin, Delphine glanced at the man's feet, barely covered with strips of leather tied with a string. When Phil's lookalike realized she was staring, he pulled his feet back into the shadows.

"What do you expect living off the dole?" the man asked, his smile long gone. "Not exactly the reception we were expecting after being brutally cast from our homes by the English, then imprisoned for years."

Delphine slowly met the man's eyes, too dark to be Phil's. His hair was too wavy and his height not nearly as tall. Yet, he wore clothes much like Gabrielle's and the other Acadians she had met in Louisiana. Was she seeing things?

"Phil?" she asked, her voice cracking.

The man's eyebrows deepened. "Think you're mistaking me for someone else."

Now that she heard his voice again, she knew Phil didn't stand before her. But who was this Acadian, conjured up from her thoughts in her time of despair? She nodded to the man, fighting back the sobs threatening to erupt, then moved to leave. For all her prayers, God was playing a mean trick.

Delphine headed back in the direction of her home, but not before another carriage turned the corner. Delphine felt a sudden hand on her elbow. "A lady such as you shouldn't be out on the streets alone." The mysterious man led her back towards the shadows until the carriage passed. "Let me see you home."

She didn't want to look at him, didn't want to be reminded of the man she loved sailing on the other side of the ocean. Sailing without her. In the state she was in, Delphine knew that one look at this man's face might send forth a torrent of tears.

"Please, mademoiselle, you have nothing to fear from me."

She didn't know why she accepted; it was dangerous allowing a man to accompany her and viewing where she lived. But Delphine agreed, somehow comforted by the image of Phil standing beside her, even if she refused to look at him.

"My name is Delphine," she said as they walked quietly down the street. "I'm sorry if I appeared startled, but you remind me of someone."

In the darkness of the street, Delphine made out a slight smile from the corner of her eye. "I've been told that on numerous occasions," the man replied. "But then, I've family from here."

"Are you Acadian?"

This time, passing a lamplight, Delphine caught his dashing smile that caused her heart to quicken. Even though his features differed slightly, he was charming like Phil. "At your service, mademoiselle."

In the light, Delphine made out his clothes, threadbare and ragged. Aspects of his dress reminded her of Gabrielle's homespun fabric, but heavier like wool. Other parts of his outfit appeared more European, but unmatched and in disrepair, as if received as charity.

When Delphine stared at his clothes his countenance changed and his face fell back into shadows. "Of course, I'm Acadian. Who else would be dressed in rags in this fine city?"

Delphine caught the sarcasm in his voice, but she knew nothing of Acadians in St. Malo. Her year in France had consisted of balls and parties and hours in her grandmother's library. For the past year, she had been isolated from everything that wasn't aristocracy.

They reached her door in minutes but Delphine didn't want to say goodbye to this mysterious Acadian who resembled the man she adored, the man she despised. More than anything, she didn't want to break the thread, however distant, she had with home. And she wanted to know his story.

"Would you care for coffee?" she asked him.

The man gazed at her suspiciously, wondering, she was sure, why a woman of her station would be offering refreshment to a peasant refugee.

"I'm from Louisiana," she confided. "My father is married to an Acadian." Delphine smiled thinking back on her home colony and the family she left behind. "Although my American uncle calls her a 'Cajun' because he mispronounces her nickname."

The man stared dumbfounded. "I had heard some had traveled there."

"Many. The Spanish have welcomed hundreds of them, given them land grants and tools to begin anew. They are calling Louisiana the New Acadia."

The Acadian gazed back with a look Delphine understood all too well. She had seen it numerous times before when her father had brought Acadian refugees into the colony. So much heartache. Too much separation. A glimmer of hope that perhaps they will see family and friends again.

Delphine touched the man's sleeve, its fabric worn. "You must be cold. Please, come in, let me get you something to eat."

The man's eyes darkened and he straightened. "*Non, merci.* I am weary of charity."

"But it's not charity." Delphine stopped, fearful she would begin crying again. How could she explain to this man that offering him coffee and clothes was a chance at healing her lonely heart? She wanted to speak to him, to hear the cadence of his unique French, to close her eyes and pretend she was sitting in Gabrielle's kitchen.

The mysterious man said nothing, but took her hand and raised it to his lips. Bowing before her as a knight would his lady, he let her hand go and moved to leave.

"Wait," Delphine whispered.

Just then, the front door opened and Etienne rushed out. "Countess, we have been so worried."

Several servants followed the butler into the courtyard, all in equal states of distress. Delphine admonished herself for being so selfish. Her servants were grieving as much as she was, needed her now, and she had deserted them for the comfort of the sea.

But she had to know the Acadian's name, she had to know if there were others. When she turned toward the street, she glimpsed the back of his gray coat disappearing behind the gate.

"Wait," Delphine called to him. "Tell me your name."

In his path, there was only silence.

# CHAPTER FOUR

"MY NAME IS JEAN BOUCLAIRE and I must see the Countess."

It was the first time Phil had used his partner's name as a guise and the words felt strange upon his tongue. But it was his only course of action entering St. Malo, the city that had once left him for dead. As far as he was concerned, Philibert Bertrand was dead to the residents of this dreadful town.

The butler studied Phil's dress, beginning with his knee-high leather boots and saber hanging from his side, up to the ruffled shirt and long, flowing coat that allowed free movement and helped conceal weapons when necessary. Phil thought to don more appropriate clothes to approach the Countess Delaronde, but he was more comfortable in his regular, sea-faring attire. Considering his anxious state, the last thing he needed was a suffocating waistcoat, dandy stockings and buckles on his shoes. And he never, ever traveled without his sword.

"The Countess has company, monsieur. Is it urgent business?"

Hell yes, Phil wanted to shout. It had been more than a year since Delphine had left for France and it was time she came back to Louisiana. If he had to drag her kicking and screaming from this granite monstrosity, then so be it. But his first tactic was to approach the Countess, convince her that Delphine was needed at home.

"It is of importance," he told the butler. "I shall not take up much of the Countess's time."

The butler hesitated, clearly suspicious of Phil. Then he opened the door to the library and motioned for Phil to enter. "May I offer you some refreshment, monsieur?"

Phil desperately needed a drink, but he shook his head. The butler exited the library, closing the doors behind him, and headed down the hall to a room where voices were heard.

Leaning back against the fireplace mantle, Phil rehearsed the speech he had practiced during the two-month voyage from America, the arguments that would convince the Countess to send her granddaughter back to the colony.

In truth, he had no business being there. He hadn't even Jean's approval. He had returned from Havana, found Delphine still not home and took it upon himself to retrieve her. Jean had been upriver on business, so Phil announced to a startled Gabrielle that he was sailing with the tide, to expect them both home by summer's end.

Phil did have an excuse. Governor Galvez had imparted business for him in France, and time was of the essence. A wealthy Frenchman wished to donate arms and money to the American cause and Phil would be its transport. There was also a group of Acadians ex-patriated back to St. Malo after being imprisoned by the English and Galvez wanted Phil to convince them to settle in Louisiana.

It was just the excuse he needed. The ink wasn't dry upon the parchment before Phil weighed anchor and headed east toward the Mother Country.

None of that really mattered. He had to see his Phiney, had to breathe in her youthful beauty and hear her sweet voice. Had to see those adoring black eyes, that playful smile.

Had to heal the wound he had thoughtlessly created.

More than a year and not a day had passed when he

wasn't haunted by his actions in his cabin that night, when he wasn't reminded that he had ruined the finest friendship he had ever known. More than a year and not a day had passed when he hadn't wanted to relive that kiss, God help him.

Gazing around the elegant library, the expensive leather-bound books and rich tapestries reminded Phil of the differences between he and Delphine and the title she would inherit. She was his Phiney, the girl he had vowed to protect, yet she was on the verge of becoming untouchable. And there was nothing he could do about it.

Despite his best intentions, Phil poured himself a drink and downed the liquid, enjoying the burning sensation it left down his throat. Since his humiliation at Marie's wedding, Phil despised the aristocracy. His Phiney might be one of them now, but he'd be damned if he'd let the Countess corrupt her with their patronizing ways. Another year among these people and she might fancy herself above all others, agreeing to a loveless marriage and a frivolous lifestyle that would only bring her misery. He had to get her home. Back to the colonies where liberty lingered in the air, where equality wasn't an empty idea tossed around by philosophers.

Hurried footsteps sounded in the hallway and Phil imagined the butler had sent a servant to dismiss him. No doubt the Countess had refused to see him and was sending him away. He braced himself for the news, ready to insist upon an audience with Madame Delaronde, when the doors flung open. Standing on the threshold, the light from the hallway casting a halo around a head of soft brown curls, stood Delphine.

At first, Phil forgot the name he had announced to the butler, forgot that Delphine had rushed to the library to see her father. All he could make out beneath the eager smile and glistening eyes were the reams of black silk gracing her form, spreading out like fountains at her hips atop wide, exaggerated hoops. Her hair was piled high above her head, curls spilling down majestically, complementing jewels upon her ears and neck. And for all her childish eagerness, Delphine stood before him gracefully like a queen.

She gasped at the sight of him and stood frozen to the spot. Her smile disappeared and her eyes took on an astonished glare.

"Countess," the butler beckoned from the hallway. "Do you need assistance?"

With an authoritative tilt of her abundant head, Delphine raised her chin like a woman of title. "*Non, merci,* Etienne. He is an old family friend."

Phil heard the butler retreat down the hall as Delphine closed the library doors. Now that they were alone, Phil wanted nothing more than to pull her into his arms. But the woman standing before him was not the Phiney he knew.

"I asked to see the Countess."

Delphine slowly turned to look at him, puzzled. "So, you haven't come to see me?"

"I came to bring you home. I wanted to speak with the Countess first."

Delphine moved forward, every movement graceful and precise. She seemed stronger somehow, more confident. Gone were the adoring glances she used to give him, replaced by a cold, aristocratic stare of a grown woman he didn't recognize. "I don't understand."

"Oh, I think you do." Phil walked around her to examine her expensive gown, accented with fine black lace. She appeared as a stranger, a woman of another world, and it angered him. "I think you know why I've come."

They stood close now and Delphine met his eyes, hers as still as the Sargasso Sea at midnight. "More than likely business on your part." Her tone was edgy and cold.

"I have come on business, yes. There are Acadian refugees in St. Malo and I plan on transporting them back to Louisiana."

At this, Delphine's eyes lit up. "Acadians?"

Too busy living a life of leisure to notice the poverty around her, Phil thought, like the other members of her despicable class. "There are Acadians here, people who need our help. You might have known this had you not spent so much time at trivial things."

It didn't seem possible for Delphine's black eyes to darken, but they did. He had meant to injure her and the arrow met its mark. "That's not fair. What do you know of me?"

Taking her in from foot to head, he smirked. "I know what I see."

She crossed her arms before her chest proudly and her eyes narrowed. "You know nothing."

He knew everything of Delphine Bouclaire Delaronde and he would be damned first before he let the aristocracy have her. "I've come for you."

At this, Delphine laughed. "Have you, now? Have you missed me that much?"

Her statement briefly took him aback, but he pressed on. "The question, my pet, is who you have missed." Nodding to her gown, he added, "You seem to be living well under the circumstances. I suppose now that you've had a taste of society you're planning on taking up residence here."

"I've never planned to stay."

"It's been over a year, Phiney."

Her eyes blared, matching his anger. "What difference does it make how long I've been in France. My grandmother needed me."

"You mean to say you needed your grandmother and all that the connection allowed. You seem to be enjoying the benefits of being a Delaronde quite nicely."

She uncrossed her arms, prepared to fight. "What is that supposed to mean?"

"Tell me, Phiney, have you denounced the name of Bou-claire as well?"

Phil was a master at reaction, an expert with the foils and the flintlock, always sleeping with one ear tuned to his surroundings, never surprised by anyone. But he didn't see Delphine's slap coming. She smacked his face with brute force. "How dare you?"

He lifted his hand to his stinging cheek, wondering which insult she had retaliated for, his remark on her family name or the liberties he had taken with her in his cabin that night. "I suppose I deserved that."

Tears burned in her eyes, tears she would never release, he was sure. She tilted her chin up and for a moment, the old Delphine emerged. "Hell yes, Philibert Bertrand, you deserved that."

He reached for her, ready to apologize, but she moved toward the table and glasses of sherry and brandy. She poured herself a drink and sipped the first swallow of brandy, then tossed the remaining liquor back. Staring into the fire, Delphine placed a hand on her hip and sighed, no doubt feeling the power of the brandy in her veins. "More than a year and no word from you. Now, you march in here as if you own me."

A spark ignited in his heart, a hope that she still cared for him, but that was fruitless considering the span of classes that stretched between them now. As he had done over the past year, Phil knew he must keep his distance. "I thought it best."

Delphine turned and her dark eyes sparkled with unshed tears. Or fury. "You thought it best to dismiss me from your life."

The familiar anger returned and Phil reached for his own glass of brandy. "What did you expect me to do?" He refilled his glass, praying the liquor would ease his aching heart. "You must marry a man of wealth and breeding now. The last thing you need is a commoner reminding you of past mistakes."

"Past mistakes?" Delphine stared at him incredulously. "Is that what I am to you, a past mistake?"

Phil wanted to say Marie was a past mistake, that Delphine meant more to him than his own life, but he was angry at the situation her inheritance caused, angry at how little his life was worth in the grand scheme of things. He said nothing, leaned an arm upon the mantle and stared into the flames.

Delphine smiled sadly and glanced down into her empty glass. "I see."

"No, you don't."

"It was silly of me to think you cared as much for me as I for you," she said softly, pain lurking behind every word.

Phil turned toward the woman he had known for years, the child who had nursed him body and soul in his darkest hour. She was still his Phiney, wasn't she? The same courageous girl he had taught to sail, to shoot, to navigate the West Indies? He placed a hand at her cheek letting his thumb explore its soft reaches, and Delphine closed her eyes, unshed tears lingering on her lashes. God, but she was beautiful, so delicate and so strong at the same time. Even dressed like Marie Antoinette.

"I love you, Phiney."

He shouldn't have said it; the confession solved nothing, could only cause more heartache. But the words freed him somehow.

To his surprise, her eyes flew open and she pulled away. She glared at him with a mixture of grief and anger. "Stop calling me that. My name is Delphine."

He didn't know what to say, couldn't fathom why she was angry.

"I know you love me, *Noncle* Phil," she continued, using her childhood nickname of him. "But that's not the kind of love I desire."

Phil attempted an explanation, but couldn't locate the

right words. While his mind rambled for an adequate retort, a knock came at the library door.

"Delphine, dear, is everything all right?"

Something in that voice made Phil's breath quicken. An alarm sounded in his brain, although he couldn't justify why. Delphine, too, reacted to the woman's voice, visibly cringing. Was it possible?

"*Oui*, Marie, everything is fine."

Dear God, Phil thought, it couldn't be. But when he stared at Delphine for a denial, her eyes softened, glancing upon him now with pity.

"May I come in?" the voice asked.

Delphine inhaled deeply, still staring at Phil with regret. "*Oui*, Marie," Delphine answered, exhaling with defeat. "Do come in."

The world suddenly slowed when Phil turned toward the library opening and Marie Labarthe, the goddess who had once set his heart aflame, the woman who had brought scandal on his good family name and ruined his life, floated across the threshold. The brandy glass slipped from his fingers and crashed to the floor.

Delphine watched in horror as her dearest friend and her present mentor, two lovers brutally separated by class and scandal, met each other's eyes. She heard the glass smash upon the stone the same time Marie gasped and placed a hand upon her gaping mouth. Ignoring her heart shattering like the glass at her feet, Delphine called out to Phil and rushed to Marie's side, seconds before her eyelids fluttered and she fainted.

Phil caught Marie in his arms, carrying her to the settee all the while staring down into her exquisite face like a boy madly in love. Delphine had seen it numerous times from the lovesick men of St. Malo, the suitors Marie had teased, loved and then cast away after the death of her husband, dismissing them all with a flick of her wrist. Yet, still they followed. Still, they adored her. Now, Phil's eyes brimmed with that identical lust.

He took Marie's hand and patted it gently, whispering her name with a reverence that had not lessened over the years. All hope she carried that Phil might still care for her disappeared. Delphine knew that Marie had, and always will, own his heart.

Phil glanced at Delphine, his eyes filled with questions. She had a lot to explain, to both of them. For now, she had a fainted woman to contend with and an audience growing at the door.

"What has happened?" she heard Charles say at her back. "May I help?"

Delphine turned and found her butler and two servants nearby. "The Countess had a fainting spell, but she is fine now. Etienne, please bring the Countess a glass of water and Charles, would you please instruct Gilbert to bring Marie's carriage around?"

Charles bowed gallantly, always eager to please, then left in search of her stable boy. When Delphine looked back at Marie, her eyes flitted open and she attempted to sit up. Then she caught sight of Delphine and remembered the reason for her lightheadedness. She glanced askance at Phil and Delphine feared she would faint again.

Etienne handed Delphine the glass and she pressed it into Marie's hands, but the Countess's eyes were locked on Phil's.

"You're dead," she whispered. "Or am I seeing a ghost?"

To his credit, despite the shock of their meeting and the memory of that horrid day, Phil smiled grimly. "No, my dear, I'm not dead."

"But how...?"

Remembering the audience and his need for anonymity, Delphine whispered, "Marie, this is a friend of my family. His name is Jean Bouclaire."

Marie's chestnut eyes, usually so soft and indifferent, turned upward toward her student, piercing Delphine. The animosity pouring forth was acute. Delphine might have been surprised that such a delicate creature could exhibit such wrath, but Delphine had always suspected a darker side to the Countess, as had her grandmother.

"The carriage has come around," Charles said, then herded her guests back to the ballroom with a final glance her way.

Thank God for Charles, Delphine thought as she sent him a smile of gratitude. Always saving her in her time of need. Too bad she didn't love the nobleman; with his caring nature and constant devotion he would have made a wonderful husband.

But the man she did love still held Marie's hand, still gripped the past like a lifeline. Delphine wanted to rip them apart, to insist that his love was wronged by this woman. Instead, she stood proudly and did what her grandmother would have expected. She acted like a Countess, like a woman descended from the noble families of Delaronde and Magon.

"Your carriage is here, Marie," Delphine said, amazed at the steadiness of her voice. "I'm sure Monsieur Bouclaire will see you home."

Phil glanced up to Delphine, appearing as if he should reject the offer but looking as if he was powerless to do so. He started to speak, but Marie stood between them and straightened her gown.

"I would appreciate that, Monsieur Bouclaire." Sending Delphine a look laced with needles, Marie added, "*Bonsoir,* Delphine. I pray you will sleep well tonight."

Delphine couldn't help herself. Not only was the envy of all St. Malo walking out the door with her heart, but she was blaming her as well. It was too much to bear.

"I shall sleep fine tonight, Marie. I pray you will too."

Marie instantly caught her meaning. Handing Delphine the glass of water, she leaned in close so only Delphine could hear. "I believe I shall not sleep at all."

Breezing by, a smug smile gracing her lips, Marie headed for the front door. If there hadn't been witnesses present, Delphine would have pulled out her dagger and shown Marie what society's latest attraction was capable of.

Phil paused by her side and reached for her hand, but Delphine shirked away, refusing to meet his eyes. "I'll be right back," he said.

Delphine shook her head. "I will see you in the morning, Monsieur Bouclaire. We'll discuss our business then."

Phil hesitated, and she felt his stare boring into her. Delphine finally braved a look, but Phil's eyes revealed nothing. Gone was the adoring admiration he had given Marie and the fury he had spent on Delphine. In its place was resignation. And that scared Delphine most of all.

He attempted to speak, but words seemed lost on his tongue. "In the morning, then," he whispered and followed in Marie's wake.

Delphine felt Phil leave the room, heard the front door open and close, then the sound of carriage wheels on cobblestones. Forgetting that she still had an audience in Charles, she flung the glass of water into the fireplace, shards flying among the stones, the water sending up a torrent of smoke.

She tried to breathe deeply, but someone had stolen her air. Fury beat at her temple and tears burned at the back of her eyes. Suddenly, two enormous hands rested on her upper arms, turning her around and pulling her into a male chest. Delphine stiffened at the contact, still furious over being bested by the perfect Marie. But slowly, calmly he wore down her defenses, stroked her hair lightly, whispered words of empathy. Delphine finally surrounded and leaned into the comfort of his embrace.

"So that was the reason you were moping on the ship."

Delphine wanted to soften the blow that she loved another, but a large lump prevented her from speaking. She nodded into his chest while tears stung her cheeks.

"I knew it was a man."

Funny, Delphine thought, he didn't appear hurt by the news. She pulled away slightly and Charles smiled down at her.

"I'm sorry," she said anyway, worried she might be bruising his heart the way hers had been brutally wounded. "I'm so sorry I don't love you, Charles. I really am."

Charles smiled, then touched her chin like a big brother. "I adore you, Delphine, but I'm not in love with you either. I'm sorry too."

Delphine was at a loss. What was he saying? He had asked for her hand.

"My mother wanted me to marry a French woman," he explained. "I asked you because you knew Louisiana and would want to live there. I'd hate to have a wife who despised my home. I'm afraid I'm quite fond of that swampland plantation."

Now, Delphine understood. "And it helped that I had a title and fortune."

Charles grinned. "Yes, it did help. I do so much business in St. Malo and the West Indies. Our marriage would have been profitable in all aspects, including your father."

Delphine's smile faded. Was he speaking of Jean or the Count Delaronde?

"I know who your father is, Delphine," Charles answered her unspoken question. "I live outside New Orleans and know of every man who sails the river. And no, that man was not Jean Bouclaire. I believe him to be Philibert Bertrand, your father's partner."

The sound of Phil's name caused her heart to quicken and the agony, briefly relieved, to return full force. She turned toward the fireplace, watching rainbows dance about the floor from the broken shards of glass.

"He's in love with Marie."

Charles took her hand and pulled her down on the settee beside him. Then he placed an arm about her shoulders, making Delphine glad Charles was there. "Who isn't in love with Marie? The woman has half this town in the palm of her hand."

"Phil has been in love with her for more than a decade." Delphine leaned her head upon Charles's shoulder. "He was in love with her before she married. It was silly of me to think I could compete with her."

At this, Charles straightened, placed a finger on her chin and forced her eyes to his. "Marie Labarthe doesn't hold a candle to you."

They were the same words her grandmother had spoken. And Charles wasn't a man of idle words. Still, at that moment, Marie Labarthe, Countess de la Candelier was riding home with the man she loved. And it was doubtful he would sleep on *La Belle Amie* that night.

# CHAPTER FIVE

THE CARRIAGE ROLLED FROM THE Delaronde courtyard and Marie gripped the sides for support, no doubt still reeling from the shock of their meeting in the library. They stared at one another, as if both expecting their visions to evaporate like specters.

Only Phil knew the breathtaking beauty before him was no apparition. He spent years dreaming of Marie's delicate face, reliving the touch of her skin and the sound of her angelic voice. The goddess before him now was definitely made of flesh and blood.

"How is it possible?" Marie finally broke the silence. "They told me you were dead."

No, he wasn't dead. By God's divine intervention, Phil had lived to see another day in her presence. Yet, his heart felt hollow, his feelings for her long disintegrated by time and distance. To Phil's amazement, he found himself smiling. "They told you wrong."

Marie's pale brown eyes widened and he wondered if she still commanded men's hearts with a mere glance. He certainly had been such a slave, obedient to her every demand. But then he had been a naive lad of seventeen, ready to take the world by storm. Class differences hadn't matter to those in love, he had told his family and friends. Words Marie had taught him.

Hell, class differences did matter. They always would.

"They said they threw you in the harbor," Marie continued. "That you had drowned."

Phil might have winced thinking back on that fateful night, when several noblemen beat him senseless and cast him off to die, but Philibert Bertrand the boy had died that night. The Philibert Bertrand sitting before her now was a new man, one who would never make the same mistake twice.

"I was rescued."

"Then my prayers were answered," she whispered, placing a hand upon her chest. "An angel came down from heaven and found pity on my grieving heart."

How ironic that the angel who found pity on his mutilated heart was probably grieving at this moment in that enormous library of her grandmother's, a family who had no business claiming her. How ironic, too, that thoughts of Delphine made him want to bolt from the carriage and rush back, even though Marie Labarthe sat across from him now. Marie Labarthe.

Something in those magical eyes shifted. Guilt perhaps? Did members of the aristocracy own consciences?

Or was it something else? As a boy, Phil rushed into every situation blind, his impulses ruling where his brain should have. Approaching the Comte de la Candelier's house the night of Marie's marriage was a good example. Marie had sent for him, begged him to steal her away before her wedding and he had obliged, charging into that household like a Musketeer. Now a seasoned captain and smuggler, he waited and watched, studying the signs, examining the possibilities.

"Oh, Philibert," Marie whispered. "How is it possible I can be so fortunate after all these years? To have you back, safe?"

She placed a hand upon his arm but Phil wasn't ready to forgive. He moved slightly, letting her hand fall away. "How is the count?" He tried to keep the anger from his voice, attempted to remain calm, but self-possession was not his virtue. Poor Delphine had seen the worst of his faults that evening. "I suspect you have a house full of children by now."

Marie returned her hand to her lap and gazed out the carriage window. "I have none. Georges took to his bed after the duel. A month later he contracted a fever and was never the same."

"My condolences."

Again, the words emerged bitter and resentful. Marie's lips turned downward in a pout and she seemed genuinely bruised by his remarks. "He died several years ago."

The pained look finally turned his heart. He reached for her hand and squeezed, relishing the feel of her smooth skin. "I am sorry."

When she met his eyes, they brimmed with tears. "No, Philibert, I am sorry. I never meant to hurt you."

Remembering that horrid night, Phil pulled his hand away. "Why?" he demanded so sternly she leaned back in her seat. "Why did you call for me the night of your wedding?"

A small tear fell down her cheek as she shook her head. "I sent for you the day before. You arrived too late."

So many thoughts flooded his mind at once. The boy running across his ship's gangplank that night, asking for Monsieur Bertrand. The lad had been out of breath, as if he had run all the way from the de la Candelier house. The parchment with Marie's handwriting, the ink blurred as if written in haste. The date. Had he not noticed the date in his eagerness to save her?

While he pondered her words, Marie moved to his side of the carriage, sliding an arm through his elbow and resting her chin on his shoulder. She smelled of lavender, the way he remembered, and her hair felt like silk against his cheek. Phil couldn't help himself. He leaned his head toward hers and savored the moment, closing his eyes to breathe in the scent of his boyhood, when a touch from her hand had lifted him into heaven.

"I always loved you," she whispered. "And I always will."

Phil turned to gaze into the eyes that had once stopped his heart, eyes that now beseeched him. Could he forgive her? Did he still love her? Her lips were so close, so seemingly eager to meet his. Before he had time to think, Marie slid a hand around his neck and drew him forward, erasing what defenses he had managed to possess, and pressed her lips upon his.

She tasted of wine and felt like the sea at full sail. So soft, so alluring, so powerful. He placed a hand at her waist and Marie moved closer, slipping her hand down the front of his shirt and tightening her fingers around a clump of fabric. When she parted her lips slightly, encouraging Phil to deepen the kiss, he took the bait.

Marie had learned a lot since their last meeting. Their lovemaking had been awkward, the passion mostly on his part. Now, Marie was meeting his tongue with hers and rubbing her foot up his leg. Phil felt the world tilt and all common sense disappear. Like the seafaring stories of old, he had reached the ends of the earth and was falling off the other side.

The carriage rolled to a stop and Marie pulled away discreetly. The lamplight of her front door reflected off her eyes and something in her gaze gave Phil pause. Still, when she leaned forward again, brushing her lips against his ear, he closed his eyes, enjoying the feel of her love once more.

"Stay with me tonight."

The coachman opened the door and Phil stepped outside, then reached for her hand and helped her to the pavement. She emerged like a queen, confident and commanding, relaying orders to the servants around her. It was just the moment Phil needed to regain his senses.

When she put out her hand for Phil to accept, he placed the petite fingers in his and kissed them, then he bowed.

"*Bonsoir*, Countess," he said, then disappeared into the dark St. Malo night.

Marie's kiss still lingering on his lips and the brandy's heat still burning his veins, Phil headed for the center of town and a safe harbor. He needed to restore his equilibrium, to reclaim his sanity. He needed to contemplate what had just happened between both women and plot a new course of action.

He needed a drink.

Yet, what he needed most of all existed at *205 Rue St. Vincent.*

Phil paused at a corner, wondering if what he was pondering would be wise — for both of them. Thirteen years. And he had been rumored as dead. Would either fact work in his favor? Would his brother welcome him home or cast him away?

He had to know, had to at least attempt a glimpse of his younger brother. Thirteen years he had spent without family, thirteen years without his sidekick pointing out his faults, nagging him about every possible thing, punching him in the arm. His father had called them salt and pepper in reference to the differences in their hair color, but Phil knew the differences in their personalities were just as diverse. They had fought constantly, nearly killing each other in the process and routinely confessed to hating one another. God, he missed his annoying little brother.

Inquiries told him Alain Bertrand had married well, worked as stable master to one of the best families in St. Malo and lived in a modest townhouse on the far side of town. The news made Phil proud, relieved that his scandal had not ruined Alain's life. But would he be glad to see him?

Phil approached his brother's townhouse from the rear, entering the courtyard and pausing at the back door. If his brother did emerge, it was best to keep Phil's identity secret, especially from Alain's family. No one need know Alain's notorious brother lived, smuggling goods into Louisiana and running guns to the Americans.

He stood at the kitchen window, fearing the worst, praying for the best, waiting for a sign. He received one, in a body that reached no further than his waist.

"Are you a pirate?" the small voice asked.

Phil glanced down at a boy dressed for bed, carrying a pail of soapy water almost as large as he. The lad couldn't be more than eight or nine, Phil thought, but stood fearless before him.

"Why do you ask?" Phil returned.

"You're dressed like one."

As if the boy suddenly realized he might be in danger, he threw the water into the bushes and backed up the stairs toward the door. "You're not here to plunder us, are you?"

"I'm not a pirate," Phil assured him. At least, that was partly true. "I'm a captain of a ship."

This deterred the lad, whose eyes lit up at the news. "My great grandfather was a captain, used to sail to Newfoundland. He never came back, though."

Phil smiled, remembering the stories of Francois Bertrand, who left one autumn morning and never returned. Of the two grandsons, Phil was the one who had inherited Francois's seafaring traits.

"I'd like to think that Francois fell in love with a beautiful woman in Newfoundland, and that was why he never came back to France." Phil leaned down on one knee, noticing that the child resembled his father, upturned nose and freckles included. "Or perhaps he heard the songs of the sea sirens and vanished beneath the waves with a smile on his lips."

The boy rolled his eyes. Obviously, too young for romance. "He joined the Indians and fought grizzly bears. Then he struck it rich on a gold mine."

Phil smiled at both the boy's innocence and the popular myths French people had of the New World. "Sounds like a good story to me."

Suddenly, the back door opened and a woman appeared, one hand wiping her apron, the other cautiously holding a kitchen knife. Phil was ready to reassure her he meant no harm, but her face softened at the sight of him. "Lawrence," she told the boy, "go get papa."

Rising, Phil met the eyes of Alain's wife, a stout woman with a lovely face. But the moment she studied his, her eyes turned cold. "You're not Francois."

Who was Francois? Phil thought. Their grandfather, even if he had returned, would be long dead by now. And on the off chance his relative was still alive, he wouldn't be mistaken for an elderly man.

The boy bounced back through the door, no doubt running ahead of his father. "He's a pirate," he announced to his mother.

The woman placed her free hand possessively on her son's shoulder and drew him close, but something in Phil's gut told him she wasn't afraid. The more she studied him, the less frightened she became. "He's not a pirate, Lawrence," she whispered to the boy. "I think he's your uncle."

Before he could respond, Phil heard Alain's footsteps in the hall, then saw his tow-headed brother walk out the door. The look Alain sent him as his brother stepped into the courtyard was one of shock, his eyes widened in horror. He stood before him, frozen, tension working his jaw.

Phil braced for the worst, waited to be dismissed and ordered away. He berated himself for being so selfish, for invading Alain's happy home for his own comfort and peace of mind. He started to say as much, but Alain approached him, myriad emotions crossing his countenance.

It all happened so quickly, Phil backing up expecting Alain's wrath while his brother grabbed his shoulders and pulled him into his embrace. It took several moments before Phil realized what has happening, that his brother, his best friend and only relative in the world, was crying and squeezing him tight.

"You're going to suffocate me," Phil said, returning the hug. "You always were emotional."

When Alain pulled back and stared at Phil, one hand still gripping his neck with affection, Phil felt his own tears emerge.

"I thought you were dead." Alain grabbed his upper arms, as if checking to make sure Phil wasn't a ghost. "They told me you were dead."

Phil pulled his brother's thick blonde hair, tied at the nape and hanging down his back. Since Alain had managed to produce such a mane at an early age, Phil had repeatedly tugged at it to tease his little brother. "You know us Bertrands. We're hard to get rid of."

For the first time, Alain smiled, the trademark chin dimple appearing. He resembled their father, a light-haired man whose face burned in the sun, who avoided the sea despite his famous Corsair father and who never left the house without a hat. Phil made out Alain's freckles in the faint light emanating from the kitchen, knowing that no matter how old Alain would be or how established he would become in his career, he would always be Phil's little brother. Forgetting all his earlier hesitations, Phil pulled Alain back into his arms and the brothers savored their reunion.

Phil leaned back in his chair, fat and satisfied. Alain's wife, Virginie, had paraded a long line of delicacies before him — onion potage, a fish fricassé with artichokes à la crème followed by fresh fruit and creamed cheeses. Now that he had eaten his fill, Phil felt like a hog fresh from the trough.

But it was the warmth that only family could offer that filled his soul. Gazing around at the meager yet comfortable home and the three faces watching his every move, Phil felt content, something he hadn't experienced in a very long time.

"Do you plunder enemy ships in the Gulf of Mexico or do you prefer the Caribbean?"

Phil smiled at the enormous brown eyes of his nephew, recognizing that curiosity as once his own. St. Malo had an elaborate history of pirating, producing some of France's notorious corsairs which resulted in nearly all the wealth of that region. Most boys Lawrence's age were fascinated by the tales. It was what had drawn Phil to the sea, but his path had been a different one. "I told you, Lawrence, I'm not a pirate."

"Then why do you have a dagger in your boot?" The boy looked pleased with having obtained such secret information. "And why do you have that sword?"

"Lawrence," Virginie admonished him. To Phil, she added, "He hears too many stories about your grandfather."

Phil leaned forward and withdrew his dagger, then handed it handle first to his nephew. "I'm not a pirate," he repeated, watching the boy study the knife with glee. "I transport goods from the Caribbean and Mexico into Louisiana, sometimes at such a large profit people have accused me of pirating. But at best, I'm a privateer. I sail under a letter of marque from the Spanish Governor of Louisiana. Should an English ship attack or attempt to interrupt my business, I am free to retaliate and plunder its merchandise and weaponry in the name of Spain. And I carry a sword because one should always be on his guard in such a dangerous occupation."

"Have you ever killed anyone?"

At this, Alain rose, took the knife from Lawrence and handed it back to Phil. "Time for bed, Lawrence."

The boy's eyes turned to Phil, pleading for assistance. "It's late," Phil concurred, which resulted in the largest pout he had ever seen. "We'll continue this another time." Lawrence brightened at those words. "Can we visit your ship?"

Phil had hoped the reunion would continue, but he couldn't press the issue, especially since boarding his ship would be done in public. "We'll see."

Virginie took Lawrence's hand and bid them all good-night, then kissed Alain who responded with a gentle hug. It was clear the two loved each other deeply and Phil felt a sharp pang of both relief for his brother's happiness and envy for the lack of his own. He missed having a family to share his life, missed dinners with Gabrielle and Jean and their growing family, missed having Delphine bring him coffee every night while he recorded the ship's logs. For a moment, before logic brushed the feeling aside, Phil wanted the life around him, desired a son who would carry on his name and bring him joy, a wife who would sail with him, be his partner, share his bed.

But that was impossible. Two women in his life and by God one was a countess and the other on her way to becoming one.

"So, did you kill anyone?" Alain poured Phil another glass of wine, then waved his hand. "Never mind, I don't want to know."

Phil had to agree; some things were better left unsaid.

Alain sat on the other side of the table and crossed his hands before him. "There is something I need to tell you, something unpleasant we must discuss."

Phil knew what was coming. No one had mentioned the scandal, yet it hung between them all night like a hangman's noose. "I know." Phil gazed into his glass of chardonnay. "I saw Marie tonight."

Phil didn't think Alain could appear more surprised than he had in the courtyard, but his mouth dropped open and his eyes widened. As shocking at that news seemed, Phil couldn't help but laugh at his brother's comical face.

"How can you find humor in this?" Alain asked.

How indeed? He had surprised himself in that regard. "I'm not a boy anymore, Alain. I won't make the same mistake." Yet, even as he spoke those words, he remembered all too vividly Marie's warm, sensuous lips and he doubted his declaration.

"Stay away from her." His brother poured them both more wine, his jaw tense. "I don't trust that woman."

Phil had many reasons not to trust Marie Labarthe, but his good-natured brother? Still, servants heard and saw things most of society did not. "What have you heard?"

"Lots of things."

His brother's eyes grew cold and Phil fought the urge to shiver. It had to be rumors. Marie Labarthe might be a heartbreaker, but she possessed a heart of gold.

"After the duel, the Count took to his bed," Alain began. "He only suffered a shoulder injury from your well-intentioned blade and the doctors predicted a full recovery."

Phil took a long drink remembering the Count and his insults the night of Marie's wedding, not to mention that as a gentleman he lost a duel and ordered his opponent killed anyway. "Too bad," Phil whispered into his glass.

"But he never recovered." Alain leaned forward as if the walls had ears. "He started getting fevers and having stomach problems. The doctors couldn't comprehend it. Then Marie tells them all, servants included, that the Count is recovering nicely and she will see personally to his needs."

"I thought you said he never recovered."

Alain leaned closer still. "He died the next day."

Phil saw his brother's point, at least he thought he did. But he wasn't convinced. "He took a turn."

"He died, Phil. Alone. Without witnesses. Without his last rites."

The last piece of news hit home. Surely, Marie would have realized the man was deathly ill and sent for a priest.

"That's not all. After they buried the Count, Marie

began selling his prize stallions and family heirlooms and disappearing for months at a time. Some claimed she went abroad."

Now, this seemed odd. What would Marie be doing outside of France? She hated to travel, absolutely abhorred the sea, not to mention foreigners. "Doesn't make sense."

Alain leaned back in his chair, taking a sip from his wine. "No, it doesn't. She never remarried either, which is odd as well."

"Maybe she was waiting for her lover to return." He meant it as sarcasm, but something deep in his gut hoped that that was true.

Alain shook his head, not catching the meaning of Phil's words. "She needs the money. Rumor has it she's broke."

Odd, Phil thought. Dressed in her usual lace and silks, she hadn't appeared as if financially strapped, but what did he know about such things?

"So, what brings you here to St. Malo?" Alain asked, breaking him from his thoughts. "Tell me it isn't Marie."

Feeling his familiar agitation, Phil stood and gazed out the kitchen window. "No, it isn't Marie. I've come on business and to retrieve my partner's daughter."

"Partner's daughter?"

Phil heard the merriment in his brother's voice so he avoided his eyes. "Before you get any wild ideas, she's the next Countess Delaronde."

Alain rose with both glasses, handing Phil his and leaning against the window ledge. "Now, that is interesting. You and the dagger woman." Phil studied Alain, puzzled at his remarks. "I help with their horses on occasion," he added with a shrug.

Phil had to laugh. Servants may be uneducated, but they were the smartest people in France. "Is there anything you don't know?"

"I know everything about Delphine Delaronde," he said proudly. "She's the talk of the town."

Suddenly, instinct to protect Delphine returned full force. "Like what?"

Alain visibly reacted to Phil's stern tone. "Dear God, don't tell me you're in love with her too."

Phil ignored the insinuation. "Alain, what are they saying?"

"Nothing as bad as all that. When she was fitted for clothes by her grandmother, they found a dagger on her leg tucked inside her garter. Now, she's the toast of society. Everyone wants to hear her stories of pirates and alligators and whatever exotic creatures you have in that God forsaken place. Apparently, the Countess is more than happy to oblige them. It's talked about that she never, ever removes that dagger."

Delphine, the toast of St. Malo aristocracy with his dagger in her garter? The one he gave her on her fifteenth birthday, then taught her how to use it? Phil tilted his head back and laughed, filled with both pride and admiration. But he should have known. Delphine could conquer the world if she wanted it.

Despite his laughter, Alain sobered. "Do you love this Louisiana Countess?"

Countess? This was a title bestowed upon women like Marie, not his dagger-wearing shipmate. If all went well, Phil would sail in a few days, Delphine in tow sans that hideous title. They would return to Louisiana, restore some semblance of normalcy and head back to the way things were before one kiss had disrupted his world. As soon as he talked to her grandmother and convinced her to find some other relative to bestow that honor upon.

Phil tossed back his wine. "Why do you insist on calling her Countess?"

Alain looked at him then, studying him hard. "Haven't you heard? The Countess Delaronde, her grandmother, died two weeks ago."

The world did tilt at that moment, water pouring over

the edge, carrying Phil and all his hopes with it. He was too late. The inheritance was complete. And he had lost Delphine forever.

# CHAPTER SIX

DELPHINE SPOTTED THE MASTS OF *La Belle Amie* before the ship came into view, the French flag swinging from the top in the early morning breeze like a call to freedom. Emotions choked her and she longed to run down to the harbor's edge, but she remembered her grandmother's instructions. She was a countess now and had a reputation to uphold. Delphine aimed to do just that. Until the ship weighed anchor and headed west.

She approached the ship quietly, watching the men at their various tasks. Mathurin Hébert, her father's second in command next to Phil, leaned against the railing of the quarterdeck barking orders in a good-natured way. Sebastien Charré tended to the spring line while Vincent Nerault poured water on the deck, their eyes more focused on the beautiful weather than on their work. Once in port, the men kept to their chores, but did so at a leisurely pace, each taking turns visiting the town at night. Sebastien must been the lucky one, Delphine thought, for he leaned his head against the foremast and sighed.

"Looks like you tied on a good one last night."

Vincent spotted her first, calling out her name and heading toward the gangplank in a trot. Delphine beat him to the deck, however, jumping onboard as he reached her side. Immediately, he pulled her into his enormous hairy arms, squeezing her hard, lifting her up and spinning her around.

"Let that child go before she stops breathing," Sebastien called out. "And give the rest of us a chance."

Vincent released her and Sebastien offered one of his usual, shy embraces. As close as the two of them were, he was always timid expressing emotions. "Glad to have you back, Phiney," he whispered in her ear.

When Delphine looked over at Mathurin, the auburn-haired Acadian she had known almost as long as Phil, she found tears in the older man's eyes. "She's no child," he said, gazing upon her with pride. "She's all grown up now and quite the beauty."

Delphine instantly threw her arms around her old friend, enjoying the smell of salt on his clothes and a hint of tobacco. "I have missed you all so much." Tears fell without warning and she buried her face into his shoulder to hide them.

Mathurin held her tight, then pulled back and tilted her chin up with his callused fingers. "You're home now, *mon amie.*"

Despite everything Marie had taught her, or maybe in defiance to it all, Delphine wiped her nose upon her sleeve and laughed. "Yes, Mathurin, I'm home."

"You sure look fancy," Sebastien said. "Are you a countess now?"

Mathurin studied her gown and frowned. Delphine prayed they wouldn't treat her differently because of her unwelcome title. "Why are you dressed in black, *cher?*"

Suddenly, the tears returned. More than anything, Delphine wished her grandmother was here to meet them all, to stand on the deck herself and breathe in the sea air, to live a day in her shoes. "My grandmother passed away a fortnight ago."

She felt Vincent's hand on her arm. "I'm sorry, Phiney."

Sebastien seemed equally concerned but Mathurin's eyes turned stern. "Did you like this Countess? Was she good to you? Did she treat you well?"

Realizing that her family consisted of a generous grandmother with a hefty inheritance and several protective
big brothers, none of them blood-related, made her smile.
"*Oui*, Mathurin. And I loved her very much." Taking his
hand, she added, "Just as I love you all very much."

Nothing seemed more surprising than three grown deck
hands with tears in their eyes. But then, these were no
ordinary men. To avoid further embarrassment, Delphine
changed the subject. "Where's Phil?"

Mathurin slid his own sleeve against his nose, glanced
up and smiled as if nothing had passed between them. "He
tied on one himself. Came in only a couple of hours ago."

"Still sleeping," Sebastien said.

Everything she had feared had come true. So, Phil had
spent the evening with Marie after all. Her heart plum-
meted, even though she had braced herself for the news,
lying in bed awake all night forcing herself to face facts.

Delphine tried valiantly to keep her composure steady.
She recalled Phil's Pirate's Rule Number Seven: "Never let
them see you sweat." She had no intention of letting him
know she was suffering inside.

"I think I'll surprise him," she said with a forced smile.

"Wasn't he at your house last night?" Sebastien glanced
from one to the other. "He said he was going to speak to
the Countess about bringing you home."

"Yes, he was." That much was true. "I thought it would
be fun to surprise him now, on ship."

"Well, he's still dressed," Mathurin said with a chuckle.
"Stumbled in and didn't bother to remove his boots."

"So, what's new?" Vincent asked. "He was born with
those boots on and will be buried in them as well."

"And his sword," Sebastien added.

They all laughed at the image and Delphine headed
for the stairs leading below deck. "Let's see how keen his
senses are after a night of ale."

She tiptoed down the stairs to the main cabin, knowing that it was more than ale that caused the heavy snoring behind those doors. She lifted the latch without a sound and entered quietly. If Phil owned an acute sense of awareness, Delphine's talent was in her blithe movements. She slipped silently to the side of the bed like a snake.

Phil lay sprawled across the bed on his back, fully clothed including the infamous boots. His thick hair, free from its tie, was tossed about his forehead and shoulders, begging for Delphine's touch. Gazing down upon his sleeping form, she noticed new lines on his tanned face, worry lines they called them, around the eyes. His nose cocked slightly to one side, the result of being broken in a fight in Hispaniola, and the scar he received defending her from an English rogue in Pensacola stretched above his right eye. All in all, it was a handsome face, chiseled features like a Roman statue yet warm, alluring eyes that turned women's hearts when he smiled. And a few scars to prove he lived an adventurous life.

Delphine examined the length of him, long legs stretched out almost past the foot of the bed. His hands rested upon a chest thick with muscles after years of hard work at sea. He wasn't anything like the men Delphine had danced with over the past year, noblemen who felt heavy from brocades and silks. Philibert Bertrand was real, solid. But he wasn't hers.

His sword lay next to him, always close within reach. As a challenge, Delphine slid her fingers beneath it, attempting to pull it from the bed. Within seconds, Phil's hand tightly captured her wrist, his dark gaze piercing her.

"Glad to see Marie hasn't ruined your reflexes."

Phil frowned, released her wrist and sat up on an elbow. His eyes cleared taking in the sight of her. "Don't you know better than to touch my sword?"

Delphine placed her hands at her hips and sent him a sly, seductive grin. "Are you sure that's what you want?"

His eyes widened at the comment, seemingly wanting to smile at the insinuation but still playing the protector. "Is this what you've been taught all this time in society? To talk to men this way?"

She traced her fingers down the length of his sword, remembering the woman who had given the lessons. "Learned everything I know from the best."

In one quick movement, Phil sat up in bed, took Delphine's hand and pulled her down next to him. "I'm sorry," he whispered, his face so close to hers she could smell his tonic. Something store-bought and French. Had he purchased it last night before coming to her house or was it something he picked up from Marie?

She turned her head, not wanting to think of what had transpired between them the night before. "Sorry for what? Sorry was barging in on me last night, barking orders or sorry for kissing me in the first place?"

Delphine felt a hand brushing back her curls, then sliding down her arm until it met her hand. He squeezed. "I'm sorry about your grandmother. I didn't know."

Delphine still refused to look at him. He was too close, yet too out of reach. The knowledge of both was ripping her in two.

"And I'm sorry for intruding into your home and making demands. You know how I feel about the nobility. I was afraid you had become one of them."

Delphine wanted to dispute this fact, plus argue that not everyone in the nobility fit Phil's description of the class, but she remained silent.

"As for kissing you, God help me but I'll never be sorry for that."

Delphine met his eyes then, his face so close he could have easily kissed her again. But all she could think of was Marie.

"Philibert Bertrand, you are the most insufferable man I have ever met." She caught the shocked look on his face just before she rose from the bed and began pacing the room.

"I realize that, Delphine, but what did I say?"

There was true concern in his voice, but she didn't care. She rested at the port window, one hand draped outside, as she stared at the rooftops of St. Malo peeking above the harbor. "You speak of kissing after spending a night with Marie."

The bed creaked loudly as Phil rose and Delphine heard his boots heading for the desk and the pitcher of water. The cabin offered many luxuries, but space wasn't one of them. Everything in the small room doubled in use. The chest containing clothes was used as a dining table and the desk became a washstand in the mornings when it wasn't being used.

"I didn't spend the night with Marie."

Anger burned in her veins; he had never lied to her before. But when Delphine spun around, she halted at the sight of him. Phil had removed his shirt and was splashing water on his face and neck, his back muscles tensing as he moved. She had seen him bare-chested before, but forgotten how broad his shoulders ranged and how rugged he was beneath those loose shirts he wore. When Delphine eyes followed his form, the rest of him seemed equally revealed. His beige breeches hugged his legs, allowing Delphine a glimpse of the man underneath his clothes, leg muscles taunt like coils of rope. And those boots. She wondered if he made love in them.

When he turned and gazed at her, grabbing a towel to wipe away the soap and water, Delphine felt the fire of her anger turn to a blush. "Don't lie to me," she tried to say with fury, but it emerged weak and laced with pain.

Phil pulled on a clean shirt that was draped across the end of the bed. "I'm not lying to you."

"Mathurin said you came in two hours ago. Plus, I doubt Marie would let you out of her grip now that you're back."

To her surprise, he smirked at that comment, but he didn't falter. "I didn't spend the night with Marie." He fumbled with the buttons on his shirt, missing one in the process. "I was with my brother."

This was something new. Either Phil had been keeping secrets all along or he was lying again. She folded her arms across her chest. "You never said you had a brother."

Finished with his shirt, he looked up, a lone tendril falling across his eyes. "You never said you knew Marie."

"When should I have told you this? Answering all the letters you wrote to me?"

Phil rubbed his eyes and swayed slightly, still feeling the effects of the ale, no doubt. "I'm sorry, Phiney...Delphine. I honestly thought it best."

There was something in his voice that tore at her heart, something that rang true. Phil had never lied to her before, why would he start now? Despite the kiss that was ruining their friendship, he would be upfront about his relationship with Marie. Wouldn't he?

"What's his name?"

Phil looked at her and sighed. Delphine swore the old Phil gazed upon her as he always did, love shining back from those unfathomable eyes. "Who?"

"Your brother."

"Alain Gabriel Joseph Firmin Bertrand."

Delphine uncrossed her arms and came to his side, fixing the lone button at his neck. "I guess I have to believe you. You're not clever enough to make up a name that fast. Is this Alain the reason why you're here?"

He watched her fix his collar, his breath hot upon her ear. "I'm here to retrieve you."

Her fingers trembled at the closeness of him, causing the button to slip twice before sliding inside its hole. "You're here on business. You said so last night."

He captured her hand and his lips lingered on her fingertips. "There is a resident in St. Malo who wishes to contribute arms and money to the American cause. I'm here to transport this shipment, plus a family of Acadians, back to Louisiana."

She met his eyes, searching for truth. He was never one for heroism and glory; profits were the bottom line. As if he read her mind, Phil placed his hands upon her shoulders. "I'm here to retrieve you," he said softly. "Everything else is a convenient excuse."

She needed to move back, leave the warm comfort of those enormous hands and the seductive power of his voice, but she felt powerless to do so. She decided to focus on something else than his intoxicating smell. "Then you're not a patriot."

At this, Phil smiled. "You sound disappointed."

In fact, she was. After spending a year reading Voltaire and other French philosophers and watching France align itself with the Americans and the idea of liberty, she had hoped he felt the same. "I am. I rather like the idea of independence, something I learned from you. I would have thought you'd feel the same."

Phil's eyes sparkled. "You haven't changed a bit."

She tilted her chin forward, aggravated that he would have thought otherwise. "Of course, I haven't."

He pulled her closer. "I missed you," he whispered.

She didn't trust herself to look at him, afraid of what might transpire again. She had damaged a great friendship with a heedless kiss and would not make the same mistake. She stepped back before she answered, "I missed you too."

They were still too close, she could feel the heat emanating from him. Or was it her own? She couldn't tell. Delphine decided to change the subject. "I can make you a tea for that headache."

Phil reached up and touched her cheek, his gaze boring into her soul. "What I really need is a hug."

All defenses disappeared as she gave in to her desires and threw her arms about his neck. Phil needed no encouragement to do the same, enveloping her in a tight embrace. They remained that way for several moments, holding on to each other tightly, Delphine savoring the feel of his unshaven cheek against hers and the musky smell that was all masculine, all Phil.

He reached up and laced a hand through her curls while his hand at her back pressed her even closer, if that was possible. Delphine closed her eyes and relished the moment, wishing the world away, praying she would stay in his arms forever.

But Phil's embrace grew slack and he pulled away enough to meet her eyes, leaning his forehead against hers and exhaling. They were the best of friends, comrades in arms for more than a decade. She knew the bond that existed between them would never be broken, despite her foolish actions in the cabin that night.

Still, something in his eyes gave her hope. A dark passion lurked there, as if he desired her as much as she did him. Encouraged for the first time since he had deposited her on shore more than a year before, Delphine's spirits lifted and her old unvanquished essence prevailed. She slid a hand down the front of his shirt, resting above his heart.

"Since you enjoyed that last kiss," she whispered, "how would you like another?"

Conflicts raged inside him; she witnessed the struggle within his eyes. But it was a battle Delphine could win. Raising herself on her toes, she closed the distance between their lips while Phil leaned forward to meet hers. They were a breath away when Mathurin sounded from the stairs.

"Captain, there is someone here to see you."

They both jerked away, each trying to regain composure. Phil appeared as if he wanted to explain or offer an apology, but Delphine wanted none of it. "Your hair," she offered.

Phil nodded and retrieved his tie, pinning the hair behind

him at the neck. Delphine found his coat and helped him put it on. He turned once again to face her, to try and justify what had been about to take place, but Delphine interrupted. "You need a shave. But it's not too bad. I think you're presentable enough."

Phil stared at her so intently, Delphine felt her insides melt. What on earth had she been thinking, trying to sneak another kiss? He loved another; he had professed as much. But for all her good intentions, Delphine couldn't let him go. "Must be your contact," she said, straightening, trying desperately to return to a normal state. "The man who wants to help the Americans."

Phil tucked in his shirt and checked his watch. "Ten o'clock. I believe you're right." Toward the hallway, he shouted, "Send him in, Mathurin."

Footsteps sounded on the stairs and Delphine watched the door, anxious to learn which resident of St. Malo lived a secret life of American co-patriot. The figure who finally emerged was the one person she never would have expected. This patriot was also the last person Delphine wished to see gracing the decks of La Belle Amie.

"*Bonjour* Delphine," Marie said, breezing into the cabin. "I'd say we're even now as far as delivering surprises."

For the second time in twenty-four hours, Phil stood speechless. Each time he opened his mouth, words refused to come. Finally, he resorted to courtesies. "Have a seat?"

Marie offered her most gallant smile and descended upon the only chair in the cabin like a queen. Even on a ship in the smelly St. Malo harbor, the woman had grace.

"I think you know why I'm here," she said to Phil. "I believe we have business to discuss."

Phil pulled a hand through the hairs lingering around his forehead. "The flag...?"

"The green flag you have at the bow of your ship, the marker." Marie straightened her skirts. "I have been waiting for it for two weeks now. What a nice surprise that you are the one to be my transport." With a coquettish smile performed for both their eyes, she added, "You could have told me this last night. But then we had other things on our minds."

Delphine couldn't help herself; she gasped as a rush of air filled her lungs. Marie sent her a challenging glance, then quickly dismissed her. All her focus remained on Phil. "May we speak in private, Philibert?"

Phil shifted uncomfortably, but Delphine knew what was coming. "Delphine, why don't you get us some coffee."

Coffee! He lied to her about his evening, said he enjoyed her kisses, even considered stealing another, until Madame Perfection floated into the cabin. Now, she was relegated to making coffee while they, no doubt, would discuss business.

Delphine tried desperately to contain her anger, not wanting Marie to have the satisfaction of viewing her discomfort, but in her nonchalant stroll to the door she gave Phil a good shove. She closed the door a bit too harshly, then stormed down the hold to the galley.

"What's bothering you?" Mathurin asked as she entered the makeshift kitchen.

Delphine couldn't speak, could only grind her teeth and expel her frustrations through a harsh groan. She wanted to smash something. Better yet, wipe that smug look off Marie's face or punch Phil was allowing her to think he still cared.

"Sit down Delphine," Mathurin said in a soft voice.

"I can't." She began pacing the tiny area they used to cook their meals. "That's the woman Phil spent the night with. She's the reason he was so late coming back. And he had the nerve to say he was with a brother. A brother!"

"The Captain? Spent the night with that well-dressed woman? She looks like nobility."

Delphine breathed deeply and prayed some of the anger would leave her body when she exhaled. Her heart pounded so loudly she swore she could hear it. "She's Marie Labarthe."

With this news, Mathurin sat down. "*The* Marie Labarthe?"

Delphine nodded and began pacing again. How would she ever compete against a legend?

"*Mon dieu.*"

The fury unabated, Delphine felt her temple burn. She needed to regain composure, but felt helpless to do so. Still pacing the room, she felt a tug on her hand. "Sit down, *chèr.*" Mathurin stood and gave her his own. "I'll make some coffee."

Delphine exhaled and fell into the chair. "I've known her for a year. All this time I've never really seen..."

Mathurin assembled the coffee pot and began grinding the beans. "Seen what, *'tit monde?*"

Delphine sighed, thinking back to that day in her grandmother's library, when she promised not to emulate Marie. "What my grandmother saw."

Mathurin placed cups on to the table in front of her. "Which was...?"

"Nothing really." It was hard to explain, hard to pinpoint. "That something wasn't right with that woman. Something more felt than easily explained. But I felt it last night. And I felt it today."

The older Acadian put a sugar bowl out and Delphine immediately dipped a finger into the sweet granules. Like he had in years past, Mathurin tapped the top of her hand in protest. "I haven't had sugar in a long time," she complained.

"Doesn't matter," he said with a sparkle in his eyes. "Manners is manners."

Suddenly, Delphine began to relax, feeling like a child again, free to speak her mind and be pampered by a host of men so dear to her. When Mathurin sat before her, she told him all about the past year, how Marie had instructed her and introduced her to society, the promises she had made to her grandmother, the proposals she had received from Charles and others. At this last piece of news, Mathurin's eyes lit up. "You take any of these proposals?"

The old pain gripped her heart as she thought of the only man she would ever love, the man who stood captivated in the other room by St. Malo's personal goddess. "I'll never love anyone else."

Mathurin took both her hands and squeezed. "She doesn't hold a candle to you."

God knew he meant well, but Delphine cringed at the words. She groaned and dropped her head upon her chest.

"What did I say?"

She raised one of his weather-worn hands to her cheek and felt her curls fall loose upon her forehead. One prime example of how inferior she was to the other Countess. "I appreciate the thought, Mathurin, but I've been told this before. How can I possible be better than the best? I've never seen the woman when she wasn't immaculately dressed, every tendril in place, every nail perfectly buffed and even. When Marie walks into a room, every head turns. Men have been known to wait outside her window hoping for a glance. Her feet, tiny, graceful..."

Mathurin put up a hand. "Beauty isn't nails and tiny feet, Delphine."

She believed that, she truly did, but she wasn't the one sitting in Phil's cabin at present, his eyes glued in reverence. Nor was she the one he had spent the evening with, made love to. Then there was that one, indisputable fact. "He loves her," she whispered, tears threatening to consume her.

Mathurin stood and poured her a cup of fresh coffee, dumping two spoonfuls of sugar inside the way she liked it. "If he loves this Marie so much, tell me this. Why has he been so tormented since you left New Orleans?"

Delphine stirred her coffee, watching the dark liquid churn like a waterspout. "Because I threw myself at him one night. I kissed him on the boat the night of Gabrielle's birthday party."

Joining her at the table with his own coffee, Mathurin grinned knowingly. "That explains everything."

Several moments passed and still Mathurin didn't venture further. "Explains what?"

Mathurin shrugged. "What difference does it make if he loves Marie like you say?"

Curiosity was killing her. She was never one to let things pass. "Mathurin, tell me."

He placed his coffee down and folded his hands on the table the way he always did before a lecture. "He's been working us real hard this past year, Phiney. Can't get out of New Orleans fast enough. Then, when we make the Caribbean and pull in our load, he rushes us back to Louisiana. Says it all on account of Governor Galvez, but we know better, know something's up between you two, we know it in our gut. Because this last time, as soon as we hit New Orleans and he finds out you're still not home, he's ready to weigh anchor. Only now, we're headed for France. Didn't even bother bringing a load with him. If we don't get a sponsor heading west, we might run out of provisions by Havana."

This wasn't like Phil, to sail anywhere without a full hold. The man was notorious for making a hefty profit. "Why didn't he take on merchandise before he left? Sugar, for instance?"

Mathurin stirred his coffee and smiled smugly. "Why indeed?"

Feeling more confident, Delphine gave Mathurin a hug, then gathered up the cups and the coffee pot and placed them on a tray. She headed toward the great cabin, pausing at the door to knock.

"I hope that's coffee," Marie called out.

Delphine bit the inside of her cheek to fight back the urge to pour the freshly brewed liquid on Marie's coiffure.

Instead, she entered the cabin and greeted them both with a smile.

"So, that's settled," Phil said from his place by the window. "We'll meet tonight and make arrangements."

Delphine dropped the tray roughly on to the desk, causing some of the coffee to spill. "Careful, dear," Marie said softly. When Delphine met her eyes, she could have sworn they offered a challenge. One Delphine eagerly accepted.

"Phil," Delphine said, "may I have a word with Marie?"

"Certainly." He poured himself a cup and headed for the door. Before he left the cabin, he hesitated, glancing back at Delphine.

"We won't be but a minute," she assured him.

When the door clicked shut, Delphine sat down upon the corner of the bed so the two women faced each other. "Marie, I want to apologize. This must appear quite puzzling, but keeping Phil a secret from you isn't what it seems."

"Of course, it is, my dear." She picked imaginary lint from her skirt. "You're in love with him."

Ignoring the remark, Delphine forged ahead. "I thought it best not to mention, considering the history between you. I never dreamed that you two would ever meet again."

At this, Marie looked up and her eyes held anything but friendship. "You *hoped* we would never meet again."

"You're wrong. I may care for Phil, but I only want what's best. His happiness means everything to me."

The smugness returned. "Then you will not stand in our way? You will stop this foolishness and let us be happy together? You see, I plan on making the voyage with him, Delphine. And I don't want your silly jealous antics coming between us."

The knowledge hit her like a hurricane in August. "You're coming with us to Louisiana?"

Marie's chin tilted upward. "He loves me, why shouldn't we be together?"

Delphine attempted to swallow, hoping to dislodge the lump in the throat. While her mind scrambled for something to say, Marie rose and loomed over her by the bedside.

"Don't get in my way, Delphine," she said menacingly. "I always play to win and I won't abide by any chit trying to steal my lover. Do I make myself clear?"

At this, Delphine smiled, almost laughed. Was delicate Marie Labarthe threatening her? Delphine slowly stood, her height allowing her to look down upon her nemesis. Marie stepped back slightly, but held her ground.

"I appreciate all you have done for me, Marie. Your friendship and guidance has made my year in St. Malo that much easier and I am indebted to you for that."

Marie's countenance shifted slightly, as if Delphine was about to acquiesce. She opened her mouth to retort, but Delphine continued, each word spoken slowly and succinctly for emphasis, her gaze boring into hers. "But you're on my ship now, Countess. No one threatens me on *La Belle Amie*. Do I make myself clear?"

To her credit, Marie didn't vacillate, but it was clear she got the message. Delphine marched from the cabin and headed up the stairs to the deck, anxious to rid herself of the suffocating company. When she reached the top, breathing in the fresh sea air and feeling confident for the first time that morning, she found Mathurin, still holding his precious cup of coffee. He smiled, then moved to the quarterdeck where Sebastien and Vincent were working. As he passed, he whispered in her ear, "That a girl, Phiney."

She might have felt the conqueror, had not Marie appeared on deck and required Phil's assistance to shore and her waiting carriage. Before she lifted her skirts and entered the coach, Marie wound her arms about Phil's neck and kissed him for all the world and Delphine to see.

Whatever wind had propelled her to confront Marie, it had deserted her sails. It would be a long voyage to Louisiana. And she doubted she would arrive the victor.

# CHAPTER SEVEN

DELPHINE TURNED FROM THE ROMANTIC scene and sat at the bow of the ship, the place where the boat's seams met in a steeple while the red hair of the female figurehead peeked over the railing. When Delphine was a child, spending hours at that very spot, Jean claimed the wooden maiden was a mermaid he captured off the coast of Barbados. Later, the red-haired goddess was renamed Gabrielle when his new bride became a permanent member of the ship's crew.

The blood still pounding in her veins, Delphine wondered what Gabrielle would think of her jealous actions that morning, of her angry tirade. Her stepmother and she were much alike, yet Gabrielle owned an even temperament, a more graceful air and steady mind when confronting adversity. When it came to passions and the rush to justice, Delphine more closely resembled Phil with his immediate rage. They both seemed to suffer from an endless attempt to manage their fitful emotions.

Then there was her grandmother, the woman who spent hours trying to shape Delphine into a presentable countess, despite her ill health. How would she judge her angry, irrational behavior?

Delphine had to regain her composure, had to control her outbursts if she was to sail to the New World with Marie on board. But deep down she knew it was going to be a long, horrific voyage.

Two boots appeared at her side, but Delphine refused to look at him. She had to first tame the fiery beating of her heart, to refrain from committing further embarrassment to herself. She couldn't let Phil see her angry nor view her heartache. Delphine raised her chin the same time she straightened her spine.

"It's not what you think."

Delphine ignored Phil's plea and stared off into the harbor.

"Delphine, I had no idea."

Breathe, she commanded herself. Stop acting like a spurned lover. Phil loves Marie and she wants him back and that is the end of this story.

She almost believed it, almost uttered the blessing that she wished them both happiness, but as Delphine raised her eyes to his, Marie's stinging words came rushing back and her vow to remain unemotional disintegrated. "You can't marry her."

To her surprise, Phil laughed, then turned his eyes into the late morning sun and squinted. "Who said anything about marriage?"

Now, Delphine was thoroughly confused. Didn't everything lead to marriage? "Then what are you two planning?"

Phil squatted down, rubbing his head in the process. When the sun met his eyes once more, he grimaced.

"Pirate's Rule Number Five," Delphine whispered, pushing the loose tendrils of hair flitting across his forehead. "Avoid too much spirits. It fogs the brain."

The corner of Phil's lips curled up as his eyes met hers, closer now and gleaming in the light. God, but the man still managed to capture her heart with a simple smile. In an instant, Delphine knew she couldn't bear watching him exchange kisses with Marie over a two-month voyage, couldn't fathom them marrying in her presence. In an instant, she knew their friendship was over should the courtship continue, and a profound sadness filled her heart.

Suddenly, all the fury and rage beating in her chest turned to lead and Delphine had trouble letting a breath escape. Phil seemed to notice her discomfort, taking her hand in his and rubbing a thumb over her knuckles.

"The plan is to transport guns to Louisiana," he said seriously. "Nothing more."

"Transport guns along with Marie."

Phil sighed. "She's offering to pay a good deal of money, which we need. Plus, she insists on making the trip with her cargo."

Delphine fought the urge to smirk. "She wants to be with you. She said so in the cabin." Delphine should have let it go at that, should have kept quiet for fear of being perceived as a jealous lover, but Phil's precious heart was at stake. "Marie said she wins every game she plays. She threatened me if I got in the way."

Phil's eyes grew dark, but unreadable. "Delphine…"

"What you plan to do with Marie is your own business," Delphine stubbornly continued. "I won't get in the way. But as a friend, I must warn you, she's not to be trusted."

A profound silence followed in her rush of words and as Delphine watched a lone hair dance before Phil's eyes, she heard the eleven a.m. call to Mass at the cathedral on the other side of town.

Finally, Phil spoke, his tone cold and unnerving. "Warning received."

At this, Phil stood and attempted to stretch out the kinks from a night of drinking and little sleep, groaning as he did so. When he glanced down and noticed Delphine watching, he smiled and held out his hand. "I'm not the man I used to be."

Delphine accepted his hand, always amazed that despite her long fingers and broad palms, Phil's hands always swallowed hers. As he raised her to a standing position, Delphine noticed the dark circles under his eyes, and something else.

Confusion? Did he still love Marie? Was he happy at the turn of events or was he saddened to be cast back into the fire of heartache?

Delphine squeezed his hand. "You're ever bit the man you used to be. You're my hero."

When Phil leaned forward, Delphine swore he would kiss her right there on deck before the residents of St. Malo and the deckhands. As much as she wanted him to, she couldn't risk her reputation the way Marie scandalously had at her carriage. Delphine was about to remind Phil of her duties to her new title when his lips met her forehead instead. They lingered as long as proper society allowed, given their friendship, then he released her and headed toward the opposite side of the ship.

"Are you coming?" Phil asked her over his shoulder.

"Where to?" Delphine answered, but she followed him all the same.

"We have business to attend to."

He paused at the gangplank, shouting orders to Mathurin who acknowledged them with a salute of his coffee cup. Then, Phil moved aside, waiting for Delphine to walk ahead. Just for spite, before Delphine's foot touched the gangplank, Phil asked, "Need a hand, Countess?"

One hand on the railing, one foot headed toward shore, Delphine turned and gave him a scathing look, one she was want to bestow upon him as a child when he teased. "I believe you have me confused with someone else, captain."

She tossed back her head and bounded down the gangplank, but Phil's words followed her to the dock. "No comparison."

No comparison indeed, Phil thought watching Delphine effortlessly descend the ship, her posture perfect, her head held high. He had sailed halfway across the world and had yet to find a woman the match of his Phiney.

She paused on the dock and looked back at him skeptically. He knew what she was thinking and damned if he had an answer. What on earth had possessed Marie to kiss him in public? Was it only a claim of female territory, a chance at one-upmanship, as Delphine had suggested? Or was Marie serious in her declarations of love?

Doubtful, Phil thought. More than likely, Delphine was correct in her assessment that something wasn't right with Marie, that the Countess couldn't be trusted. But even though his rational mind agreed, Marie's kisses lingered in his mind. A tiny flame in the deep recesses of his heart, despite his better judgment, made him hope Marie still loved him.

Delphine placed her hands on her hips and frowned, either impatient to get back home or busy reading his thoughts. He was a fool to even think of Marie and her sensuous lips, but that label had been branded upon him years ago. Now, he had two countesses to consider. Of all the dangerous situations he had thrown himself into within the last ten years, this was by far the most treacherous.

Shaking the images from his head and forcing himself to concentrate on matters at hand, Phil descended the ship and took Delphine's elbow, leading her toward town.

"Where are we going? Your brother's house?"

He glanced over and realized Delphine suspected a lie considering the sarcastic tone of her voice. She was in for more than one surprise that morning. "Yes, my brother's house."

"Alain Bertrand. I must hand it to you, Phil, you are more clever than I thought, dreaming up such an impressive name on the spot."

Phil tightened his grip on her elbow as they entered the crowded street facing the harbor, a lane filled with crates and cargo and men in various dress conducting business. "It really wasn't so hard, being that I was at his christening."

Delphine attempted a rebuttal but Phil suddenly realized he was escorting the current Countess Delaronde through the harried streets of St. Malo by foot. He whistled to a driver standing beside a carriage and called him over.

"Where are we going?" Delphine asked again as Phil opened the door and motioned her inside.

Phil gave the man instructions and joined Delphine, pulling the door shut and falling against the seat as the carriage took off in a trot. "I told you, my brother's house."

Her eyes never softened and Delphine's countenance remained stoic. She pulled on her gloves, clasping the pearl buttons, and for a moment Phil wanted to grab each hand and plant kisses at her wrists, still tanned slightly despite her year behind doors.

"What is this business you speak of?" she asked.

Phil tore his gaze from her elegant fingers and other enticing aspects of her figure that had developed nicely over the past year and watched the harbor disappear from view. "The Acadians. There is a group of twenty-two people in St. Malo who were sent to English prisons after being exiled from their homes in Nova Scotia. The French interceded on their behalf and brought them here, but have done nothing more for them except offer six sols per person of charity and…

"Empty promises," Delphine finished.

Phil looked back and smiled. So, his socialite hadn't been as preoccupied with society as he thought.

"There have been efforts to help establish them on estates in the region," Phil continued. "But Galvez is hoping I can convince them to come to Louisiana instead."

Delphine straightened out her skirt, smoothing out the black cotton. "There are hundreds here, Phil. Not just twenty-two."

"Hundreds?"

"They came over a few years ago from England, aboard cramped ships where many of them succumbed to small pox." Delphine looked up, pain reflected in the depths of her black eyes. Like her father, the plight of the Acadians was personal, given that half her new family in Louisiana suffered through *le grand dérangement* twenty-four years before. Twenty-four years and still thousands lingered in exile.

"They've had little assistance from the King except for being placed on the dol," Delphine continued. "As for establishing them on estates, these Acadians owned their own farms in Canada and do not wish to become subjects to France's feudal system. They helped carve a nation out of the wilderness, lost their homes and loved ones when the English took over and now France wishes to thank them for their troubles by making them peasants."

Pride rushed through him listening to Delphine continue her passionate speech. How could he have imagined she would change and become an uncaring member of the leisure class? He was so enraptured watching her animated argument, Phil failed to realize they had arrived at Alain's house. Delphine, too, didn't stop talking until the coachman opened the door.

Phil hoped from the carriage, then reached for Delphine's hand and helped her to the pavement. At the same time, Alain opened the front door and reached their side immediately, then pulled Phil into a massive embrace.

"I was beginning to wonder if it had all been a dream," Alain said, when he released his brother.

"A nightmare is more like it," Phil said, gripping Alain's upper arms affectionately. "Your scandalous brother returns from the dead."

Alain noticed Delphine and paled. Then he bowed politely. "Countess Delaronde."

"Alain, I'd like you to meet Delphine." Phil turned to Delphine who looked equally shocked. "Delphine, this is my brother, Alain Bertrand."

"It is an honor, Countess," Alain uttered, his head bowed

in reference.

Delphine recovered well, her eyes glued to the blond head bowing before her. "Please, Monsieur Bertrand, call me Delphine."

Alain finally looked up, but his eyes darted. "No, Countess, I could not do that."

"Why not?" Phil asked. "I do."

Alain sent Phil a frown, a combination of distress and censure. Titles and class could be ignored in Louisiana, but never on the soil of the Mother Country.

Delphine smiled warmly and took Alain's elbow. "It's only a title, Monsieur, one I never imagined holding until this year. I was raised onboard ship with your brother, so we are almost family, *n'est ce-pas?*"

"But I tend your stables, Countess," he stammered.

Delphine's eyes lit up with the recognition. "Of course, I knew I had met you before. You're the dear man who tended to my lame horse last month."

"I trust he is well."

"Very well, thanks to you, Monsieur."

They walked into Alain's home, arm in arm, chatting about carriages and the price of stallions, her brother the epitome of politeness. At the threshold, Delphine glanced back at Phil with a puzzled expression.

"What?" he asked, although he hated to hear the question.

"You're not at all like your brother," she answered with a smug smile, and Phil got the implication immediately.

Virginie greeted the threesome in the hallway, bowing before Delphine like royalty. When Delphine looked over her shoulder at Phil with a pleading expression, he returned the smug smile, charging into the living room to find his favorite nephew.

Instead, Lawrence found him. He felt two small arms encircle his legs, followed by childish laughter that seemed to emanate all the way from the boy's toes. "Gotcha, pirate,"

Lawrence said with glee. "You're my prisoner, now."

With one quick movement, Phil grabbed Lawrence and flipped him upside down, then shook him repeatedly until the boy squealed with laughter.

"Put that child down," Delphine admonished him. "Chances are he just had breakfast."

Virginie stifled a smile, her eyes shifting among them as if uncomfortable resting on such an honored guest. "We were getting ready to sit down for lunch," she practically whispered.

"Dear God," Phil said. "Are we that late?"

Virginie took Lawrence and righted him, then delivered him back to earth. "Well, you and your brother were out fairly late last evening."

"More likely this morning," Alain said with a blush.

"But come," Virginie said, opening the door to the kitchen. "Please join us."

They all waited for the Countess to walk through, but Delphine kneeled before the tyke and offered her hand. "What is your name, sir?"

"Lawrence," the boy said as he gingerly accepted her hand.

"Please to meet you, Lawrence. My name is Delphine, but you can call me Phiney."

Lawrence shifted from one foot to the other. "That's a silly name."

Virginie paled and Alain grabbed Lawrence and pulled the boy behind him. "My apologies, Countess. Lawrence is a bit outspoken and impertinent."

Delphine rose, but managed to reach behind Alain and tousle the boy's hair. "I was much the same way as a child. Besides, it's a Bertrand trait, is it not?"

Phil thought of himself at that age and his heart constricted. "For your sake, Alain, I pray he takes after you."

"Doubtful," Alain said. "More than likely he will follow in your footsteps. Or Francois's. He's enamored with the sea."

"Who's Francois?" Delphine asked, but Virginie ushered her into the kitchen where an elaborate array of food stretched before them.

"My apologies again, Countess," Alain said. "Had we known we were entertaining such an esteemed guest, we would have prepared something more appropriate."

Delphine let her fingers slide along the table as she gazed at all the specialty foods, simple but hearty dishes she had probably not enjoyed since leaving the colony. Phil sensed what she was feeling. The same thoughts he had had about family — or the lack of — the night before.

"This is lovely," Delphine said. "I couldn't have asked for a more delightful repose. I'm truly honored.

"But," she continued, raising her head stubbornly. "I will not eat a bite until you call me Delphine."

Alain and Virginie exchanged uncomfortable glances, clearly nervous at speaking to a Countess on such a casual basis. Phil thought to come to her aid, to argue that Delphine was as much a part of his family as Alain, but he never got the chance.

"Perhaps this will help." Delphine placed a foot on to a chair and lifted her skirt to the top of her boot. There, tucked inside, was a dagger, the red handle peeking out the top.

"Hooray," Lawrence cried. "She's a pirate too!"

They all laughed at the reference, the gesture breaking the tension between them, then settled down to dinner. By the time Virginie brought out dessert, the word Countess was never mentioned again.


"So where is Francois?" Phil asked as he sipped his coffee.

After three courses of food consisting of a freshly killed chicken, artichokes from Virginie's garden, paté and fresh bread, followed by fresh fruit for dessert, the group moved to the courtyard for coffee. Delphine hadn't felt so comfortable in months, relishing the sweet nature of Phil's brother and wife and their adventurous child. Although life with her grandmother was a time she would cherish forever, she missed the camaraderie of a large family, missed the laughter of Gabrielle and Jean's children, of the endless cousins, children of Gabrielle's two sisters, Rose and Emilie. More than anything, she missed being simply Delphine.

"He said he would be here for lunch," Alain answered, "but Francois is not known for his punctuality."

Delphine placed her cup on to the table in front of her. "Who is Francois?" she asked for the second time that day, but again, received no answer.

"Uncle Francois," Lawrence offered as he played with imaginary friends among the foliage.

Delphine looked at Phil. "Another brother?"

"Not exactly," Alain said, placing his own cup down and rising. "Delphine, I'd like you to meet our cousin, Francois Bertrand."

Before Delphine turned and met the eyes of the dark Acadian standing behind her, she knew exactly who Francois was. She didn't comprehend how or why Phil's twin had turned up in St. Malo as an Acadian refugee, but at least one mystery had been solved.

Francois Bertrand, still dressed in threadbare wool and ragged shoes, bowed politely before her. "Countess," he said, his eyes twinkling as they had that night at the harbor. "A pleasure to meet you again."

"The pleasure is all mine, monsieur," Delphine countered, offering her hand, which Francois discreetly kissed. "I never thanked you properly for escorting me home that evening."

At this piece of news, Phil rose, his imposing height bearing down upon the two of them. "You've met before?"

His possessiveness almost made Delphine laugh; he had always been that way. She doubted he was jealous, but she thought she'd had some fun. "Now, really, Phil, do you honestly think your twin could walk the streets of St. Malo and I wouldn't find him?"

Phil crossed his arms and gave his cousin a scrutinizing glance. "How did you two meet?"

Francois smiled slyly, no doubt having as much fun as she. This Acadian was a charmer, Delphine assessed, and a handsome one at that. "That will be our secret," the debonair man said with a wink to Delphine. "A secret between the Countess and me."

Phil's eyes narrowed and he was about to retort when Alain cleared his throat. "We have business to discuss, gentlemen, do we not?"

Francois's eyes remained intent upon Delphine's face, as if she was the business he wished to discuss. "My cousin, Countess, wishes for me to return to Louisiana with you. I was opposed to the idea when he approached me last night, but in the light of day I may change my mind."

Delphine ignored his flirtations, using the opportunity to press the point. "I do hope you do, monsieur. You will find Louisiana more hospitable than France has been, a haven for you and others to start anew. And with the current politics, Governor Galvez will be pleased to have more Catholic residents willing to stand against the English should they breach their boundaries."

At this news, Lawrence picked up a tree branch and began running circles around the group. "I'll fight the English. I'll help you keep them away."

But Francois didn't take news of the English as lightly. The light disappeared from his eyes as he sat down and Virginie handed him a cup of coffee. "Tell me, cousin," he said, turning toward Phil. "Are you transporting other goods to Louisiana besides our small group?"

Phil's gaze shifted among Delphine and his brother, but

he refused to speak the words aloud. He sat down and leaned forward as if the courtyard walls had ears. "Yes. But I'm not at liberty to say what those goods are."

"Do you realize the English are attacking ships leaving this city, confiscating cargo on ships heading to the colonies as they round the tip of Britain?"

"I had heard that. Now that France has sided with the Americans and is at war again with England, it is to be expected." Francois paused, gathering his thoughts. "There is word among the harbor that a spy has been betraying our ships to the English. Being that I spend most of my days near the sea, I hear a lot of things."

"Like what?" Alain asked.

"There are speculations," Francois answered. "Some claim a man by the name of Charles Armand is responsible for the recent raids on French ships."

Delphine nearly choked on her coffee. "Charles Armand? That's impossible."

Phil eyed her curiously. "You know this man too?"

"He's a good friend," Delphine assured him. "Lives upriver from New Orleans, travels to St. Malo on business quite often. In fact, he knows…"

He knows too much, Delphine suddenly thought.

Phil leaned forward some more, his eyes narrowing. "What does he know, Delphine?"

"No, he can't be a spy," Delphine said more to convince herself than the others. "Not dear Charles. But he does know that Jean is my father."

"Who's Jean?" Francois asked.

"That's a secret between the Countess and me," Phil said, sending Francois a harsh glare. Perhaps Phil was jealous after all, Delphine thought, her heart skipping at the idea. A little jealousy could work wonders, even among cousins. If she happened to be that sort of woman, she reminded herself as the image of her grandmother came to mind.

"I must inform you, Charles Armand asked to return

home with us," Delphine told the men, bringing the attention back to the problems at hand. "He approached me last night, said he would pay handsomely for the trip."

"That doesn't sound wise," Francois said. "Refuse him."

"I'm afraid I have to agree," Alain offered. "I've heard the man is extremely secretive and comes and goes through the port often. He fits the description."

"No," Delphine insisted. She couldn't believe Charles capable of such actions, even if he did know every man who traveled the Mississippi. "If he was a spy, which I'm sure he is not, why would he ask to join us? Wouldn't he inform the English and let them charge our ship? Why would he wish to put himself in danger by being on board?"

"Delphine has a point," Alain said. "Or perhaps Charles will jump ship at that point, after he signals the English."

To everyone's surprise, Phil smiled broadly and shook his head. "You're all forgetting an important element here. No one boards *La Belle Amie* without my say and never against my will. There will be no English taking anything."

Francois put his coffee down and grew stern. He was clearly unconvinced. "That's all fine and good, cousin, but you're asking me to risk the lives of twenty-two people and the Countess on the basis of your boast."

Phil rested his elbows on his knees and his eyes drew dark. "No one boards *La Belle Amie*," he said so sternly Delphine almost shivered. "No one."

Nodding toward Delphine, he added, "And as for the Countess, I'm perfectly capable of taking care of her."

Again, Alain cleared his throat to ease the tension building between the two men. "Phil, I believe you wish to set sail at the earliest date?"

"As soon as Delphine has made arrangements to her estate," he said, his voice still carrying an edge.

"Consider it done," she answered, hoping to steer the conversation back to cordial terms. "My cousin has agreed to take over the country estate and I have hired a manager to address my financial concerns in town."

"Your cousin?" Phil asked. "I thought you were the only one."

A very distant cousin, Delphine thought, remembering the dear, plump man who had attended the funeral with his army of children. He was a Magon, descended from her grandmother's first cousin, and the only living relative apart from Delphine, but not on the Delaronde side and unable to inherit the title. She liked Pierre Magon instantly, found his laughter warm and friendly and his loving family a welcome relief from the grief assuaging her heart during those awful days following her grandmother's death. When she had presented him with the key to the chateau, she thought the poor man would collapse on the spot. A farmer of limited means, the chateau provided him with plenty of room for his eleven children and the opportunity to rest for the first time in his middle-aged life.

"I assure you, my cousin doesn't resemble me as yours resembles you," Delphine said. "But I like him just as much."

Francois's eyes twinkled again as his face erupted into a deep smile, a bit too familiar for polite company. At the same time, Phil frowned, clearly displeased with Francois's demonstrations.

Yes, the twin was extremely charming, Delphine thought, and quite attentive. Then there was Charles, her dear, equally attentive friend who might well be an English spy. Suddenly, the dreadful, two-month journey in which she would have to endure a courtship between Phil and Marie seemed a lot more interesting. Suddenly, Delphine had a mystery to unravel and Phil's family to inhabit her townhouse.

Glancing at Phil and watching his gaze bore into hers with concern gave her hope. Things were beginning to look up.

# CHAPTER EIGHT

THE WEEK FLEW BY IN a haze for Delphine, filled with trips back and forth from *La Belle Amie* and endless signing of documents and concluding affairs. The manager Delphine had hired, by recommendation of her grandmother, turned out to be a godsend, finalizing her probate in a timely manner and arranging her finances. All the servants would continue their employment with generous bonuses to take care of Alain and his family. Convincing the Bertrands to take charge of her household had been a more difficult endeavor, but when Delphine argued that she needed someone to manage her stables in her absence, Alain acquiesced. Little did Alain realize that when he moved into the spacious townhouse, she had instructed the servants to treat them like royalty. Their lives were about to become easier, especially with a new babe on the way.

Etienne, the butler, vowed to stay on in case Delphine returned to St. Malo. His eyes glistened in the candlelight with unshed tears when she told him the news of her departure and handed him personal items of her grandmother that she wished for him to have. Even though Delphine had no intention of returning to France, it was comforting to know that Etienne would be there, helping Alain manage the property, carrying on her grandmother's legacy.

Funny, she thought glancing around the library now shy of a few books, she would miss the place, cold rooms, tight corsets and all. She would miss the friendships she had established, miss the fine wines and rich desserts, even miss those damned social engagements with her hair arranged so high it nearly scraped the ceiling. Most of all, she would miss the conversations she had had in that very room, discussions about books and adventures that she would remember for the rest of her life.

Delphine took one last look around, then cast her eyes skyward and silently thanked Sandrine Magon, Countess Delaronde, for one of the finest years of her life. She then thanked God for the pleasure of knowing such a woman.

Charles Armand peeked into the library. "Ready, my dear?"

Delphine wiped her eyes and nodded, then followed Charles into the hallway where the servants were lined up as they had been on the day of her arrival.

"I feel like George Washington, addressing my troops," Delphine said, recalling the details of the Continental Army in that week's newspaper. "I want to thank you all for making my visit so pleasant. I appreciate all you have done for my grandmother and me."

Turning toward Etienne, standing proudly despite his tears, she threw her arms around his neck and kissed his cheek. "I will miss you," she whispered, then hurried out the door and into the waiting carriage.

Delphine felt the buggy tip when Charles entered, but she comprehended little else as the tears blurred her world. What was wrong with her? She was going home, should be happy at the prospect, yet sobs consumed her.

Charles took her hand and placed a handkerchief there. Then he placed an arm about her shoulders and held her close. Despite Phil and Francois's suspicions, Charles couldn't be guilty of treason. Could he?

Delphine managed to fight back the tears. She blew her

nose soundly and laughed when she realized she was heading back to a place where no one cared if she did.

"What's so funny?" Charles asked, brushing the hair from her face.

"Nothing, really. I was thinking what my grandmother would have said to that."

"Doubtful she would have approved."

He was smiling at her, so comfortable in her presence, so loving and caring. And yet, for all she knew, Charles Armand could be murdering her countrymen as they headed for home.

Shaking off the shiver that suddenly ran through her, Delphine had to ask. "Charles, how do you stand on France's position with the Americans?"

His eyes dimmed and his countenance grew stern. She had touched a nerve somehow. "Why do you ask?" he finally said.

"I'm curious, considering that we're now heading back."

Charles straightened his sleeves and frowned, clearly uncomfortable with the conversation. "I'm a son of Louisiana and therefore a son of France. I stand beside her. Always."

It wasn't the answer she was hoping for, but Delphine knew more information was not forthcoming. They rode in silence toward the harbor until finally Delphine couldn't stand the quiet, couldn't bear the chasm that had opened between them.

"I'm sorry you have to share a cabin with Phil," she offered. "It is the main cabin and the finest part of the ship. My father uses it when he captains *La Belle Amie*. The bed was bought for my stepmother and a most comfortable one at that, although I've never slept there myself."

Charles's countenance shifted and the familiar friendly smile emerged. "It makes no difference, Delphine. I'm perfectly content to share a cabin. I would have had to wait a month for the next ship to Louisiana so I am grateful to you and Monsieur Bertrand for any assistance you can give me."

Assistance? Hardly. They were short on cabins due to Marie and her personal maid. Delphine had her own cabin, once she always used when aboard ship, and the Acadians had been relegated to bunks in the massive hold. Still, Phil insisted Charles sail and share his cabin so that he might keep a watchful eye on his suspect. Should Charles betray their actions, Phil would be the first to know and the first to take appropriate action.

Francois and Alain voiced their disapproval of the plan, but Phil was intent to capture the traitor. Knowing that Charles had once asked for Delphine's hand had nothing to do with it, she was sure.

Delphine bit her lower lip and stared out the window, watching the masts of *La Belle Amie* come into view in the darkness of the predawn. She had let that piece of information slip when Marie had visited one night, when the Countess had leaned against Phil and whispered secrets into his ear and made him laugh. As hard as she tried, Delphine couldn't deny an acute desire to gauge the woman's eyes out.

"What are thinking about?" Charles asked. "You're about to draw blood."

Delphine slid a tongue on her lip and found it swollen. "It's going to a fitful journey."

Charles's eyes took on that nervous look once more. "I agree. But what makes you say that?"

The carriage abruptly halted and the coachman jumped down and rushed over to open the door. Delphine thought it best to ignore the question and exit the carriage, but as soon as she descended and stood before the gangplank, Charles captured her elbow and pulled her back.

"Should you ever need me, I am here," he whispered.

Through the corner of her eye, Delphine saw Phil standing at the quarterdeck, clearly in view. When he barked orders to the men, Charles must have made the connection as well, for he bowed forward and gingerly kissed her lips.

She wasn't sure, but it appeared as if all activity ceased aboard ship, or perhaps it felt as if the world stopped moving. Delphine wanted to look, but her eyes were glued to Charles, trying to decipher his intentions.

"We had an understanding that night."

Delphine nodded numbly, but hadn't they agreed to be friends?

"I know you will never love me, Delphine, but don't throw your life away if the person that you do love doesn't love you back. You deserve better than that."

At this, she tried to speak, but Charles cut her off. "As I said before, I consider you a dear friend. If nothing else, we will make good partners."

Charles slid his hand to her elbow and motioned her toward the gangplank. She felt others staring but her mind registered only on Charles's words. "And, if for nothing else, if you need me to make a certain man jealous." Charles paused, bowing before her with a smile. "I am your man, Countess."

*Mon Dieu*, Delphine thought, things were getting more complicated by the hour. She returned the smile and removed her elbow from Charles's grip, then walked on the ship where deckhands and some of the Acadians were preparing the sails, Phil was supervising the action and two small boys were chasing each other through the melee. She felt Phil's eyes on her but she refused to look at him. Instead, she grabbed Lawrence as he ran past and felt a boy of equal weight and size slam into her backside.

"Lawrence, Michel!" Virginie shouted.

Delphine tickled Lawrence for punishment and he giggled, but when she turned to see who the other culprit was, the boy stared in horror. Virginie reached her side and grabbed Lawrence by the arm.

"I'm sorry, Delphine, these two have been incorrigible all morning."

"No harm done," Delphine replied, looking at the shy lad about the same age as Lawrence. "Who is this young fellow?"

She posed the question to the boy, but he backed off, then ran away, Lawrence hot on his heels.

"His name is Michel Fontenot," Virginie explained. "He's one of the orphans."

"I thought there were four and all over the age of twelve. I've never seen or heard of Michel."

Virginie smiled and took her hand, pulling Delphine out of the way of two men loading a chest on to the deck. "He's not part of the group. He was with some of the other Acadians, apparently orphaned recently, keeps wandering the docks looking for his mother."

"Oh, the poor boy," Delphine said, searching for the shy tyke among the deck's crowd, but he was nowhere to be seen.

"Francois found him and they've become friends. He couldn't bear to leave him behind."

"No, of course not." Finally, Delphine spotted the top of curly brown hair behind a skiff on deck. "I will personally see that he's comfortable."

As if he heard her, Michel peeked out from behind the boat and studied her. She offered him a smile but he withdrew, then disappeared once more.

"Where is Francois?" Delphine asked.

"Helping bring your blasted chests on board."

The sparkly-eyed Acadian struggled behind her with the chest Delphine knew contained most of her books. "Let me help," she shouted, but Francois pushed her aside.

"Don't be ridiculous. But what do you have in here, gold?"

"Not gold, Francois, but its equivalent."

"Glad to hear it," he said, sweat pouring down his brow.

"I would have hated thinking I was struggling with petticoats."

Delphine felt useless. She imagined she resembled Marie the day before, standing like a queen upon deck supervising the deckhands bringing aboard her things. "I should do something," she said to Virginie.

"Don't bother. I have already asked twice and Phil said the best thing for the women to do is stand out of the way."

Heat prickled up from Delphine's toes to her nose. Best thing a woman could do? She folded her arms and glanced at Phil, but when he turned and gave her a wink, Delphine's wrath receded. He was as excited as she was to be going home.

"Where's Marie?" Delphine asked.

"Below deck. Phil told her to get out of the way and she gladly obeyed. She didn't appear well. I don't think traveling agrees with her."

Delphine would have laughed had not the thought been absurd. "Virginie, we haven't left port yet."

"Still, she looked green to me."

Images of Marie remaining below deck for the entire voyage came to mind, but Delphine refused to be glad for Marie's discomfort. She had to get past her invidious passions and her desire to make Phil jealous, despite Charles's offer and Francois's continuous flirtations.

"I think I'll go see to her," Delphine told Virginie.

"You're not going to poison her, are you?" she asked with a grin.

"Poison?" As much she envied Marie and disliked her for threatening her that day, Delphine still considered her a friend, was still grateful for the instruction and companionship Marie had offered over the past year. She would stand tall and watch her back, but never inflict harm on the woman. Not if she could help it. "I would never think of such a thing," Delphine said as if offended, placing a hand on her chest and batting her eyelashes.

"I forgot," Virginie said with a laugh. "You prefer the dagger."

"I prefer she wasn't here!" Delphine concluded, then headed for the ladderway leading below deck.

Delphine flattened herself against the wall as men bustled back and forth with supplies, then she knocked at Marie's cabin. At first, there was no answer, but upon the second knock Marie's maid opened the door.

"I was checking on the Countess," Delphine explained. "Is she well?"

The maid hesitated anxiously, no doubt told to send visitors away but helpless to assist her employer.

"Is she ill?" Delphine asked. "I can help."

The maid opened the door wider to allow Delphine entrance. Squeezing into the small cabin, she made out Marie in the darkness, lying on the bed with a wet handkerchief over her eyes.

"She gets seasickness very bad, madame," the maid whispered.

Delphine approached the bed, sat in the chair beside it and took Marie's delicate hand.

"Who's there," Marie asked.

"Your hands are cold, Marie. You should be on deck in the fresh air."

"I should be home in my warm bed."

Made perfect sense to Delphine. For the life of her, she couldn't fathom why Marie would make the journey to such a rugged place as Louisiana. "It's not too late. I'm sure Phil will take good care of your cargo."

Marie slipped the handkerchief from her eyes. "You'd like that, wouldn't you?"

Delphine dropped her hand and began pacing the somewhat spacious cabin that now felt crowded with three tense women. "I don't want to argue, Marie. I want us to be friends."

"You deceived me and you want to be friends?"

"I meant you no harm. I honestly thought I would return to Louisiana and you would never see Phil again."

Marie managed to sit up on an elbow. "You *hoped* he would never see me again."

Delphine decided to be honest. "Yes, I hoped he would never see you again. Can you blame me? My father nursed him from death's door. He was lying in that very bed when I first met him, his entire body covered in…"

"Stop," Marie ordered. "I wasn't responsible for my husband's actions."

"He's my best friend," Delphine continued. "I don't want to see him hurt again."

Marie glared, ready to issue more fighting words, but the ship shifted bringing on cargo, and she fell backwards on the bed with a groan.

"I'll bring you some tea," Delphine offered. "Or coffee. Drink it in small doses, a teaspoon even. Plain bread will help, but again in small doses." When no further sounds came from Marie, Delphine turned to her maid. "Try to coax the Countess above deck. The air gets stale down here and will only make her sicker."

The maid curtsied, and Delphine headed for the door, but Marie rallied once more. "I will recover," she vowed.

Delphine took one more look at the suffering figure on the bed, conscious, at last, of what her grandmother had indicated. Jealousy, competitiveness, vindictiveness. None of it was admirable, especially in a Countess. Suddenly, Marie wasn't the beautiful goddess Delphine had worshiped all those months. Suddenly, she didn't desire to be like her anymore.

"As you wish," Delphine said, then headed back above deck.

The light had improved in the few minutes she was gone, a soft pinkish glow piercing the sky. Before the sun would break the horizon, they would set sail. Delphine's heart lurched. In two months' time, Delphine would be sur-

rounded again by family. She would no longer be required
to wear the latest fashions nor bruise her ribs with suffocating corsets. Delphine closed her eyes and faced the sea,
breathing in its comforting scent. She was finally heading
home.

"It's time," she heard Phil whisper in her ear. When Delphine opened her eyes, she witnessed the same excitement
in his eyes, until he turned and gazed at his family.

Alain and Virginie must have sensed that the time had
come for they approached them solemnly, Virginie biting the inside of her cheek to fight back emotions. Phil
kneeled down to bid his goodbyes to Lawrence first, pulling a sailor's hat from inside his coat and placing it on the
boy's head.

"For me?" Lawrence exclaimed.

"I'll be back one day," Phil said. "And I expect you to be
worthy of that hat."

"I will," the boy said eagerly. "I'll be ready to captain my
own boat by then."

Phil smiled, but it was a weak one. "There are more
important things than sailing into the morning sun." Phil
paused, swallowing hard. "Take care of your family first."

Lawrence nodded, then threw his arms around his uncle.
"When you're old enough, I'll talk your parents into coming to Louisiana," Phil whispered.

"You won't have to talk us into it," Alain said. "We will
come as soon as we're able." Glancing at his wife with love,
he added, "As soon as the baby comes."

Phil straightened, still holding Lawrence's hand. "When
the time is right, you let me know. I will send you the fare.
Or I will retrieve you myself."

Virginie couldn't stand it any longer. The tears poured
down her cheek and she rushed forward to embrace first
Delphine, then Phil. Then she silently took Lawrence's
hand and walked off the boat.

The two brothers stared at one another, Phil pulling

the hair away from his eyes. Then, without a word, they embraced one another, held each other tight, and then Alain patted Phil on the arm and backed away.

"Be careful," he said hoarsely. "Come back to us."

Phil didn't answer, only nodded. To Delphine, Alain added, "It's been a pleasure, Countess, and I thank you for all you've done."

"It has been my greatest honor," Delphine managed to say, despite the lump lodged in her throat.

"Please take care of my big brother," Alain said in a whisper.

Delphine slipped her hand through Phil's arm and leaned her head against his shoulder. "He's in the best of hands."

Alain placed his hat on his head, went to reach for Phil once more, then turned and followed his wife to shore. Phil finally found his voice, although it remained shaky. "Take care of yourself," he shouted at his little brother, who didn't look back but waved his hand. "Take care of that boy. Don't let him grow up to be like…"

Phil faltered, and Delphine felt his body tense.

"Like you?" Delphine finished. "He should be so lucky."

Phil's cheek rested on her forehead and the morning sun sent red streaks across her hair. He reached down and caressed her cheek. "I'm the lucky one," he whispered.

Before Delphine had a chance to digest his words, Phil straightened, regained his haughty self and began shouting orders. "All visitors to shore. Prepare to set sail." Within minutes, the ship pulled away from the dock and headed out to sea, the silent faces of the Bertrand family growing fainter with each breath of wind. Within the hour, St. Malo passed from view.

Delphine spent the morning addressing the needs of the Acadians, helping the eight women settle into their bunks below deck and assisting Mathurin with breakfast. The four children on board refused to settle anywhere. They played on deck and watched the sailors at work or lined the railing searching for dolphins or any type of fish that would rear its head. The nine Acadian men helped scale the ratlines and furl the sails, while Sebastien and Vincent gave directions, then they all took turns enjoying their first meal at sea.

"The fresh bread, sausages and fruit are a gift from Delphine," Mathurin told them repeatedly. "But don't expect more like it."

"This is our third ship voyage and the first a friendly one," Francois reminded him, savoring his second orange. "I'm sure whatever gruel you will serve us will be a luxury compared to what we've experienced."

When Mathurin forced Delphine to sit on the quarterdeck and take her own plate, she finally realized she was back at sea, the waves sighing beneath her feet, the sun basking her forehead. She slid her legs underneath her like she used to sit as a child, then leaned back and devoured her plate. She was extremely hungry, and for the first time in more than a year, it didn't matter how much she consumed.

"Happy?" Phil didn't turn from his place at the wheel but she knew he was smiling.

"Yes, very," she said with a mouthful of sausages. "I shall dance when my feet hit Louisiana mud."

"Has Marie eaten anything?" he asked.

"Doubtful. She was quite green the last time I saw her."

Phil turned then, his eyes questioning.

"I tried to help, but she would have none of it."

"She's a proud woman, Delphine."

"She's a stubborn woman," she said, pointing her fork at him. Heavens, a few hours at sea and her manners were deteriorating. But she didn't care. It was Phil, after all. "You two make a good couple," she mumbled after another large bite.

When he glanced back again, she couldn't decipher if his frown was in regard to her last comment or because she had abandoned the Countess in her hour of need. "I'll check on her shortly," Delphine said with a sigh.

Around noon, Delphine knocked again at Marie's door and insisted she take a turn above deck. Marie again declined, but accepted the plate of food which, to Delphine, was an improvement.

"How come you're not sick?" Marie asked from her bed.

"I never get sick," Delphine answered.

"Everyone gets sick sometime." Marie sat up, glanced at the food, then fell back upon the bed. "Especially at sea."

"I don't get sick," Delphine reiterated. "And never at sea. I suppose I'm lucky in that regard."

"More than you know," Marie mumbled.

Her duty done, Delphine decided to look for Michel. She had given him time to find his peace on ship, as her father used to say, but the lad had to be hungry, if not a bit scared. When she entered the hold and began searching among the crates and chests, Francois tapped her on the shoulder.

"He's fine. I've made sure he ate."

Now, that everyone seemed settled and well fed, Delphine felt useless. Charles had risen from his nap — he and Phil had to take turns using the bed — and began helping Mathurin with dinner. When she entered the galley and attempted to brew coffee, both had shoed her out the door. The Acadian women were napping or tending to their children and Sebastien and Vincent were setting the sails aweather as the wind shifted from the east. Delphine finally planted herself at the railing and stared out into the sunset.

"I'm going to caulk the deck," Phil said to her as he left the wheel and walked past.

"Ah huh," Delphine replied, registering his comment to take a nap but watching the sun play games with the water's surface.

Phil paused at the steps leading below deck. When Delphine looked up, she realized he was waiting for her.

"Coffee?" he asked, like a boy asking for seconds on dessert.

Suddenly, her heart lightened and an enormous smile spread across her face. She had forgotten her duties serving him coffee while he entered the day into the ship's log, but Phil hadn't. How long had it been since they had performed that ritual — a year, two? And he had remembered.

Delphine passed him at the rail, trying hard not to show her excitement, and bounded down the stairs. "Meet you in your cabin."

She practically ran to the galley and quickly put together a tray, ignoring Mathurin's knowing grin. Then she entered the main cabin and found Phil at his usual place, describing the day's events into a massive book with his spectacles perched on his nose. She placed the tray upon the desk to his left and poured him a cup of coffee, black with a pinch of sugar. Phil watched from the corner of his eyes and smiled, but he didn't look up.

"I don't suppose the Countess will do this for you."

The smile disappeared and Delphine kicked herself. Why did she have to mention Marie? Now that she thought of it, what was she doing in Phil's cabin anyway? She was twenty-two, a titled heiress who should be expected her second child as Virginie was, not following around her father's partner who had made it clear he loved another.

As much as she wanted to stay, to talk about the day as they had done for years, Delphine decided it best to leave, best to stop reminding her heart that Phil was as far removed as France would soon be.

Delphine headed for the door, but something caught her skirt. She turned to dislodge the material and found Phil holding the cotton fabric. "Where are you going?"

"I shouldn't be here," Delphine replied.

His eyes darkened and he frowned, but he never released her skirt. "Why not?"

"Because…"

The sun was setting at the bow of the ship, but its final rays cast an orange glow about the cabin, reflecting off Phil's eyes still staring at her with concern, as if afraid she might bolt out the door. And Delphine wanted to. Her mind was traveling places it shouldn't, and she felt in danger of succumbing to his charms.

Phil's hair was loose from its tie and tendrils curled about his neck, making her ache to touch them. His coat was draped upon the chair allowing her to make out his chest through his sweat-stained shirt. One long leg stretched out from the desk, brushing against her, causing her heart to quicken and other feminine spots to react shamelessly. She needed to get out before she did something foolish, before she repeated her embarrassing actions in his cabin that night almost two years before.

Yet, somehow she moved closer. Whether it was Phil pulling her forward and she acting on her own, she didn't know, but in seconds Delphine's hands were on his shoulders and his hand at her waist. Suddenly, he released her skirt and reached for her cheek, then gently pulled her down into a passionate kiss.

It was reminiscent of the night when they had both thrown caution to the wind, only this time Phil didn't start slowly. His hunger was evident, his kiss deep and penetrating from the first. As his tongue circled her lips, inviting her to taste more, Delphine thought to slip into his lap and let nature decide their fate. But everything came to an abrupt halt when a forceful knock came at the door.

Delphine straightened and Phil bolted up from his chair, pulling on his coat self-consciously.

"What is it?" he shouted.

"Captain," Vincent answered. "You're needed on deck immediately."

Before either could ask as to the cause of alarm, Vincent answered all questions.

"The English are on our starboard bow. And they are preparing to attack."

# CHAPTER NINE

T HE ENGLISH FRIGATE APPROACHED FROM several leagues, nearly a spot on the horizon, yet Phil and the crew knew exactly of her intentions. Through his spyglass, Phil spotted the Union Jack flapping at her stern while men scuttled about deck preparing for action, the cannons poised and primed.

He slammed the glass together and handed it to Mathurin. *"Merde."*

"My thoughts exactly," Mathurin answered. "I'd say twenty-four guns."

"Twenty-four cannons?" Francois asked, his voice laced with panic. "How can we ever hope to match a ship of that size?"

There was no other option than to meet the English head-on. They had traveled too far from St. Malo to turn back in time; the hearty frigate would outrun them within hours. *La Belle Amie* never lacked speed, but the English ship far outnumbered them in crew, guns and dimensions.

"Captain," Vincent said from his rear.

"What?" Phil answered, his eyes glued to the English frigate.

"There's another ship gaining on us."

Phil turned to find a ship of equal size bearing down from the stern. He opened his spyglass, but the ship was too far to decipher.

"All men on deck," Phil announced.

Mathurin began shouting the order, then walked to the top of the ladderway and yelled below.

"I want everyone above decks." Phil handed Vincent the glass so that he might better study the ship to their rear. "All women, children, everyone. I want the English to see who we are carrying here."

Francois grabbed his arm. "I told you this would happen. You have put all these people's lives in danger."

"And I told you that no one will be in danger as long as I captain this ship."

Francois backed up, his dark eyes blazing. "You are putting us all at risk because of your damned arrogance?"

What was it about his cousin that made his blood boil, Phil wondered. He flirted with Delphine, he argued with his decisions and challenged his authority. He was too much like family, always critical, never knowing when to keep his mouth shut unlike his crew, who followed orders unconditionally.

"My damned arrogance, Francois, has kept this ship afloat for more than a decade," Phil bit out. "My damned arrogance has not lost a man yet." From the corner of his eye, Phil saw Charles climb the stairs and head toward the quarterdeck. "If you want to blame someone, blame him."

Charles anxiously strode toward the group. "Is it the English?"

"Yes, Charles, it is the English." Phil wanted to throttle the aristocrat, right before he strangled his cousin. "Strange, how you should know this."

Anger, closely guarded and controlled, passed over Charles's features. "We are passing England. Why wouldn't I surmise such a situation?"

With their sails windward, the English frigate would be on them in minutes. The ship astern would be facing the wind as they were and unable to overtake them as quickly, allowing them a chance to fight one ship beside the next, if their luck held. But first, Phil had to clear the deck of all aggravations.

"Sebastien," Phil called out. "Put Monsieur Armand under guard."

"What?" Charles shouted. "Are you mad? I'm not the enemy here."

Quick to conclusions, Phil thought. Too quick. "What made you think that we thought you were?"

"Why else would you guard me?"

Sebastien grabbed Charles's arm and attempted to lead him toward the main mast, but Charles struggled. "You're making a big mistake."

"If you have put anyone on this ship at risk," Francois bellowed to Charles, "I will personally kill you."

Delphine rushed to Phil's side, tugging on his sleeve. "Don't do this. He can't be guilty."

"Just taking precautions, my dear."

"It's not right," she answered, pulling harder.

Phil had had enough of the varied opinions around him, all spoken with personal reasons. Phil's only objective was the safety of his ship and passengers, no matter how right any of it was. He took Charles's arm himself and led him away from his jury of peers.

Charles glanced aside at him, his eyes burning. "It's not me," he whispered.

"It's not you what?" Was the man this stupid? He exposed himself with every word.

When they reached the main mast, Phil released Charles's arm so that Sebastien could tie him up. "Not too tight," Phil said. "We want him well enough for his hanging when we reach Havana."

Charles stood proudly as Sebastien began to wrap the ropes about his waist, his eyes never leaving Phil's. "Trust no one," he said. "Especially those you fancy."

Phil wanted to demand what the hell that meant when the Acadian women and children scattered above deck, their voices anxious and fearful. Delphine helped group them in safe places where they loaded weapons while the men tended the sails and primed the cannons. As in years past, the ship became armed within minutes, although the weaponry was well concealed. Now, they all waited as the frigate bore down upon them.

"Let Charles go," Delphine whispered to Phil as they stood at the railing watching the ship slowly come into focus. "He can't be guilty of this."

"If he's not, then he has nothing to worry about."

"But what will the English think of us with a man tied up at the main mast?"

Phil huffed. "I don't give a damn what the English think."

He felt Delphine's fingers on his sleeve and he remembered all too well how he had lost his senses in the cabin. How had he come to kiss her once again? Would he never think before letting his heart rule his actions?

"Please Phil." She looked up at him, her brown eyes sparkling in the moonlight. Heavens, but he wanted to kiss her again.

"Think with your head, Phiney." He meant the advice for himself as much as for her. "We are at war. We take no chances."

A silence settled among the ship's inhabitants as the English frigate drew close. Phil half-cocked the flintlock in his belt and adjusted the sash holding his sword.

"Where is the Countess?" A lantern swung above Charles's head, casting eerie shadows about his features, but Charles appeared as calm as the sea about them. "Are we not all present and accounted for?"

Phil glanced around the deck and the Countess was nowhere to be found. "She's ill."

"Of that, I have no doubt." Charles glanced toward the ladderway. "But surely, she won't want to miss this."

As if Charles was there to announce her entrance, the Countess appeared, ascending the ladderway like royalty,

wearing one of her finest gowns. Still owning a pale countenance, she nevertheless held her head high and made her
way to Phil's side. "The English are here?"

No one answered as the frigate moved alongside *La Belle
Amie*, the English sailors shouting to reef the sails. There
were fifty men to their two dozen, Phil assessed, but now
that there were broadsides, his smaller ship had an advantage of stealing away if he could sail out of reach of their
cannons in time.

"I speak English," Marie said. "Would you like me to say
something to them?"

"Trust no one," Charles shouted out.

"Put a muzzle on that man," he shouted to Vincent, who
gagged him with his handkerchief.

"Tell them we carry only passengers," Phil said to Marie.
"Tell them we have women and children onboard."

Marie leaned against the railing and spoke to the English
captain. After a long discourse, the Englishman shouted
back.

"He doesn't believe you," she said to Phil. "He wants to
come aboard and inspect your ship."

"Over my dead body," Phil yelled.

Marie paled and grabbed his arm. "We are outnumbered,
Phil. Let him come aboard and look around. They will find
nothing, then we will be on our way."

Was it arrogance, Phil thought, or intuition that something wasn't right here? He never let anyone board *La
Belle Amie* and he certainly wasn't going to start now. But
as he looked at the fearful eyes of the Acadians, he wondered if arrogance would win the day. The weapons for the
Americans were carefully hidden. Even the finest pirates
would be hard pressed to discover them buried inside the
hold. Still, if Charles had indeed betrayed them, the English
would know the guns were on the ship and refuse to leave
until they were uncovered.

"No," Phil commanded. "No one boards my ship."

"They will fight us," Marie whispered. "Don't be a fool."

Phil cared not for being called a fool. He cared less for her tone and the glint in her eyes, a deadly combination that reminded him of another day, when Marie had denied knowing him and allowed her new husband to challenge him to a duel.

"Tell him they will not board my ship." When Marie hesitated, Phil glared, causing her to step back. "Tell him."

Marie finally did as she was told, parlaying instructions to the English while Charles fought against his ropes and gag.

"Someone shut him up," Phil barked, and Sebastien landed a fist across Charles's face. The blow silenced him, but he remained conscious. To his back, Phil heard Delphine gasp.

The English captain yelled instructions back to Marie, who swallowed hard. "They say that you must allow them to board or they will open fire."

"Open fire?" Phil looked at the Englishman, one knee resting on the inner railing, his perfunctory face lighted by the glow of several lanterns. If anyone was arrogant in putting innocent lives at danger, it was he. "Is he mad?"

"He says he does not trust us," Marie added, her voice shaking. "He says if you let him inspect the ship and he finds nothing, he will let us pass."

"I don't trust him, Marie." Phil glanced around at his men, standing on deck, poised for action. "Have you no knowledge of what the English do to confiscated ships and their passengers? Do you not think that these English will put the Acadians back into their prisons?"

Marie leaned close, brushing her bosom against his. Dear God, Phil thought, the woman was playing seductress at a moment like this. "Who cares about them," she whispered. "Think about us. I'm an aristocrat. They will hardly think of hurting me and I will make sure no harm comes to you."

For a moment, Phil's entire life came into focus. In that brief amount of time, he wondered how he had destroyed so much being in love with Marie. Looking at her resplendent face now, all he felt was contempt.

"No one boards my ship," he repeated, his tone cold. "Tell them if he insists on putting the lives of my passengers in danger, I will draw fire."

Marie straightened, then turned to the others behind them. "Your captain refuses to let the English board our ship. They want to come in peace, but he's too stubborn to allow it. Are you going to let him put you all in danger?"

The Acadians remained silent, staring at Phil with conflicting eyes. So much separation, so much heartache. They were all so hopeful, sailing to the New World to start anew, to rebuild their culture and start new homes. And now the English were once again waiting to rip it apart.

Phil glanced at Delphine, a pistol tucked inside her belt, her feet braced for action. Their eyes met and he knew where she stood, despite the dangers. He turned to Francois, wanting his approval, hoping for acceptance, but waiting for another argument. What he found surprised him.

"No one boards *La Belle Amie*," Francois said. "We will fight the English before they will take us again."

For the first time since they met, Francois smiled, pulling his own coat aside and revealing a pistol. Then he walked to the Acadians on the other side of the ship and stood before them as their protector.

"Don't do this," Marie pleaded. "For God's sake, Phil, you'll kill us all."

Phil faced his opponent and raced his chin defiantly. What little English he knew was all that mattered. "I refuse."

The English captain straightened, placing both feet on to the deck. He appeared surprised and glanced at Marie with a frown. He spoke English to her and she rattled off a quick conversation Phil couldn't dream of following.

"What did he say?" Phil demanded.

"What he's been saying all along." Marie removed a handkerchief from her sleeve and began to wipe the perspiration from her neck. "Let him board."

"You're sweating, Marie." When Marie turned astonished eyes to his, he almost laughed. "Never thought I'd see the day."

"Are you mad?" she said, close to hysterics. "We're about to be fired on by the world's greatest navy and you're talking about my..."

"Now, now, Marie." Delphine reached their side, her eyes focused on the ship before her. "Some words are not meant to be spoken in mixed company."

Marie began to back away, her handkerchief still clutched to her chest. "You're both insane."

"Maybe it's best you go below deck, Countess," Delphine offered. "Things may get hectic once the cannons start firing. The smoke alone might cause you to faint, not to mention what may follow."

Marie's face paled as white as the moon, but she wasn't ready to give up yet. She turned to the English captain and shouted and the Englishman shouted back. Finally, the captain relayed an order and the soldiers on deck raised their rifles.

"He said he will shoot us," Marie translated.

Phil pulled the pistol from his waist, a gesture that sent the crew into action. Vincent and Sebastien pulled blankets from the loaded cannons on deck and rolled them to the railing, and Delphine pulled out her own flintlock. With one quick movement, Phil pushed Delphine behind him. "Not unless I shoot him first," Phil said as he lowered his pistol and aimed it carefully at the captain's head.

They all faced each other for several moments, the English soldiers poised with their rifles and *La Belle Amie* with its motley but seasoned crew ready to fight back with any means necessary. While they remained in the standoff, the ships rolling with each wave as the moon cast shadows about the water, the ship astern could be heard making its way toward them both.

Phil could hear his heart beating as he waited and watched the English captain, who waited and watched him. All the while both men were cognizant of the approaching ship with its British flag waving in the night. The English captain smiled smugly as the ship came into view.

"Surrender," the Englishman yelled to Phil. "You are surrounded."

Phil understood the words, but he refused to believe the worst. He couldn't be outnumbered. Not here, not now.

"Captain," Sebastien whispered from his right.

Without moving and breaking eye contact with the English captain, Phil answered, "What is it, Sebastien?"

"The other ship."

"Damn it, I know the other ship has arrived."

"Surrender," the Englishman shouted again. "You have no choice."

"The other ship, sir," Sebastien insisted.

"I know about the other ship," Phil retorted. "Get some men to our rear."

"But sir…"

Before Phil had time to bark at Sebastien's insubordination, a cannon fire blasted through the calm night. Phil turned astern to find one of the ship's cannon barrels smoking and braced himself for impact. But the explosion came from the English ship that faced him as the cannon ball smashed into its starboard bow.

"What the…?" Francois asked.

As if to answer his question, the ship astern lowered the British flag and raised another, this one sporting red and white stripes and stars floating inside a corner. Then it fired again, blasting the yardarm off the English ship's mizzen mast.

"Well, I'll be damned," Phil heard Mathurin shout. "It's

an American ship."

With the English focused on their attacker, Phil wasted no time. "Fire," he shouted.

Vincent, Sebastien and Francois lit the fuses on their starboard cannons and three cannon balls flew across the water to tear apart the frigate's sides. Another cannon ball from the American ship tore through the English ship's mainsail, setting it and parts of the deck on fire.

The English captain shouted to his men and sailors climbed the ratlines to release the sails. With the Americans still firing from its rear, the English set sail and quickly took flight. Without a single shot fired from *La Belle Amie's* rifles or pistols, the Englishmen were gone.

The men on the American ship cheered, and the Acadians quickly joined them. Phil released the lock of his pistol and replaced it into his belt, breathing a sigh of relief. When the American ship sailed broadside to *La Belle Amie*, Phil finally met its co-patriots in arms.

"My regards," shouted the man who appeared to be the captain. "I hope I am among friends."

"You have my deepest appreciation, sir," Phil shouted back. "And friends we will be forever for your aid this night."

"Are you friend or foe to the American cause?" the captain continued, speaking French with a distinctive accent that Phil was hard-pressed to name.

"He's a patriot, sir," piped Delphine with a smile. "As am I."

"We all are," Francois added. "And we thank you for your assistance."

"I am happy to fire upon any English ship," the man continued. "But tell me, who am I speaking with?"

"Captain Philibert Bertrand of France and her colony, Louisiana." Phil bowed politely. "At your service."

The ruddy-faced captain bowed as well. "John Paul Jones at yours, sir. I am in service of the American navy, with the generous assistance of France. This ship is a present of King Louis."

"And a fine ship it is," Phil said.

The captain smiled proudly. "I call her the *Bonhomme Richard*, after the patriot Benjamin Franklin, for it was he who arranged my commission."

Captain Jones began shouting orders in English and the men dressed in uniforms of different nationalities trimmed the sails in preparation of chasing the frigate.

"Do you mean to follow that English ship?" Phil asked him.

Even through the darkness of night Phil made out a sly smile on the American's face. "My dear sir," he said, "I have not yet begun to fight."

# CHAPTER TEN

HOURS PASSED BEFORE THE SHIP'S passengers finally settled down to sleep. Around midnight the Acadians slipped below deck to their bunks, grateful for the peace that had finally descended upon their waters.

The children were too stimulated to sleep, so Delphine let them lounge above decks, singing soft ballads as they lay beneath the stars, the sails swaying in the breeze as if accompanying her tune.

Francois watched the children listen in rapture to Delphine's story of Indians and alligators, then one by one the tiny bodies grew still as each child slipped into slumber. Two of the smaller tykes nestled against Delphine's side and she hugged them close as she, too, closed her eyes and nodded off, the gentle sea breeze blowing dark curls about her forehead.

The maternal role seemed natural to Delphine; she appeared to relish in the chore. Watching her face light up as she sang lullabies and stroked the children's hair reminded Francois of a simpler time, of an era when he raised his family without fear of the English government or their politics, when he and his neighbors vowed to remain neutral in the European wars, to simply farm their lands and practice their religion. The image seemed another lifetime away.

When Michel appeared from behind a crate and hurried

to his side, placing his head in Francois's lap, the familiar pain returned, threatening to steal his breath. How long had it been since he lost Marguerite and Jean Pierre? Years now, so many he had lost count. Yet the agony felt as fresh as if it had been yesterday.

Michel sighed and closed his eyes, his petite head round and precious as Jean Pierre's had been. Francois slid his hand through the fine brown hair and tried to exhale, but the emotions choked him. The last thing Francois wanted the orphan to see was his own debilitating grief, but tears blinded his eyes.

"Are you not feeling well?"

Francois blinked to make out Charles through the wavering shadows of the listing lamplight. Charles remained tied to the mainmast, but Phil had requested a guard to watch over him until they had cleared the coast of England. Francois had volunteered since sleep was the farthest thing from his mind after the near battle. Now that Michel had returned and memories assaulted him, Francois knew he would be up half the night.

"I have nothing to say to you, traitor," Francois bit back. "If you know what's best for you, you'd mind your own business."

To his credit, Charles never flinched. He sat up proudly despite the tug of the ropes at his waist and wrists.

"I'm not the enemy," Charles said.

"Tell that to the governor when we get to New Orleans."

At this, Charles laughed. "Governor Galvez and I are old friends. He will think this quite humorous."

Francois shifted to allow Michel more room in his lap, at the same time providing better access to the gun in his belt. "We shall see."

Charles leaned his head back against the main mast, studying Francois in the meager light coming off a quarter moon. "You've lost someone. I can read the hurt in your eyes."

If it hadn't been for Michel, Francois would have pulled the knife from his boot and slit the man's throat. He never spoke of the past. Never! And he would kill any Englishman who dared force such torture upon him again.

"I'm sorry," Charles quickly said. "I didn't mean to pry."

"As I said before," Francois answered in a cold, menacing tone, "leave it be."

In the darkness, Francois saw Charles nod, then heave a long sigh. "I was engaged once," he began softly. "It was an arranged marriage, but the moment we saw each other we fell madly in love. I was the happiest man in the world."

Francois looked away, doubtful the nobleman knew anything of true suffering, no matter where his story was leading.

"She died two years ago, from the fever that plaques Louisiana in the summer." Charles's words faded into a whisper and when Francois gazed back, he noticed tears in the man's eyes.

"I'm sorry." Francois tried to conjure up feelings for the man's loss, but Charles Armand had threatened the entire crew only hours before.

To his surprise again, Charles smiled. "No, you're not."

Francois leaned forward so that his eyes were clearly visible. He felt the fire burn up his spine, a mixture of anguish, hatred and fear. "I lost everything I owned," Francois said sternly. "Everything. My farm, my livestock, my livelihood."

"I know…" Charles began.

"You know nothing," Francois spit out. "They hauled us onto ships and sent us all over the colonies, innocent people who wanted nothing to do with their conflicts and wars. So many were taken ill on the trip to New York, we weren't allowed to land. So they forced us to sail to England where every day another person died from smallpox and exposure."

Charles's eyes widened and a voice inside Francois told him to stop. God knew he wanted to. He vowed to never speak of the past, to never mention his beloved family, but his voice betrayed him.

"My son died first," he continued, tears burning his eyes. "Died in my arms, his eyes begging me to explain why, as if I had an answer as to why the English would treat us no better than common cattle. Then my wife stopped eating, withered away. They buried them both at sea." Francois paused, forcing himself to swallow the emotions building in his chest, thinking back on that horrid day when their forms disappeared beneath the waves. "Tell me, Monsieur Armand, are you able to visit the burial site of your intended? Are you able to place flowers on her grave?"

Charles said nothing, simply stared. Shut up, the voice inside Francois demanded. He was speaking to a traitor, a man no better than the ones who killed his family, a man incapable of sympathy.

"I'm not the enemy," Charles repeated.

The fire spent, Francois leaned back against the railing, making sure Michel wasn't disturbed. "How the hell do I know that?"

"Because I am loyal to the French crown." Charles lifted his chin. "And I know who the spy is among us."

Francois smirked, glad to be speaking of other things, even if they were ridiculous. "And who might that be?"

Was it the light swaying above Charles that made his eyes glimmer with sincerity? Or was fatigue playing tricks with his mind? For a moment, Francois believed the man to be telling the truth.

"You see, Monsieur Bertrand," he said softly, "I speak English."

The moon descended toward the horizon but Phil refused sleep. He preferred keeping watch with his men as they rounded the coast of England. In a day or two, when they veered southwest toward the Azures, Phil would relax and relinquish more control to his men. For now, he needed to be alert, on deck.

As he gripped the wheel and steadied the course to fill his sails, he glanced back at Delphine, peaceful in slumber with one child beneath each arm. His heart filled with the sight, wanting to protect his angel, wanting to give her what she desired, a home and family.

"You're a fool."

Phil grimaced at the sound of Francois's voice. Tired beyond measure, he was in no mood for his cousin's criticisms. "Aren't you supposed to be watching our spy?"

"I was. I am." Francois leaned upon the quarterdeck's railing, looking equally tired. "That's what I wanted to talk to you about."

"And this has something to do with me being a fool?"

Francois frowned as if not making the connection, then he glanced at Delphine. "No. Yes."

For not the first time, Phil wondered if the two had anything in common besides the resemblance. "Go to bed, Francois. You're not making sense."

"I'm not making sense?" He righted himself. "I'm not the one in love with the wrong woman."

So, now they were discussing women? Was there no end to his cousin's inquisitions and reproach? "What do you know about it?"

"More than you think."

Something in Francois's tone made Phil imagine his cousin was as suspicious of Marie as he was. But that was impossible. Francois knew nothing of Marie's history, nor had he heard of Allain's skepticisms. "Speak plainly, Francois. It's too late for riddles."

"Plainly?" Francois asked. "I don't trust her."

"Who?"

Francois smiled slightly, then met Phil's eyes. "Now,

who's playing riddles?"

Chalk one up for his cousin, Phil thought. The man was cautious, he'd give him that. "Why do you distrust Marie?"

"I think you should ask your spy that question."

Phil glanced at Charles a few feet in front of them both, but out of earshot of their conversation. Charles shifted in his bound state, clearly awake and clearly uncomfortable. He suspected the answer to his question, but he asked anyway. "What does he have to do with it?"

Francois walked to Phil's side and leaned in close. "He thinks she betrayed you," he whispered.

Hell yes, she betrayed me, Phil thought, but that was long ago. Yet, despite all that had occurred years before, what Marie might have done aboard his ship that night, putting his passengers and his beloved Phiney in danger, fared far worse. But that was a fear brewing in his mind, born out of heartache, no doubt. The Countess couldn't be a coldblooded, murdering spy. It wasn't possible.

"Ask him," Francois said. "Ask Charles what he knows."

Thoughts battled inside him, fears urging him on, his rational mind insisting Marie could not be at fault. In the end, Phil decided to be sure, to at least hear what Charles had to say.

"Vincent," Phil called out. "Come take the wheel."

Francois and Phil approached Charles, then sat against the railing opposite him where Michel was sleeping, his body carefully covered by Francois's coat.

"First of all, this conversation means nothing," Phil stated. "I don't trust you and I doubt that what you have to say will change my opinion."

"Granted," Charles replied. "I respect that."

"Then what is it you want me to know?"

Charles attempted to stretch but the ropes held tight. "There's no chance of one man taking over this ship. Do you think you might release me from this prison?"

Now, that they were alone in the middle of the Atlantic,

Charles had a point. Phil leaned behind him and released the ropes. Charles sighed and rubbed his wrists that were raw from the contact. "My thanks, Captain."

He didn't appear the traitor, Phil thought. Despite all that had happened, Charles seemed almost agreeable. But Phil wasn't easily impressed. "What is it you want, Charles? My time is precious here."

"Of course, Captain. I will make this brief."

"He speaks English," Francois inserted.

Phil smirked. "I'm sure he does."

"I speak English because I do business with the English." Charles adjusted his clothes and smoothed down his hair. "I have a plantation upriver near Baton Rouge. In fact, one of my neighbors, Oliver Pollack, is an American."

"I'm familiar with Monsieur Pollack," Phil answered. "I would not speak of him lightly, for I will be able to check your statements here."

"Then you know he is a patriot, spending his own fortune to aid the Americans in their fight."

Phil said nothing, but merely stared hoping to see some trace of insincerity emerge. But Charles's countenance never faltered.

"I have been traveling to and from St. Malo purchasing and arranging transportation for guns to America," Charles said softly. "Since the death of someone close to me, I have been eager to leave Louisiana and its memories. The challenge of helping the Americans was also a great lure. Believe it or not, Monsieur, I am a great believer in liberty and all the freedoms it brings."

"I'm sure you are," Phil said sarcastically.

Charles ignored the comment. "I am here this time to negotiate a shipment for a Monsieur Moulineaux, a blacksmith who has been forging weapons with two other tradesmiths. Monsieur Moulineaux has a distinct brand on his weaponry. He marks the butts of each rifle with 'RM,' his initials, and a star floating above. It's very distinctive."

"And what has this to do with me?" Phil argued.

"The night I saw you at Delphine's, I knew you could be trusted to carry the weapons to Louisiana. I know all about you and your partner's work in Louisiana. So, I visited Monsieur Moulineaux that night to speak of it, but he had been murdered and his shipment stolen."

A silence fell upon the trio, until the ship fell forward in the lull of a wave and the sails flapped lightly in the shifting of the wind.

"Again, what has this to do...?"

"Everything." Charles grew stern. "Does a green flag on the bow mean anything to you?"

Now, things were starting to click. Galvez had given Phil instructions that no one else was privy to.

"Your contact was to meet you at ten in the morning after you set the flag on your bow," Charles whispered. "And you flew that flag, Captain. I was there. I saw it. Only I wasn't the first one to contact you."

An arrow of fear shot through Phil, but he fought the sensation. For all he knew, Charles was lying. "Are you trying to tell me the Countess is a spy?"

Charles leaned close. "I know she is."

Again, all his fears seem to take root, but Phil forced his head to clear. "How is that?"

"I knew what she said to that English captain and she wasn't pleading for our lives."

Phil crossed his arms about his chest. "And why am I to believe you? I'm supposed to take your word at this?"

"I can prove it."

"How?" Phil and Francois said in unison.

"The weapons in your hold." Charles smiled slightly. "I know they are here and no, Delphine did not tell me. They should have the mark of their maker. If you check the rifles, you should see Monsieur Moulineaux's initials upon them."

"That still doesn't prove much," Francois said. "You

could have killed Moulineaux yourself."

"Yes, I could have," Charles agreed. "But how did the weapons come into the Countess's possession?"

"You could be in league with her," Francois offered.

At this, Charles laughed. "Hardly. I don't believe the woman has given me more than the time of day in all our meetings over the years."

That much was true. Marie had bowed politely upon meeting Charles onboard, but that was the length of it. He hadn't the money or the title to matter to Marie. Unless it was all a ruse.

"Her husband was one of the greatest supporters of France's last war against England," Charles continued. "He died mysteriously, did you know that? What's even more mysterious is his fortune has disappeared."

It was all too much. Phil shook his head to clear the conflicting thoughts inside. "You're saying she married the man so she could poison him and steal his fortune to give to England? You're insane."

Charles's eyes grew dark and foreboding. "I'm saying more than that, Captain. I'm saying she enlisted the help of an unsuspecting lover to kill her husband, then when the duel did not do him in, she finished the job."

An intense pain gripped Phil's chest as if a hand had taken hold of his heart and squeezed. "I could kill you for that insinuation."

Charles leaned back against the main mast. "I realize that. My apologies, Captain. But we are at war here. No one is to be trusted."

The mainsail flapped as the boat veered too far astern and Phil shouted to Vincent to straighten the course, caus-ing two children to wake and stare. Delphine, too, looked up with a questioning frown, then settled back down to sleep when Vincent offered his apologies.

"You don't have to believe me, Captain," Charles con-tinued in a whisper. "You can check the weaponry and see the initials and still not trust me. If I were you, I would not."

Phil managed to pull his emotions back to a calmer state. "That's precisely what I'm going to do."

Charles leaned forward again and touched his forearm. "She told them where we are headed. She specifically said Havana, right after she begged them to rescue her from your ship. Keep me a prisoner, tie me back up, but please change your course. It's a trap, I know it."

Only the crew, Delphine and Marie knew where they were heading. Phil had made special precautions for Charles to know nothing. Pirate's Rule Number Three: Keep tightlipped about what's important, only Phil should have applied that law to Marie.

"Head to any place but Havana," Charles continued. "Don't tell me where you're going. Tell no one. Just change your course. For the sake of all lives on this ship, tell no one."

It took several moments for Phil to digest the information, but he finally nodded his head. He still didn't trust Charles, but Charles's fate would be determined in time. Now, Phil had the rest of his passengers to consider and he would take no chances.

"Everything we have spoken of tonight remains between us," Phil said, looking at each man. "Nothing will be shared with anyone else, do you understand?"

Francois nodded, but Charles frowned. "And Delphine?"

"Delphine must not know any of this," Phil answered. "She is too curious for her own good. I don't wish to put her in any danger, and knowing Delphine, she would soon place herself in the middle of it."

"You do her a disservice, sir," Charles said.

His patience expired, Phil stood to leave. "I know what's best for her."

"I wonder, sir, if you do." Before Phil had time to react, Charles stood and met him eye to eye. "She loves you.

More than you know."

Phil had tired of the two, tired of the constant advice and interruptions. "I know Delphine more than she knows herself."

"Then you know her heart," Francois said. "Her heart belongs only to you."

What was it about these two men, Phil thought. And how did he manage to get saddled with such an annoying lot, Marie included. He had only wanted to retrieve Phiney from the Delaronde family and head for Louisiana.

"Perhaps, Cousin, Monsieur Armand, you have not noticed that Delphine is a Countess and I a commoner." Phil really should be off. He owed neither man an explanation. "Regardless of our friendship, there is no future between us."

"Love is more important than a title," Francois said sadly. "As you witnessed today, we could all die in a heartbeat. Why waste your time on things that really don't matter in the grand scheme of things?"

Phil began to retort but noticed Charles smiling. "Where we're going, Captain," Charles said, "titles and class differences will not matter."

A nice concept, Phil thought, spoken by a man who owned land and possessed noble blood. He would believe in liberty and all its promises. The common man hadn't such luxuries, nor even the good fortune to dream of such.

Regardless, he had to think of Delphine and what was best for her. Somehow, the two had lost track of that fact. And Phil wasn't in the mood to discuss it further.

"Good-night gentlemen," Phil said brusquely and headed for the ladderway and the lower decks.


It took Phil half an hour to silently dissect the section of the hold which contained some of the weaponry, one small area away from the sleeping passengers where no one could witness. When he finally managed to pull a rifle free, Phil held the weapon up to the lamplight and searched beneath. There, in the soft glow, were the initials "RM" beneath a floating star.

It still didn't prove Charles's innocence, but the facts began to lean in his direction. And despite the rifle with its telltale mark lying in his hands, it was the gut feeling that determined Marie's guilt. He knew who was to blame for the English ship as sure as he knew she had not sent her missive until the night of her wedding. He knew it the moment she had argued on deck, the moment she had proposed to surrender to the English in exchange for their lives.

Phil leaned back against the side of the ship and sighed, amazed at how calm he remained, considering the woman he had once loved had both used him and cast him off to die years before, then threatened to do the same that very evening. In fact, Phil felt nothing, as if he had come to that conclusion already, expecting her betrayal, expecting the worst.

He wasn't even angry, which surprised him more. He didn't wish to place Marie in a boat and cast her off at sea, let the sharks and the English save her. No, he would play this to the fullest and enjoy the game she so carefully arranged. She wanted to best him, to use him as a pawn in her international scheme? She would meet the challenge of a lifetime in Philibert Bertrand.

Phil placed the rifle back in its hiding place. Pirate's Rule Number Six: Never turn your back on an enemy.

It was time to return to deck and guide the ship into safe waters. Time to play the lovesick fool and discover what Marie would do next.

It was time to change course.

# CHAPTER ELEVEN

ANOTHER DAY PASSED AND DELPHINE felt more frustrated than the first. Where on their premiere day at sea she had kept busy tending to the passengers and crew, today everyone seemed either self-sufficient or pre-occupied.

She had waken the night before to witness Charles in deep conversation with Phil and Francois, but when she approached Charles about the matter, he had offered a platonic smile and tipped her chin, then quickly changed the subject. Delphine wasn't easily dismissed, but after three questions, Charles called out to Vincent and began helping with the sails.

Francois, too, was elusive, dodging her questions like the dolphins surfing the waves at the bow of their ship. He would not speak of their meeting the night before and, in so many words, told Delphine not to bother Phil about it as well.

Not that she would have had the opportunity to bother Phil about anything. He was too busy escorting a refreshed Marie above deck, showing her the layout of the ship and keeping her company while she ate her meal on the quarterdeck. While Delphine enjoyed what was left of her fruit and bread, she could hear Marie laughing at something Phil had said, her lilting voice ringing out over the peaceful cadence of the waves.

How could he be friendly to that woman, Delphine thought in horror. She had defied him the night before, refused to follow his orders. Even called him a fool! Yet, Phil listened intently to some story Marie related, a love-sick smile pasted on his face.

Thoroughly disgusted and no longer hungry, Delphine placed her plate down. Within seconds, Michel appeared, staring longingly at her food.

"You can have it." Delphine pushed the plate towards the child, then patted the seat next to her. "I could use some company."

Michel gingerly approached, reached out a small, thin arm and snatched the apple. Once in his grip, he rushed away to the far side of the ship. Delphine sighed. She couldn't even get small children engaged in conversation.

"What's the matter pet?" The setting sun casting a halo about his head, Mathurin stood before her, soup pot in hand.

Delphine didn't know how to explain her loneliness. She felt like a child being abandoned by her playmates. But Mathurin seemed to understand, sitting down next to her, relinquishing his duties as cook for a moment.

"I'd say you are a woman caught between two worlds," her friend said. "First, you are your father's daughter, traveling the world on this rugged ship with a cast of equally rugged men. Next, you are a countess in France, making friends with the likes of her."

Mathurin's tone turned sour when he mentioned Marie and Delphine wondered if it was from Marie's conde-scending nature toward the crew or her insubordination the night before. Before she had time to ask, he straightened and gave her a smile. "When you want something, *chèr*," the Acadian said with a wink, "you have to fight for it."

He then looked at Phil, standing proudly at the wheel while Marie recounted a story of something inconsequential, Delphine was sure. As if sensing he was the subject of their conversation, Phil turned and raised an eyebrow.

"If you let that woman win," Mathurin whispered in her ear, "I'll never forgive you."

Suddenly, all Delphine's self-doubts disappeared. Mathurin was right. She wasn't giving up without a fight. And she knew just what to do.

"Don't worry, Mathurin," Delphine said, still staring at Phil. "Marie doesn't know who she's up against."

Holding the coffee tray with one hand, Delphine reached down and straightened her skirt, smoothing out the wrinkled fabric. Then she knocked on the door.

"Who is it?" Phil asked.

"Delphine. With your coffee."

Phil opened the door with a curious look. Usually, she let herself in, always felt comfortable alone in his cabin. But tonight, she had a plan. Before he had a chance to ask, Delphine pushed past him and placed the tray on to the desk next to the ship's log. She glanced down and noticed that several pages had been dedicated to the confrontation with the English, but before she could decipher Phil's handwriting, he was at her side, closing the book.

"You must have lots of work to do, considering all that has happened since we left St. Malo."

Phil ignored her question, taking her hand and holding it against his chest. "Delphine, we must talk."

This wasn't the direction she hoped the conversation would veer. Apologies she didn't need. She slipped her hand from his and poured him a cup of coffee. "You really should get some sleep. It's been almost two days since you've had rest."

He was right behind her now, his breath hot on her neck. While she placed his one spoonful of sugar into his cup, she prayed those lips would descend upon the exposed skin of her shoulders.

"Delphine."

Hearing her name spoken, her vision vanished. His voice said he regretted his actions and now a brotherly lecture was forthcoming, something she couldn't let happen. Delphine placed the cup before him and moved toward the bed, placing a lazy hand on the bedpost and turning back to face him. "You're right, Phil. We must talk."

"About last night…"

"Terrible thing." Delphine shook her head in consternation. "What would we have done without Monsieur Jones coming to the rescue?"

Phil frowned. "I wasn't speaking of…"

"But then your courage and leadership would have won the night, I'm sure."

When his eyes met hers, a sadness lingered there. Delphine wanted to throw herself into his arms and beg him not to continue the path he was taking, persuade him to kiss her again. And again.

"Delphine, I…"

"I can't let her steal you away." She hadn't meant to blurt it out, but the words fell from her lips before she had time to think.

Amazingly enough, Phil seemed genuinely confused. "Who?"

Delphine approached the desk and poured herself a cup of coffee, adding three spoonfuls of sugar for support. "The Countess, who else?"

She felt his hand brush a curl from her face, cupping her ear lovingly. She stirred her coffee and then moved back toward the bed, back toward a safer harbor where she had courage to state her case. When the ship listed, she sat upon the bed to keep the coffee from spilling. Phil took the opportunity to sit at the desk, his long legs stretched before him and his hands locked in his lap.

"She's not right for you," Delphine finally said.

Phil said nothing, only nodded.

"She can't be trusted."

"So, you've said."

"But you don't believe me."

Phil leaned back in his chair and grimaced and Delphine feared the worse. He had to be madly in love with the Countess to not see her numerous faults.

"Do you love her?" The words emerged before Delphine had time to stop them.

A pained look passed over Phil's face and the coffee soured in Delphine's stomach waiting for the answer. She stood abruptly and placed the coffee cup on his desk. "Forget it. I don't want to know."

She felt him take her hand again, his thumb rubbing circles across her knuckles, but she refused to look down, knowing the sight of him would unravel her.

"You deserve better than the likes of me," Phil said softly. "Now, that you have a fortune, land and a title, you can have any man you desire."

Delphine turned and leaned her forehead against his, breathing in his heavenly scent. "I only desire you."

Phil's hands reached up to her waist, sliding across the fabric of her dress in reverence. He pulled her closer and she leaned forward, hoping he was finally relenting. But Phil's head cleared and he straightened, then he gently pushed her away. He turned back toward the desk, pulled his spectacles over his ears and returned to the ship's log. "I have a lot of work to do tonight, pet."

Disappointment filled her heart, but she was on a mission and she would not leave until she spoke her mind. "It won't be that easy."

Phil pulled out the quill and ink. "What won't?"

She ran a lazy finger across his broad shoulder blades. "Resisting me."

At this, Phil turned and gazed into her eyes above his spectacles. Shock and fatigue shown back and Delphine capitalized on the moment. She leaned forward and gingerly brushed her lips against his, then quickly withdrew.

"I'm going to seduce you, Philibert Bertrand," she whispered.

Phil frowned and appeared ready to retort, but Delphine refused to give him the opportunity. She raised her chin and walked seductively toward the door, exactly as Marie had taught her. Then with a coquettish nod of her head, she left him there, alone with his logs and the memory of her kiss.

Weeks passed and Delphine still delighted in watching Phil squirm whenever she approached. She had not yet crossed the boundary between friendship and seduction, but every night she moved a little bit closer and the tension unnerved him. Two nights hence she had recounted her day while lying casually on the bed, wearing her most revealing gown that offered a nice view of her bosom. The night before she had brushed against him from behind, causing him to spill his ink.

Most times, when Delphine pushed too far, Phil would rise from his desk, grab her hand and shove her out the door. But every night 'round dusk, he would glance her way when he was ready for his coffee. She knew it was only a matter of time before she broke down his defenses.

"One more song?" Delphine asked the children sitting before her that morning.

The small group of tykes shouted approval in unison, except for Michel, who watched them from the safety of Francois's legs.

"*Pont de Nantes*," shouted one.

"Make Francois dance," shouted another, which brought up a round of laughter.

"Great idea," Delphine said, and began to lead them all in the traditional French tune, while casting a side glance at Francois. Finally, the Acadian acquiesced and began to dance a jig as accompaniment. Within seconds, the adult Acadians gathered round, always great lovers of music and dancing.

Toward the end of the song, the boat listed, throwing Francois off balance. The children squealed with delight and the adults clapped and laughed as he fell upon the deck. The children then surrounded Delphine, pulling on her skirts and demanding another song, but both the darkened skies and Mathurin announcing supper gave Delphine the excuse she needed to end her day.

"Tomorrow," she told the group, "I will teach you about alligators."

Sighs of approval rose from the group as the adults led the children below deck for dinner. Her leadership role relieved at present, Delphine leaned back against the quarterdeck railing, amazed at how tiring children could be.

"You really shouldn't spend so much time above deck," Marie chastised her. "You are becoming horribly tanned."

Delphine didn't have to glance down at her arms to know her skin was turning the color of Louisiana's bayous. "I am returning to my native color," she said with a smile.

Dressed in garments that covered her entire body, her face shadowed beneath a bonnet, Marie shook her head. "Have you learned nothing during your time in France, among proper society? How will you attract a husband looking like a savage?"

Delphine glanced at Phil manning the wheel. "Perhaps I hope to attract a savage husband."

She wasn't sure, for she could only view a quarter of Phil's face, but Delphine thought he had smiled.

"You're incorrigible," Marie said with disgust. "I don't know why I spent so much time on your tutorage."

"You did it as a favor to my grandmother. And you did it because you wanted information on Louisiana. I think, in the end, it was a fair trade, *n'est-ce pas?*"

Marie tilted her chin skyward. "Hardly. What I taught you was invaluable information."

Now, that she thought about it, Marie was right. Everything she had been taught was coming in handy in her elaborate seduction scheme.

"I thank you," Delphine told her. "I assure you, it has made all the difference in the world."

A few drops fell and Marie tightened her bonnet about her head. "Not if you refuse to keep your skin pure and you associate with those below you, like these peasants. You should be in your cabin, studying your Latin or perfecting your embroidery skills."

"I should be below deck plotting to nab the richest Creole in Louisiana, you mean."

Drops began falling harder, the water cool on Delphine's face. She leaned back to enjoy the refreshing reprieve from the harsh sun, letting the raindrops cascade off her cheeks. When Marie failed to answer, Delphine turned and found herself alone for the Countess had scurried below.

"Vincent," Delphine heard Phil shout. "Man the wheel."

"Aye, aye, *Capitaine*," Vincent returned.

The rain began to fall harder, melting her clothes to her skin and causing a large curl to fall about her forehead. Delphine would have stayed there all evening soaking up what amounted to a long-overdue bath, but Phil had reached her side and grabbed her elbow, pulling them both toward the ladderway.

"One minute longer," she pleaded.

"Come on," Phil whispered. "I have a surprise for you."

She followed him down the ladderway to his cabin, then nearly stumbled upon the large iron tub inside the door.

"We collected more water than we needed from that shower this morning," Phil said. "Don't tell anyone or I'll have the entire ship wanting a bath."

Since fresh water was a premium aboard ship, baths were a luxury. And because of the amount of passengers on

*La Belle Amie,* no baths were allowed until they reached
Havana, an order particularly disturbing to Marie, who
had complained loudly.

Phil quickly shut the door behind them and grinned
slyly. "Not a word."

"I shall be as silent as the night." Delphine returned the
smile, eyed the lukewarm water and sighed. Havana was
only a week or two away, yet the thought of immersing
into a tub of water seemed as heavenly as enjoying a real
meal cooked on an open fire with fresh fruit and cream for
dessert. She couldn't wait to dive in.

Then she remembered Phil standing there. "Where will
you be?" she asked with a coquettish grin.

The smile lingering on Phil's lips disappeared. "On
deck," he stated firmly. "There's a storm coming and I will
more than likely be above decks all night, so take your
time and enjoy."

Delphine grabbed one of the brass buttons on his coat,
the same gesture she had performed more than a year
hence when they had stood in Phil's cabin and she had
professed her love. Only this time, she wasn't thinking with
her heart. "We could share this bath."

Phil grabbed her wrist. "If your father was here, I'd have
him bend you over his knee."

"If my father was here, I'd have him tie you to the yardarm for ignoring me."

"Ignoring you?" Phil's smile returned, although she
didn't trust it as being kindly. "That, my dear, is impossible."

"Then why won't you...?"

Still holding her wrist, Phil pulled her forward, uttering
each word succinctly. "You know damn well why not."

Phil released her and strode to the desk, placing his hands
on the back of his chair. Delphine could sense the tension
in his back, but she wasn't giving up.

"If the bath's out of the question, then how about a kiss
good-night?"

He turned and stared in disbelief. "You never give up."

Delphine tested the water, a bit chilly for a bath but she didn't care. "Of course, I don't give up. Surely, you know that about me by now."

"This isn't a game, Phiney."

"I never thought it was." She shook the water from her hand. "And my name is Delphine, remember? It's been a decade at least since my father 'bent me over his knee.'"

"That doesn't change the fact that you're acting like a child."

If he wanted to injure, he certainly succeeded. "You can leave now," Delphine said, trying to hide the hurt in her voice.

Phil headed for the door, but he paused at her side, taking her shoulders in his hands affectionately. She wanted to pull away, but she couldn't deny that, despite all her seductive advances over the past month and a half, she was madly, desperately in love with him.

Silently, slowly, he leaned forward and kissed her forehead, his lips lingering long on her skin as if branding himself to her. Then he pulled away slightly, burying his face into her hair and closing his eyes. "Oh Delphine," he whispered.

Delphine wasted no time sliding her hands up his chest, grasping his lapels tightly and leaning close. His lips breathed fire against her neck as he kissed the soft places beneath her ear. Delphine pushed her face against his rough cheek, savoring the smell that defined him, a mixture of sweat, salt and tonic. Then his arms encircled her and they held each other tight.

All those weeks she had focused on seducing him, never realizing that it was pure love that bound them, a passion built on years of friendship and respect. She loved him, always had. And she wanted him madly. But at moments like these, Delphine knew there was a greater element at work here, something larger than lust and physical fulfillment.

They were lifelong friends. No one, save her father and Gabrielle, had cared for Delphine as much, had vowed to protect her from harm and did so on a daily basis. A friend such as Phil would not be easily won from an exposed bosom or a kiss in the moonlight. He would care too much to see her ruined, no matter how much she enticed him. He would wish for only the best, which, in her case, would be a rich and titled man. Her grandmother had wished the same and Delphine had promised her she would inherit the title.

Thunder belted and the ship rolled with a hard wave. Both shifted their feet and managed to remain upright, but drifted apart at the intrusion.

"We're a pair," Phil said, remarking on their sea legs.

Yes, they were quite the pair, Delphine thought, an intense sadness filling her soul. Two people destined not to be one.

She pulled away from his embrace, feeling the cold air of the coming storm breeze through the porthole. "You should be on deck," she said softly.

Phil leaned forward once more and placed a kiss on top of her head, then turned to leave the cabin. In that instant, Delphine felt a rush of panic. She couldn't let him go, couldn't give up now, no matter what obstacles stood between them.

"We are a pair," she stated, as if daring anyone to deny that fact.

Phil looked back and smiled grimly, one hand resting on the doorknob while lightning illuminated the room and, in the process, his dark features. "Enjoy your bath," he whispered, then quickly exited the cabin.

As Delphine's heart constricted and tears poured forth, she removed her clothes and entered the cold water of her beloved bath. Had the waters been steaming with heat, and a bowl of Gabrielle's gumbo waiting on the desk, Delphine's malaise would have remained. She loved a man she could not have and no easy seduction would remedy the problem.

# CHAPTER TWELVE

THE CREW HAD REMAINED SILENT while *La Belle Amie* entered the Mona Passage, bypassing the English islands to the north and skirting the coast of Hispaniola. If all proved well in the night, Phil would travel through the treacherous passage, then take port at Santa Domingo by morning. The next day they would head northwest past Jamaica and on to Spanish Cuba without anyone the wiser.

In the far distance, Phil spotted the lights of Hispaniola. If the tradewinds at their stern held and they encountered no opposition, it was possible to make landfall immediately past daybreak. He could taste Carmelita's roast chicken and sweet wine now.

"I take it that land's not English."

Give it to Francois to be awake at this hour, Phil thought. The man seemed to be forever at his back, ready to comment.

"Hispaniola is Spanish," Phil answered. "The French own the western part of the island known as Saint-Domingue. We have managed to bypass the Grand Bahamas, the English islands altogether."

"Wonder what our Countess will think of this."

Phil had wondered the same thing, was anticipating the look on Marie's face when she woke that morning. Landfall on safe soil was her final test. If he had any doubts as to her guilt, tomorrow's reaction would determine her fate once and for all.

"Have you managed to find out anything from your flirtations with her?"

If Phil wasn't mistaken, Francois's tone was condemning. He was sure that his cousin would have preferred Phil had locked the Countess inside her cabin for the remainder of the voyage.

"She asked a lot of questions about Galvez and the state of Spanish rule in Louisiana," Phil explained. "Delphine had mentioned Marie had asked questions of her when in France, always curious about our colony. She did the same of me."

"That should tell you there. She's a traitor. I feel it in my gut."

"Tomorrow will tell." Phil hated discussing Marie with Charles and Francois. Even though all he felt for her now was disdain, Marie had used him, threatened those he loved for her own personal gain. The pain was as fresh as if a knife had just sliced through his heart.

He felt Francois's hand on his shoulder, but pity he didn't need. He was about to tell him to go to bed when his cousin said the most surprising thing.

"You're a lucky man."

Even though the words shocked him, when he turned and met his cousin's eyes, he knew exactly why Francois had spoken them.

"I can't have her," Phil said, grateful to be able to confide in someone, even his insufferable cousin. "I've watched her grow from a child, saved her life on occasion and now I'm the last person she should marry."

Francois squeezed where his hand rested. "You're the only person she should marry."

His cousin may have put pressure on his shoulder, but it was his heart that felt squeezed. "How? I can see no way out of it."

Francois sat down on the steps of the quarterdeck,

stretching his long legs in front of him like Phil was want to do. It never failed to amaze Phil at how physically alike they were.

"Love is the only thing that matters in this world," Francois said solemnly. "I had everything once. Land, food on the table, a warm hearth and the love of a good woman." He paused briefly as if gathering his courage and a lightning bolt shot through Phil at his revelation. How had he not known his cousin had had a family in Acadia?

"In a matter of months I lost everything." Francois cleared his throat and glanced up, his face now devoid of emotions. "So, don't throw away a gift when it is presented to you, simply because of useless titles and inheritances."

"Francois," Phil began, needing to know what horrors his cousin had suffered.

Francois sensed the question, rose and patted Phil on the back. "I shall turn in. Do let me know when we make landfall."

Phil wasn't ready to let him go, wasn't ready for him to dismiss their conversation when he had so many questions, but he honored his cousin's feelings. "You will be the first to know."

In the fading moonlight, Phil caught a sly twinkle in the Acadian's eyes. "No, allow that pleasure to the Countess de la Candelier."

Phil watched his cousin make his way to the bow of the ship, where a small bundle lay near the main mast. With slumped shoulders Francois sighed, then removed his coat and placed it over both he and Michel's small sleeping form. Remorse filled him. How had he spent months in his cousin's presence not knowing of his personal tragedies? How hadn't he conceived that Francois lost family like the rest of the Acadian passengers?

"*Merde*," Phil said to himself. He had neglected Francois, was causing pain to his beloved Phiney. But tomorrow was a new morning. They were finally on the far side of the

Atlantic, close to home. At last, things would be made right.

"We are where?" Marie shouted.

"Hispaniola," Vincent explained. "It's a Spanish island. We are safe here."

Delphine watched as Marie's face whitened at the news. Why wasn't she happy to finally be rid of the ship she had complained about since leaving St. Malo? Her reaction was peculiar.

"No." Marie shook her head as if speaking to a child. "We are supposed to be heading toward Havana. You are mistaken. That island must be part of the Bahamas."

"That island is Puerto Rico and Hispaniola is straight ahead, madame."

Vincent was tiring of the conversation; he had much to do before landfall. He glanced at Delphine pleadingly, but when Delphine attempted to intervene, Marie brushed past, heading straight for Phil.

"You said we were going to Havana," she practically shouted at him.

To Delphine's amazement, Phil stared ahead, his concentration bent on his progress through the tricky passage. Tidal currents ran through the area between the two islands, causing a number of problems for sailors, so every hand was on deck, helping bring La Belle Amie to shore.

"Phil," Marie said, stomping her foot. "Did you not hear me?"

Delphine saw the jaw muscles tighten in his face as he gazed heavenward and shouted orders to flatten the sheets. "I heard you Marie, now go below before you get thrown overboard."

Marie appeared shocked at his words, but curious enough to proceed. "How can you talk to me like that? I deserve an answer."

Holding tight to the wheel, Phil turned so strongly,

Marie took three steps back. "We are heading into the harbor of Santa Domingo. It is not Havana, Marie. But I'm sure you will find hotels of equal stature there to handle your delicate needs."

Someone chuckled near the bow, and Phil returned to his duties as captain. Marie, smarting from his remarks, turned toward Delphine for support. "Why Hispaniola? Why the change? We were supposed to go to Havana."

Why not, Delphine thought, wondering for the umpteenth time if Marie had ulterior motives for making the trip. "It's a lovely island, Marie. My father has a small house there. An elderly woman named Carmelita lives in it and cooks us delicious meals when we arrive. It's a bit rugged, but you will be treated like a queen."

A look of panic spread over Marie's face and the gesture sent a shiver through Delphine. She wasn't the only one who noticed; silently, Phil was studying the Countess too. Only he didn't appear half as surprised as Delphine at Marie's reaction.

"I'll take the hotel," Marie said, defeated. "I'll not be at the mercy of this ship or its crew any longer."

"We will drop anchor shortly," Phil said in a tone that issued warning. "We will leave first thing in the morrow. I'll expect you to be ready."

Her eyes enlarged like a cornered animal, Marie glanced at the faces around her, cowering from Phil's harsh stare. Then she retreated below decks.

"*Mon Dieu*," Sebastien said. "What do you think she wanted to do in Havana of all places?"

Betray us, Delphine thought. When she stole a glance toward Phil and saw hatred and pain shining back, she knew her intuition about the Countess had been right. The woman was responsible somehow for the English attack. Phil had known it, had discussed the event with Charles and Francois that night. There was more at work here with the Countess and her shipment of guns. If it took Delphine the rest of the voyage, she would figure out how.

José rushed down the mountainside to greet Delphine as she made her way to her father's house, only the small tyke had turned into a handsome young man.

"Phiney," the boy exclaimed.

"*Hola*, José," Delphine answered. "How is your grandmama?"

"I saw your ship arriving this morning and she is preparing your welcome dinner now."

Now that José was close, Delphine realized the young man was much more than that. For all she knew, the little boy who used to follow her father around like a shadow was long married. "*Gracias*, José. I am desperate for a home-cooked meal."

José patted her on the shoulder, then headed down the street, waving as he walked. "Must go to my house. I am needed there."

Delphine waved back and headed up to the end of the winding street where the houses disappeared until one lone chimney appeared above the thick forest. Before she had time to reach the door, Carmelita came rushing out.

"*Bonjour* Delphine," she cried out in her accented French, grabbing Delphine and hugging her tightly. "It has been so long."

"*Si*, Carmelita. Too long."

"And I'm afraid it may be longer still." The older woman wiped tears from her eyes with the corner of her apron.

"Why is that?" Delphine opened the door and waited until Carmelita entered, but Carmelita never moved.

"José's wife is expecting a baby." The older woman hugged Delphine once more. "I have put soup on the stove and there is fresh fruit on the table. I won't be back for several days but if you need me, you send for me."

This time, Delphine hugged Carmelita, then gave her a reassuring squeeze. "Go be with your family. We will tend to ourselves."

"We?" Carmelita asked. "Your father or Philibert with you?"

"Philibert is, *si*."

A sparkle gleamed in the old woman's eyes, then she patted Delphine's cheek. "I still have that old pig trough that you like so much. It's on the back porch. Clean too."

Delphine smiled thinking of Carmelita's enormous bathtub that she had nicknamed as a child. It had been two weeks since her bath in Phil's cabin and soaking in that huge tub would be heavenly, right before indulging on the fresh fruit Carmelita had spoken of.

"*Merci*," Delphine said, taking the woman's hand. "*Gracious*."

Carmelita hugged her once again, then headed down the mountainside, talking to herself all the way. Delphine watched her go, feeling the familiar malaise settle over her heart. Would Gabrielle rush away to witness the birth of Delphine's child one day? Would Delphine ever marry?

Pushing the painful thoughts aside, Delphine entered the small but expertly clean house. On the stove was a pot of steaming vegetable soup while ripe avocados, mangos and bananas lined the top of the kitchen table next to a bottle of wine and a pitcher of water. Delphine devoured the pitcher first, relishing the sweet taste of fresh, clean water. Then she extinguished the fire in the stove — since the temperature had risen considerably in the house — and placed the pot to cool.

"Now, for the bath," she said to herself.

The back porch extended across the bedroom and on the way to retrieve the tub Delphine found a light cotton dress spread out on the bed. The Spanish dress must have been made for one of Carmelita's grandchildren, but she had left the garment for Delphine's use. Delphine thought to wait for the bath, but she couldn't stand another minute trapped in her suffocating corset and heavy gown in the August heat. She peeled off the dirty gown and undergarments, then raised the white cotton over her head and let the soft fabric brush against her skin as it dropped to her ankles.

Feeling several pounds lighter, Delphine pulled the massive tub from the porch and placed it in the center of the main room, then took a trip to and from the garden well to fill it with fresh water.

First, she washed her clothes and hung them to dry, then replaced the reservoir with clean water and added lilac oil. Delphine arranged a towel, soap and plate of sliced fruit by its side, ready to take advantage of her delicious bath.

"One more thing," she said to her masterpiece, then headed back to the garden, where Carmelita grew a variety of wild roses.

Phil expected to be greeted by a talkative Carmelita as he entered the small abode, but instead he found it empty save for an inviting bath surrounded by soap and substance. He checked the stove and found it cooling, a pot of delicious smelling soup by the side. Carmelita must have known they were coming, but had pressing matters to tend to and rushed away. Looking back to the bath, Phil sent up a prayer to Carmelita, so grateful for the chance to be rid of two months of sweat and salt.

It took less than a minute for Phil to rid himself of his clothes, boots and sword. He stepped into the bath, amazed that he fit inside the large tub, his legs folding in well within the metal rim. He untied his hair and slipped lower into the cool water, closing his eyes and shutting off the world. For a few blessed moments he would forget all his troubles, forget that Marie had checked into a city hotel with only Charles at her watch, forget that the traitor still posed a threat to their safety, forget that by New Orleans he would have to watch Phiney enter society with bachelors at her heels.

Something or someone entered the house; Phil could sense their presence approaching from the garden. Listening intently, he discerned that it was a person easing their way toward the tub. There was no rustle of petticoats, yet his gut told him it was Delphine. When that person reached for his sword, Phil moved his hand and captured a wrist, then glanced up to see what foe stood before him.

"Don't you ever give up?" he asked her.

Delphine released the handle of his sword and stood up. Dear God, but she wore nothing more than a thin Spanish dress, embroidered around the neck but lacking nothing but sheer cotton all the way to her calves. Her muddy toes peered out from beneath the hem and her exposed arms were tanned a golden brown. Her brown hair, loose from its usual ties and pins and somewhat bleached by the sun, cascaded over her shoulders, which were practically bare as well.

She was the most beautiful creature he had ever set eyes upon. And Phil had witnessed the best.

When Delphine straightened, she placed her hands on her hips and grinned. "I would worry less about your sword and more about the fact that you're completely naked."

Horrified, Phil grabbed the plate of fruit and placed it over his lap. "What are you doing here?"

Delphine moved a hand over the tub and released her fingers, letting several rose petals fall into the water. "This was supposed to be *my* bath."

Phil started to rise, then thought better of it. "If you turn your back, I'll get up."

Delphine washed her fingers in the water, purposely letting her hand brush against his thigh, which caused an instant reaction. "I owe you one. Enjoy."

She headed for the kitchen, stopping at the table to

open the bottle of wine. As Phil surveyed her hips swaying through the thin cotton, his reaction increased. Knowing Delphine, she might leave him to bathe but sneak a quick look, and he didn't want her to catch him in such an aroused state. Yet, he couldn't well bathe with a plate of fruit on his manhood.

Watching her work the bottle, his imagination ran wild. The more his body betrayed him, the more he ached for those fingers clutching the bottle of wine to hold him. He imagined Delphine quite the adventurer in bed, which only added to his intense discomfort.

"Would you like some wine?" she asked.

"Damn it, Delphine. Leave me."

Again, she smiled while pouring him a glass. "I've seen you naked before, Philibert Bertrand."

Phil raked his brain trying to remember when that was. In the meantime, Delphine approached, almost laughing at the plate of fruit, and handed him his glass. Then she leaned into the tub and retrieved a slice of mango from the plate while she raised an eyebrow seductively. If he hadn't owned some semblance of control, he would have pulled her in on top of him.

"When?" he asked, clearing his throat when the words emerged scratchy.

"When I first met you." She slipped the mango slice between her luscious lips. "You don't remember it, I'm sure. You were badly hurt and I bathed you then, helped my father bandage your wounds. You kept murmuring something about angels."

"I remember it well."

Delphine shook her head and curls spilled out upon her forehead. "You couldn't have. You weren't awake."

"You were crying."

Her eyes darkened at the revelation and her smile disappeared. "It was the first time I had seen a man so badly injured," she whispered. "And I felt something…"

She looked into the tub's depths, so solemn and quiet. It wasn't like Delphine. "Felt what?"

She dipped a finger into the water, making circles around a petal floating near his knees. He shifted to relieve the pressure building under his lunch but it only increased his discomfort.

"I felt a connection," she continued. "I felt that if you died, a part of me would too." She smiled sadly and cocked her head, causing one curl to dance over one eye. "It sounds crazy, doesn't it?"

Forgetting the plate and what lay beneath, Phil leaned forward and pushed the curl away, then cupped her cheek. Delphine grabbed his hand and held it tight against her face.

"Carmelita has gone to help with the birth of José's baby. She will be away for days."

Phil released his hand abruptly, causing Delphine to lose balance and grip the sides of the tub for support. "You must go. We can't be seen like this."

But, Delphine wasn't moving. "Who's going to see us?"

"Anyone. José."

"I told you, it's José's child."

Phil felt trapped. He couldn't rise from the tub and he couldn't convince her to leave the room. Knowing Delphine, she wouldn't leave until she played her silly games.

"Delphine, you can't be here. I'm a man who's been on a ship for…"

"Yes, I know." Delphine slid one of her hands inside the water again, teasing another petal. "You've been without a woman for two months and you're randy."

He should have been shocked at her language, but she had more than likely learned it from him. He was more surprised that she imagined him with another woman while in France. Then, he remembered Marie. Of course, she would think he had been with Marie.

"I've not been with another woman since you sailed

from New Orleans."

It was the worst thing to say. Her eyes darted up, glistening in the morning light as if he had opened a door and welcomed her inside. Without warning, he felt a hand upon his thigh. The movement jolted him so, he lost control of the plate, which began to slide into the waters of the bath. In one deft movement, Delphine caught the plate with her free hand and tossed it on to the floor.

There was a loud thump as the plate hit the rug, and the distraction was just what Delphine needed. Before Phil had time to react, her hand moved upward.

"You're mine, now, *Capitaine*," she whispered.

# CHAPTER THIRTEEN

PHIL IMMEDIATELY GRABBED HER WRIST, holding tight. "Let go, Delphine."

Their eyes locked, but Delphine didn't budge.

"Damn it, let go."

His hand exerted pressure on her wrist, but Delphine was never one to back down from a challenge. She stared at him defiantly as her thumb, free from his grip, moved up and over the tip.

His grip never lessened but a profound shift occurred. She could sense sensations pouring through his body as his eyes, still intent upon hers, began to glisten with an emotion she didn't recognize. It was as if his steadfast control slowly leaked from his body with each movement of her thumb.

She did it again and again, amazed at his reaction, amazed that she could win with only a touch of her hand. Her mind dizzy with power, she slipped her index finger forward, tracing the sharp line that distinguished the mushroom-like apex.

Phil sucked in a deep breath and his grip lessened. Seizing the opportunity, Delphine slipped her hand down the length of him, only to rise back to the soft skin at the top. His jaw muscles tensed and his eyes never left hers as she repeated the action. She suspected he wanted to speak, to demand she release him, but he was powerless to do so.

The more she touched him, stroked him, the more his eyes narrowed and glistened. Delphine suspected a lesser man would have closed them from the beginning, tossed his head back, and wallowed in the pleasure. But not Phil. Never Phil. Bertrand's Pirate's Rule Number One: Never lose control.

Suddenly, Delphine felt ashamed. He was her savoir, her best friend, and her champion. And here she was resorting to a cheap method of battle, using female weaponry he was defenseless against. She saw defeat shining in his eyes, the way he struggled to keep his head level, his focus pinned on her face.

She almost stopped, almost removed her hand and offered a quick apology, but Phil's breathing became labored and he tilted his head back, so she continued the strokes. He finally shuttered, his body pulsating with waves of release, and Phil gripped the sides of the tub as if in pain. Delphine wondered if she had hurt him, besides stealing his pride.

His eyes turned toward the ceiling as he struggled to regain his breath, his chest heaving as if he had run a race. When the shuttering stopped, Delphine removed her hand.

What would she do now, she thought wildly. She had crossed a chasm one didn't bridge between friends. She had made him lose control. Remorse filled her and she wanted nothing more than to disappear on the spot.

She lowered her gaze and began to rise, but felt a hand on her arm, its grip as tight as before. When she looked up, the old Phil had returned, his gaze boring into hers.

"I'm sorry," she whispered.

Delphine expected a harsh rebuttal, or dismissal. Instead, Phil reached up and grabbed her other arm and pulled her into the bath, her chest falling flat against his and water spilling everywhere. She struggled to right herself, planting both knees on either side of his hips, but not before Phil slid both hands up the length of her legs, the wet cotton dress coming with them.

While his fingers grabbed her bottom, his lips sought out hers, hungry and demanding. Delphine leaned forward, wrapping her arms about his neck and feeling his hard chest through the wet fabric of her dress.

This time, the sensations roared through her like cannon fire. The feel of his fingers exploring her upper thighs and bottom, his tongue dancing with hers, her nipples brushing against the harsh planes of his chest — the combination was heady and provocative. A pounding began deep inside her, an ache that demanded release.

Phil's lips slipped away, lowering down her neck, nipping at her earlobe, sucking the soft skin at her nape. Delphine straightened slightly to give him more room, and he responded by leaning down and taking a nipple between his lips, savoring the nub beneath the wet fabric as his tongue circled it again and again.

Delphine gasped as a rush of pleasure jolted her, beginning at the core of her femininity and rising to the tips of her fingertips. She arched her back and leaned her head skyward, not caring if she lost control or not. She didn't mind if he won this round. She was his, and he could do with her as he pleased.

Then, with one hand, Phil tugged the dress up over her hips, caressing her thighs passionately, diving his hands forward toward that unknown place Delphine had only heard about, that spot where union took place, where exotic pleasures could be found. His lips left her bosom for a moment and, in one quick jerk, he pulled the dress up and over her head.

Suddenly, Delphine felt exposed and embarrassed. It was one thing to make love with Phil in the privacy of a dark bedroom like she had imagined time and again, quite another to be straddled naked inside a bathtub. She raised her arms to cover herself, wondering if she could flee the tub before Phil had a chance to capture her.

To her surprise, Phil's eyes turned comforting. He placed

a hand at her cheek and let his thumb slowly caress her face. "You shouldn't play with fire, pet," he said in a hoarse voice.

Perhaps he was right, but deep down Delphine wanted this to happen, still wanted Phil to make love to her.

"I love you," she whispered. "I want to be with you."

His hand still holding her cheek, Phil leaned forward and began gently kissing her face: her forehead, her eyelids, the tip of her nose, the rise of her freckled cheeks. Then he captured her bottom lip between his teeth and sucked, while his tongue ran the length of it, and Delphine felt the powerful rush returning.

As if on their own accord, Delphine's arms circled his neck and she leaned forward, savoring the soft patch of hair on his chest brushing against her nipples. Phil deepened the kiss, then moved a hand to cup one breast, teasing the bud between his finger and thumb.

Time seemed to slow, each caress, each kiss the feel of a lifetime. When his mouth took the place of his hand, Delphine closed her eyes and felt the pressure mounting once again. This time, she wasn't embarrassed. Their contact felt so right, as if each person melted into the other, their souls united as one.

With his lips and tongue still savoring one nipple, his hand reached down and grabbed her bottom, urging her body upward. Delphine had no idea as to his plans, but she did as she was bid and rose slowly on her knees. Phil's hand moved between her legs and delved inside, while his lips traveled down the length of her, kissing every inch of her wet body.

Delphine couldn't help herself. She gasped, then emitted a moan when his fingers vibrated inside her. Then, in a most shocking move, Phil urged her higher while his lips brushed lower and his tongue finally rested on a spot where lightning was born. As his tongue teased the place that caused her heart to beat wildly and her breathing to become ragged, his finger slid back and forth inside her.

Delphine grabbed his shoulders for support as an eruption of pleasure overtook her. She tilted her head back as Phil had done, but she held nothing inside. "*Mon dieu*," she exclaimed, as the sensations rocked her repeatedly and her body shuttered with the release.

Still holding tight to Phil's shoulders, Delphine dropped forward as the sensations subsided. She felt him lower her against him, kissing her repeatedly everywhere. She leaned her head into the crook of his neck, helpless to do anything, her energy spent. Phil's hands roamed her hair, smoothing the curls from her forehead while he whispered comforting thoughts. But all Delphine comprehended was an intense bliss, and a sleepiness that threatened to overtake her.

Then, somehow, through the fog of her fatigue, Phil rose inside the tub, taking her with him. She felt him wrap her in a towel, still kissing her face and brushing her hair, then headed toward the bedroom. In the dimmed light of the darkened room, she sensed the bed beneath her, felt it tilt as Phil joined her, pulling her on to his chest.

For a moment, Delphine realized they hadn't fully consummated their love, and she wondered if Phil had been fulfilled as she had, but she was helpless to discuss it. As soon as she placed her head on his chest and his arms wrapped lovingly about her, Delphine sighed and gave over to the heavenly realm of sleep.

Phil watched his precious angel nod off, the water of the tub still fresh on her eyelashes. He kissed away each drop, then kissed the rest of her face, savoring the feel of her beneath the sheets, the fragrant scent of her hair.

God, what had he done? He was her protector and he had lost all control, had defiled her in a bathtub, no less. One touch and she had conquered his desires, emotions he had fought months to tame. Yet, he adored her, had never experienced such pleasure with a woman, and was sure she had felt the same. Somewhere deep inside him he regretted nothing.

But, what was to become of them? There was no solution, no simple route for them to travel. They had reached the end of their voyage without a safe harbor to enter. Now, there was consummated passion lingering between them. They had entered dangerous territory, and there was no turning back.

"I love you too, Phiney," he whispered, as a profound sadness filled his heart.

Holding Delphine close and relishing the feel of their bodies entwined, Phil joined her in sleep, resting well past the time he intended. The sun shone through the bottom of the curtains by the time he awoke, making him wonder if Charles had already come and gone.

"Damn," Phil thought. What if Charles had seen them together?

He rose and pulled on a clean set of clothes he had brought in a satchel, then removed the remnants of the bath. The fruit had disappeared, no doubt by one of the many neighborhood cats Carmelita constantly befriended. There was a pot of soup remaining, and Phil headed toward the kitchen to relieve his hunger.

He paused at the threshold of the bedroom, watching the soft rise and fall of Delphine's bosom under the sheet, her resplendent face like an angel's in slumber. What he truly hungered for was a chance at happiness, a chance to wake every morning with Phiney by his side, to be able to make love to her properly, as a husband.

Bypassing the soup, Phil grabbed the bottle of wine and proceeded to the porch, where he fell upon the stoop with a sigh and began drinking, anything to relieve the pain gripping his heart. The wine proved no help, so he bent his elbows upon his knees and ran a hand through his unruly hair.

"I'd say you had a tough night." Phil looked up to see

Charles emerging through the foliage of Carmelita's front yard. In his present state, he didn't welcome the man, but the sight of Charles lifted his spirits somewhat, knowing that the Creole hadn't witnessed their lovemaking.

"Any progress with the Countess?"

Charles sat down next to Phil, his eyes streaked with crimson with dark circles beneath. He took the bottle from Phil's hands and swallowed a long drink. "She checked into the hotel and went to her room with that twit of a maid. I expected her to stay there all night, like I would have having been two months aboard ship, but she wasn't gone an hour before she emerged into the lobby dressed like a queen." He paused and offered a sad smile. "She is the most beautiful woman, isn't she?"

Phil remembered the time when his body ached for her presence, when Marie's image made him feel whole. Now, all he could think of was the soft touch of a young privateer who wore daggers beneath her skirts.

"You're not still in love with Marie, are you?"

Startled by the question, Phil looked at Charles, then realized he must have been wearing a smug grin thinking back on what had recently transpired in the bath. He cleared his throat. "Hell, no."

The questioning look on Charles's face remained, but he nodded. "Perhaps it was someone else you were thinking about."

Phil looked away, studying the sunset over the western ridge that led down to his ship. He didn't want to discuss Delphine with Charles, didn't want to air his problems with anyone, but somehow the thoughts slipped free.

"After my partner, Delphine's father, married an Acadian woman ten years ago, he made it his purpose to bring Acadian refugees into Louisiana," Phil began. "None of his charity comes free, so I have been the money-making arm of our operation, smuggling goods into the colony and the American interior."

Charles grinned again, wiping the remnants of wine on his lips. "I'm well aware of this, *Capitaine*. You and Jean Bouclaire are legendary to patriots like me on the Mississippi."

Phil took the bottle and tilted it back, letting the warm wine burn a trail down his parched throat. "What you don't know is that for the past year my profits have been greatly lessened."

"Due to the American efforts, I assume."

Phil stared at the man, wanting to trust the agreeable aristocrat, but wondering if he would be betrayed as he had with Marie. "Let's say, that because of certain circumstances, Jean and I are in dire straits."

Charles appeared genuinely concerned. "Are things that bad?"

Phil almost laughed. Instead, he drowned the anxious feeling with another bout of wine. "Things are that bad."

"Is this why you are reluctant to ask for Delphine's hand?"

Phil stood, gazing down to the harbor where the masts of his beloved ship peered over the treeline. "I have nothing to offer her," he said softly. "If she marries me, she will lose everything – her land, her title, and her inheritance."

"But surely you don't think these things matter to Delphine. Not when she cares for you so."

No, he didn't. But they mattered to Phil. "Jean and I are insolvent, Charles. I have made no money on this trip. There is a good chance we will be forced to sell *La Belle Amie* upon arrival in New Orleans."

A silence fell between the two men, broken only by the calls of seabirds announcing dusk. "I wish I could assist you, but I've given my entire fortune to the American cause." Charles laughed lightly, then hung his head. "And to think my poor mother thought I was traveling to and from France in search of a wealthy wife."

Suddenly, Charles's grim smile disappeared, replaced by a

frown. He looked up at Phil sternly. "You don't mean you will sit back and watch Delphine play the marriage market. You don't expect her to marry another just to keep her father's business afloat."

Over his dead body, Phil thought fiercely, but what else had he been thinking? She couldn't marry him, a commoner. To do so would mean the loss of her fortune and beloved ship, ruin to her family. To maintain her inheritance she either had to marry a nobleman or become a spinster, neither of which met with Phil's approval. It was a paradox without answers.

"Does Delphine know of your money problems?" Charles asked.

"No, and I'd rather she didn't."

Charles stood up and took the bottle, drinking the last remnants of the wine. "Don't underestimate her, my friend. You keep her in the dark on too many things."

"I'm doing what is best for her."

Charles's eyes never wavered. "Are you?"

The twilight breeze teased at Phil's nape and he fought back a shiver. He missed confiding in Delphine, longed to share his problems with her every night when she visited with coffee, but he worried that her curiosity would bring her harm. Jean had been clear that his daughter should know nothing of their problems. No, it was better this way.

"The war won't last forever, Phil."

The war had lasted too damned long, as far as Phil was concerned, and cost him too dearly. And in the most ironic of circumstances the woman who had once stolen his heart had reentered his life, only to betray him once again. Thinking back on the past year and his and Jean's many sacrifices, Phil wished he had turned Galvez down. Hell, he wished he had never let Delphine leave his cabin that night, had married her instantly and continued his business without thoughts of France and American independence.

Pushing the painful thoughts aside, Phil concentrated on

the problems at hand. "So, Marie visited the lobby. What happened then?"

Charles shook his head lightly. "Not much, as far as I could see. She took dinner, spoke with a few of the other visitors. Of course, several men approached her, asked her questions, some in Spanish which she did not understand."

"Don't assume anything with that woman."

Charles thought about this and nodded.

"Who is watching her now?"

Charles's countenance shifted as a notion suddenly occurred to the Creole, then he looked up as if surprised Phil had asked a question. "Francois. But Marie had gone to bed by the time he arrived."

"Did you make out what the Spaniard said?"

The pensive look returned. "Now, that I think about it, we may have a problem."

A pain, like a knife twisting, began in Phil's gut. Something was not right, he could sense it. "What is it?"

"The Spaniard told Marie that Spain has entered the war, has aligned with France against England. I don't know if it's true or not, but Marie might use this information…"

Before Charles could finish his sentence, Phil grabbed his coat and pulled him on his feet. "Time to go," he announced.

"But I haven't eaten, haven't slept."

Phil removed his hands from Charles's lapels and brushed his coat. "Of course. You stay here. There's soup on the stove and a pallet in the livingroom."

Then, he remembered Delphine, sleeping naked in Carmelita's bed.

"Wait here," Phil said and hurried into the house. Quickly, he closed the bedroom door after placing all of Delphine's clothes at the foot of the bed, including the cotton dress that had dried in the interim. Phil then grabbed his coat and headed out the door.

"Delphine is sleeping inside," he instructed, like a big

brother. "Do not disturb her."

Charles nodded unemotionally and Phil was thankful for no further questions. If Charles suspected something between them, he masked it well.

"Tell her nothing," Phil said as he headed toward the road. "Remember, Delphine must never know about our problems with Marie."

Delphine woke to the sound of voices on the porch — two men if she wasn't mistaken, one of them Phil — then rose when silence followed. Her clothes had been laid upon the bed, all dried and neatly folded. She pulled on her usual attire of corset and gown, wishing they were alone so she could resort to the casual freedom of her cotton dress. But, once again, because of her grandmother's instruction, she felt the need to greet the world as befitting a countess.

When Delphine entered the kitchen, she found Charles sitting at the table, enjoying a huge bowl of soup.

"*Bonsoir*, Countess," he said cheerfully. "Care to join me in some of the most delicious soup I have ever tasted."

Odd, she thought, to be greeted by Charles in her father's house, and he didn't appear the least bit taken aback by their awkward situation. Now that she thought about it, she was ravenous, and things like protocol hardly mattered on the island of Hispaniola.

"I'd love some." Delphine joined him at the table while Charles spooned the vegetables and broth into her bowl. "But I must ask, why are you here?"

To this, Charles smiled. "Your grandmother would hardly approve, I know."

Her grandmother would hardly approve of anything she had done within the last few hours. Thinking back on how Delphine had initiated lovemaking with Phil, in a tub no less, a blush burned up her cheeks.

"Don't worry, my dear." Charles lightly patted her hand. "No one, save Phil, knows that I'm here. So, no one will be the wiser."

Meeting his eyes, Delphine wondered if he meant the two of them sharing dinner alone or if he alluded to what happened before with Phil. She decided to change the subject.

"Where's Phil?" Not exactly the appropriate turn of conversation, but she had to know.

"With Marie." Charles's spoon stopped halfway to his lips, then he gazed up at her nervously. "I mean, he had to check on something in town."

Whatever bliss Delphine had experienced before disappeared with the sound of one woman's name. She had trouble breathing, trouble swallowing the tomato lodged in her throat.

"He has business in town," Charles quickly added. "Important business. He told me to tell you he would meet you at the ship at daybreak."

No longer hungry, Delphine placed the spoon on the table, her world spinning and her heart crashing to the floor. Through the intense pain gripping her chest, she felt Charles's hand on hers. "It's not what you think, Delphine."

What did she think? She had no idea. Suddenly, she became numb, deaf to everything around her, including the explanation Charles was rattling off in Phil's defense.

"Do you hear me, Delphine? It's business."

Delphine nodded, then offered a smile. Charles's shoulders relaxed and he continued eating, but Delphine still couldn't manage a bite.

"I'm exhausted," Charles said, when he finished his bowl. "Do you mind if I sleep? Phil said there was a pallet in the livingroom."

So, Phil had disappeared to conduct "business" with Marie and left Charles to share the house with her. As much as she liked Charles and would always welcome him into her home, having him there that night was an affront to all she and Phil had shared hours before.

"Of course," Delphine said. "Please make yourself at home."

Looking as if he might fall asleep at the table, Charles grinned sleepily and headed toward the livingroom. Falling on to the pallet, he fell fast asleep.

The night breeze tossed the curls across her forehead, but Delphine felt nothing, sat staring off into the darkness of Carmelita's garden. Finally, when she couldn't stand the anguish another minute, she pulled on her shoes and plotted her mission.

If Phil still loved Marie, then there was nothing in her power to stop him. But Delphine couldn't help thinking something else was at work here. If it took her all night to discover what that was, Delphine was going to find out.

# CHAPTER FOURTEEN

MATHURIN BLOCKED DELPHINE'S WAY AS soon as she attempted to board, slipping out of the shadows of the docks like a thief.

"*C'est moi*," Delphine whispered.

Mathurin straightened, letting out a breath. "What are you doing up here, Phiney? I'd thought you'd be well fed and put to bed by now. In one that doesn't rock."

In truth, so did she. "Forgot something," she whispered, crossing the plank and stepping carefully on to the ship so as to not wake Francois and the others sleeping near the main mast.

"Who is with you?" Mathurin asked. "Don't tell me you're here by yourself too. Do you women have no sense?"

Delphine waved and offered him her sweetest smile, then hurried toward the ladderway before he inquired more. When Mathurin's words sank in, she paused at the top of the stairs and gazed back at her old friend. Delphine thought to ask what he meant, but a movement on deck caught her attention. There, to the right of the wheel, huddled above the quarterdeck, sat a small bundle with eyes.

"You should be asleep," she admonished Michel in an undertone.

In defiance of his shy nature, Michel reached up and took her hand, his enormous brown eyes glistening anxiously in the moonlight. "Stay here with me," the small voice said. "I don't like that lady."

Delphine should have been thrilled that the young boy had finally spoken to her, but she neither comprehended his words nor wished to remain on deck at present. She bent down so her eyes met his, then ran a loving hand through his tangled locks. "What lady?"

"The one who always yells at us," he said so softly Delphine almost missed his meaning.

"The Countess?" Delphine couldn't help the feeling of satisfaction that ran through her. Even though she despised Marie for scaring the boy, it thrilled her that the flawless Countess de la Candelier would be less than perfect in one male set of eyes.

Michel nodded. "I'm scared of her, and I'm scared of this place."

Nearby, Francois shifted and began snoring loudly. "I doubt you will come to harm with that much noise about you," Delphine said with a smile.

The little boy wasn't easily convinced. "Are there bears here? I heard the New World has bears and alligators and all kinds of ferocious creatures."

Delphine tried to pat his troubled head, but Michel pulled away at the contact. He wasn't ready to forego his cautious nature yet.

"You have nothing to worry about, sweetpea." Delphine leaned back slightly to give him space, but remained close enough to provide comfort. "Whatever wild creatures are in the New World won't harm you here. You are still on the water and no creature would dream of coming aboard this ship. Besides, Mathurin won't let them."

"But what about the *Loup Garou*?"

It took everything in Delphine to stifle a grin. "It's an old folk tale, Michel. There is no such thing as the *Loup Garou*, no werewolves ready to devour little children. That story's been told since I was your age and it wasn't any more true back then."

Through the darkness, Delphine watched his mind dissect this information, but the tension never left his body.

"Would you feel better if I lent you my dagger?" she asked him.

Michel thought some more, then slowly nodded. Delphine removed the dagger from her garter and handed him the knife, handle first. "I'll expect it back in the morning."

Michel said nothing, retreating to the comfort of his blanket, his eyes continuing to study her, his hands gripping the dagger tightly. In that instant, a breeze stirred the reefed sails, rattling the sheets against the masts as the ship rocked gently against its ties.

The whisper of a wind brushed a loose curl on the back of Delphine's neck, causing a shiver to run violently through her. Like a skunk crawling on one's grave, Gabrielle would have said. In that instant, Delphine felt an overwhelming desire to bolt, as if the *loup garou* was indeed aboard ship and ready to sink its teeth into her.

Then she noticed Mathurin pass, pausing at the end of the gangplank and waving. Her spirits lifting, Delphine waved back, then descended the ladderway into the bowels of the ship.

She silently stole into Marie's cabin, picking the lock with a hairpin by the light of a lone hallway lantern. Leaving the door ajar to allow enough light inside the cabin, Delphine began looking around but the cabin was spotless, every article of clothing in the massive trunks upon the floor, every toiletry put away somewhere else. It was an odd sight: a woman meticulously groomed and owning trunks of articles in a cabin that appeared almost empty.

Then Delphine realized whom she was dealing with. Why wouldn't the perfect Countess de la Candelier live in an expertly clean cabin?

Her anger returning at the thought of her unconquerable competition, Delphine began shuffling things around, searching beneath the bunks and furniture, feeling behind the bureau. The more she looked and found nothing, the angrier she became. She had to find a chink in the woman's armor. No one could be that faultless.

When she realized she had made a noise in her haste and anger, Delphine sank to the floor beside the bed, tears burning her eyes. How did Marie do it? How did she capture Phil's heart when nothing existed inside hers? And how could he love a woman incapable of loving the sea, who complained and made demands the entire voyage.

No, she commanded herself, wiping her nose against a sleeve, there was something amiss here and she had to find it. She was jealous, yes, but she didn't trust Marie and she had to know why. Delphine had to prevent Phil from making the same mistake twice. If he was too blind to Marie's faults, then Delphine would be his eyes. She loved him too much to let him throw his life away again.

Brushing back a tear, Delphine made out a tiny object peering from beneath the mattress. Upon closer scrutiny, she found it to be the corner of a piece of parchment. Slowly, gently, Delphine pulled the parchment from its concealment, realizing it to be a letter addressed to Marie.

Delphine quickly glanced around to make sure no one was present, then pulled the parchment from its envelope. The letter was English, as incomprehensible to Delphine as Greek, but the signature was recognizable. Her heart lurched in her chest and she felt the air rush from her lungs. Mother Mary of God, Delphine thought, they were all in terrible danger.

"Looking for something?"

If the letter hadn't stilled her heart with fear, the sound of Marie's voice did. Delphine whipped around to find the Countess's silhouette appearing on the threshold, blocking her light. In an instant, Delphine pulled her hand behind her back, her fingers still gripping the parchment.

"Actually, I am," Delphine stuttered. "I have misplaced one of my favorite books and I was hoping it might be in here."

As Marie entered the cabin, Delphine took in the length of her. The Countess was dressed elegantly for dinner, but she held a tea tray in her arms. "Care to join me?" she asked.

Delphine had no idea what the Countess had in mind, nor why she would be interested in tea at this hour, but she sat gently back upon the mattress, slipping the letter inside the waistband of her skirt, hoping that the parchment would be well concealed in her backside.

"What are you doing here, Marie?"

To this remark, Marie smiled, then she began pouring two cups of tea. "I should ask that of you, my dear. After all, this is my cabin."

When Marie turned and handed Delphine the cup, another shiver traveled up her spine, but Delphine quickly dismissed it, trying to keep a steady composure. "I told you, I am searching for a book. It doesn't appear to be here, so I'll be on my way."

Marie picked up the sugar bowl and raised an eyebrow. "If I'm not mistaken, you're quite fond of sugar. One teaspoon or two?"

The ship shifted starboard and the light from the hallway lantern sent shadows across Marie's face. Delphine searched her features for sincerity, wondering if the Countess suspected anything. Instead, Marie smiled warmly, placing two teaspoons into her tea.

"I've missed our friendship, Delphine." The Countess sat down upon the cabin's only chair, preferring her tea unsweetened. "We had some wonderful times together."

Images of the past year flitted through Delphine's mind. All those questions about Louisiana and Spanish rule. Marie had been bleeding her dry of knowledge, information she undoubtedly used against France and the Americans. The British ship ready to attack innocent women and children as they crossed the Channel, all arranged by the good

Countess, she was sure.

As Delphine looked upon the woman she had once wished as her mentor, she felt nothing but contempt. "I suppose we want different things."

"I doubt that," Marie said, raising the cup to her lips. "I believe we both love the same man, but even that can be rectified when a dear friendship is at stake."

This, Delphine wanted to hear. "How do you propose to do that?"

Marie placed the cup in her saucer, then slowly raised her eyes. "I know where his loyalties lie," she said in resignation. "I know how much he cares for you. I will never sever the precious bond between you two. You have my word on that."

Delphine wanted to say her traitorous word meant as much to her as a promise from King George, but Marie leaned forward and touched her knee the way she had when they were friends back in France. "Do drink up, Delphine. Let us make amends and start anew."

Good idea, Delphine thought. Best to drink her blasted tea and be rid of the spy, steal to the upper decks and find Phil, show him the letter. She gulped down the lukewarm tea in one swallow, then placed the cup and saucer on the tray.

"I'll be going now," Delphine said, but Marie raised her hand in a friendly gesture.

"Let us shake on it, then?"

Delphine gazed at her outstretched hand in disgust, but she couldn't let on yet. She had to get away with the proof of Marie's guilt, had to exit the cabin with the letter intact. She rose from the bed and met Marie's hand, and the two shook.

In that instant, as she met Marie's eyes, Delphine could have sworn that the Countess was innocent. Marie placed her other hand over hers and held tightly, then offered her a warm smile. Or maybe it was the hazy feeling that seemed to overwhelm Delphine at that moment that clouded her judgment.

"Is the boat listing?" Delphine asked.

Whatever friendly sparkle emanated from Marie's face disappeared in a heartbeat. Her countenance grew stony and her grip tightened, as a wave of nausea swept through Delphine.

"No, my dear, the boat is not listing." Releasing her grip, Marie placed a hand on Delphine's shoulder and pushed her back toward the bed. "I'm afraid you are."

Nothing she could do could stop her from falling backwards on to the bed. Delphine attempted to grip the nearby trunk for support but her head spun like a whirlpool. Darkness crept into the corners of her consciousness and any attempt to speak failed.

Delphine comprehended little as the darkness threatened to swallow her whole, except the startling fact that she had been drugged and Marie was now frisking her clothes. When Marie turned her over harshly, then clucked her tongue, Delphine knew she had found the letter.

"He never loved you," she heard Marie whisper near her ear as the world turned ominously black. "And you'll never live to see the Louisiana shore."

She was trapped, falling into an abyss with no lifeline to grab. Even if she managed a moan, there was no one about to hear her below decks. A prickly sensation skittered up her arms and legs and bile rose in the back of her throat. The darkness returned full force and there was no stopping it now.

But Delphine refused to go down without a fight.

"I just came from Phil's bed," she said with every ounce of strength she could muster. "And I will see you hang in New Orleans, you traitorous bitch."

A sting burned her cheek as Marie slapped her hard, but Delphine welcomed the pain. It jolted her from the dizzying spell of the drug and plunged her into a place where she could finally feel no more.

"You'll never see another day," she heard Marie say.

Just before the darkness won, Delphine managed one last thought.

"Then I'll see you in hell."


Time had no meaning when Delphine woke. The boat rocked dramatically and the sun filtered through the boards above her bed, but for all she knew the ship was halfway through the Gulf of Mexico by now. Or heading toward the Bahamas and English rule.

Where was Phil and why hadn't anyone come? She had been strapped to Marie's bed for more than a day, it seemed, and every time she opened her eyes, Marie's nasty maid would pour some hideous liquid down her throat, causing her to lose consciousness once again. If only she had the strength to refuse to swallow, but her lips and throat were parched and her body betrayed her need for sustenance every time. The maid also made sure the liquid went down by holding her nose until she gagged. How much of the drug had she consumed? Enough to slowly kill her, she was sure.

"Have you drugged her today?"

Delphine kept her eyelids shut, mindful not to let her attackers know she was awake.

"She's had an awful lot of the laudanum, madame. She won't survive another round."

Delphine sensed Marie's presence studying her, heard the crackle of her petticoats by the bedside. "That's the point, Josephine."

"But won't the captain suspect?"

Yes, Delphine wanted to shout, Phil would rally to her defense. But, where was he?

"He's bought my story so far, but he won't for long." Marie's voice turned toward her maid and Delphine wished her hands were free so she could rise and strangle the wench. "We must do this quickly so we can bury her at sea. If we wait too much longer and get closer to Louisiana, Phil may insist on bringing her body to New Orleans for inspection. As it is, we are too far off the coast of Saint-Domingue to keep a body on board."

Dear God, Delphine thought, another day and it would be too late. Where was Phil and what story was he buying?

"Do you have to kill her?"

So, the maid had a semblance of a heart after all, Delphine thought. Still, if Delphine managed to survive the ordeal, the maid would be strangled right after her employer.

"She found the letter, Josephine. She knows of our plans with the English governor of Florida. Since our designs to deliver this ship into British hands in the Bahamas has failed, we will have to rely on getting word to the English at Baton Rouge. Time is of the essence now that the Spanish have joined with the French. For all we know, Governor Galvez is planning an attack on Baton Rouge now."

"Only if he knows of the Spanish involvement."

"Then let's hope that we get that information to the English first."

Delphine felt Marie's gaze upon her again. She prayed her slowed breathing and calm countenance would belie the fact that she was awake.

"How much did you give her last time?" Marie asked Josephine.

"Enough to kill her, I'm sure." Josephine's voice was laced with fear. "*Mon dieu*, madame, must we do this?"

"Afraid of a simple murder?" The Countess laughed. "You didn't have any problem with the English hauling everyone into chains when Captain Viceroy and his ship arrived."

"That was different," Josephine answered. "It wasn't so… personal."

Delphine felt Marie raise her hand as far as her ties would allow, then drop it back on the bed. "It's personal all right,"

Marie said. "All the more reason."

"But do we have to…?"

Marie turned back toward her maid, and Delphine could sense the tension in her body. "If you would have brought the letter with you to the hotel, like I instructed, none of this would have happened."

"I didn't know she would come searching your cabin," the maid pleaded.

"The stupid girl doesn't know when to keep her noise out of other people's business. Good thing I was here and thought quickly. But, now you must rectify your mistake."

Delphine heard the rustle of Marie's petticoats head toward the door. "I'll be above deck, placating the captain and those peasant sidekicks of his. You finish the job."

The cabin door clicked shut and a shadow fell across Delphine's face as Josephine studied her prisoner. Delphine thought of remaining quiet, continuing her ruse, but a panic spread through her like wildfire. She fought to remain calm, to tame her frightened heart, if only to see what Josephine had in store for her.

Luck was with her for the maid sighed, then fell into the cabin's lone chair. Delphine could hear her nervously twist the apron strings in her lap from the opposite side of the room. Had she been granted more time? Delphine didn't know, but she waited and listened until the sounds disappeared. When the sunlight failed to peer through the cabin's ceiling and darkness fell, Delphine knew hours had passed. When she heard Josephine's snores rise up from that side of the cabin, she realized it was now or never.

Delphine opened her eyes and studied her options. The ropes at her wrists were tied snuggly but not enough to restrict movement. If only she could retrieve her dagger and release herself, then she could easily overpower the maid and rush to deck. She twisted in the bed to feel for the blade but her leg felt barren.

Realizing she had passed her dagger to Michel, Delphine's spirits crashed. How would she remove the ties now? How would she defend herself?

Delphine closed her eyes and bit her lower lip, feeling the sharp taste of blood in her mouth. She refused to cry, refused to give in to defeat and despair. She had to break free of this prison, had to find a way out.

Concentrate, she demanded herself. Then, calling upon the spirits of her family, she asked for their assistance. Her proud, strong grandmother who faced death with dignity. Her brave father who met the cruelest of enemies again and again. Gabrielle, her true mentor, a woman who had taught her to believe in herself and her abilities to overcome any obstacle. She thought of Phil, of the many pirate lessons he had conveyed to her over the years.

"Bertrand's Pirate Rule Number Eight," Phil had said. "Never, ever give up, no matter what the odds."

Delphine pulled at the ties, slowly, methodically twisting the ropes until they grew slack. Finally, after what seemed an eternity, she removed one wrist from its bounds. With catlike dexterity, Delphine reached over to free the other hand. Then, ignoring the world spinning out of control, she reached down to remove the ties at her ankles.

"Going somewhere?"

Before Delphine could comprehend that Josephine was at her side, the maid grabbed her hair and yanked her backwards on the bed, then slid a cup of liquid against her lips. Delphine fought her with one hand, but the maid slapped her hard, sending a shower of stars before her sight. In that instant, as Delphine gasped for air, Josephine poured the liquid into her mouth, enough to drug a horse, she was sure. Then the maid held her nose shut.

As hard as Delphine tried to spit the liquid from her mouth, most of it slid down her throat, adding to the numbing sensation already devouring her body. But, she wasn't going to give in yet. With her free hand, Delphine grabbed the teapot by the side of the bed and sent it smashing against Josephine's head. The maid's eyes rolled back and she slumped to the floor.

The darkness came hard and fast this time. Delphine knew she had little time to save herself. She had to get above deck, had to expel the drug from her body, let someone know what was happening. With pain jolting her every step, she rose from the bed and staggered to the hallway. Then, slowly, each step threatening to be her last, Delphine inched up the ladderway.

When she finally felt the sea breeze on her face, Delphine allowed herself hope. She leaned over the railing and slid a finger down her throat, expelling remnants of the drug she had swallowed. Her body weak from lack of water and food, it barely obeyed. Instead, she only managed to spit into the black water, then collapse on deck. The last thing Delphine witnessed before the deathly gloom took her soul was Michel's caring face.

"She's a spy," Delphine whispered to the boy. "The *loup garou* is here on this ship."

Then her world turned to night.


Almost two days, Phil thought. What on earth could be keeping Delphine below deck for close to two days?

"I told you, Philibert," Marie said with the sweetest of smiles. "It's female problems."

Francois must have overheard them, for he turned toward the couple, one eyebrow raised. Phil knew what his cousin was thinking, the same thing he had imagined since leaving Santa Domingo. Something was amiss on ship and Delphine had been caught in the middle. He knew Delphine must suffer from the same maladies as most women, but he had never seen her sick a day in his life.

"I need to see her, Marie." Phil had carefully concealed the emotions from his voice, but truth be told, he was ready to tear down the walls of her cabin to make sure

Delphine was safe.

"You're being ridiculous, Phil." Marie toyed with a button on his sleeve. "She said something had happened between you two and she needed time alone, especially now that she's not feeling well. Let's not embarrass ourselves by discussing this further."

God, had he hurt her in their lovemaking, had he crushed their friendship as well by seducing her in Carmelita's cabin? Wild thoughts flitted through his mind, but guilt reigned supreme. If he had caused Delphine any semblance of pain, he would never forgive himself.

"I have to talk to her."

"Phil, I've told you, she doesn't want to see you right now."

A rage of protectiveness surged through his body. "I need to see her now, Marie."

Several of the Acadians turned and stared and Phil realized he had raised his voice. Francois refused his eyes, but he knew his cousin was listening intently. Both he and Charles had argued endlessly about Delphine's condition, not believing a word of Marie's story.

"She is still suffering from her cycle," Marie whispered in Phil's ears. "Perhaps she is suffering from more than that?" Phil stared down at the Countess, noticing lines of jealousy in her forced smile. "What do you mean by that?"

The Countess shrugged, straightening her skirt as if she discussed these things daily. "She mentioned that the two of you had shared intimacy. I can only assume the rest."

Phil wanted to strangle the traitorous spy, wishing for not the first time that he had insisted Marie be arrested in Santa Domingo and left for the Spanish authorities to deal with. But he had no proof, even after waiting and watching her hotel room that night. Galvez would take him at his word and incarcerate her. He had to wait until New Orleans.

For now, all he could think of was Delphine. He had to

see her. If she indeed had misgivings about their lovemaking, he wanted to hear it from her lips. She had never shied away from confronting her problems and he doubted she was doing so now. Something wasn't right with this picture and he was damned if he wasn't going to find out why.

Before he had time to make those demands, Phil felt a small tugging on his left pant leg. When he turned abruptly toward the intrusion, Michel gasped and ran to hide behind Francois.

"What is wrong with that child?"

Phil didn't mean to scare the tyke, but he had no patience today for games.

Francois gazed down at the boy, but Michel refused to show himself. Instead, he merely pointed a finger toward the portside railing.

# CHAPTER FIFTEEN

ALL HELL BROKE LOOSE UPON the sight of Delphine lying defeated against the railing. Every person above deck leaped to her assistance, but Phil reached her first, holding her dear head between his fingers, his eyes widened in shock at her limp form.

Francois didn't know who hurt worse, the poor girl lying pale and ill by the ship's edge or the man who carried her life in his heart. Francois put out his hand to place on his cousin's shoulder, to offer Phil some comfort, but Phil suddenly straightened, turning his icy eyes upon Marie.

"What have you done to her?" he shouted.

Marie backed up slowly toward the ladderway, ready to bolt to her cabin, but Charles blocked her way. "If you hurt Delphine, so help me God…," Charles said, emotions choking his words.

"I told you she was ill," Marie began nervously. "She must have come up to get some air."

Phil cradled Delphine's head in his lap, stroking her hair and calling out her name. Francois felt his heart splinter as he watched his cousin kiss Delphine's face, begging her to speak to him.

"She must have gotten worse," Marie offered, but the eyes that turned her way were anything but sympathetic. "I did all I could," she added defensively.

Charles knelt by Phil's side, examining Delphine

closely. Francois took her hand to check for a pulse. They exchanged worried glances while Phil continued to plead her to respond.

"There's a pulse," Francois said, "but she's barely alive."

"I don't see what could have made her so ill so quickly," Charles said.

"She was fine this morning," Marie interjected, and there was something in her flippant tone that struck a nerve with all those present. Francois could feel the tension mount among the group. "She was laughing and telling stories, without a care in the world."

Everyone grew quiet as they watched Delphine for a sign, hoping and praying that the limpid form before them would rally and offer her trademark dimple. From the corner of his eye, Francois saw Marie head for the stairs once more. Somehow, he knew that wretched woman was the cause.

"You're not going anywhere," he shouted at the Countess. "Not until you tell us exactly what has been going on."

Marie lifted her chin and sent Francois her usual patronizing air. "I have nothing to say to you, peasant. The girl became ill, that is all."

Francois leaped up, grabbed the Countess by her arm and held her captive. "That is not all and you know it. By God's will, I will know what you have done."

"Let go of me," she demanded, sending a harsh kick to Francois's shin. He howled in pain, but his grip never lessened.

Just then, Michel bolted forward, sending his own, albeit small kick to Marie's leg. "Take that, you *loup garou*," Michel shouted at Marie, then he kicked her again. "Take that, you spy."

Francois pulled the tyke aside, his arms and legs still flailing. "Easy boy."

The Countess seized the chance to pull free, but Francois only tightened his grip, enjoying the opportunity to bruise her arm. She began to yell obscenities at Francois and the boy, while Michel screamed and yelled back. Charles stood and demanded order but none came, only more questions and yelling from others on deck.

Finally, the captain's voice rang out over all the others and a silence descended upon the deck. Phil placed Delphine's head gently upon Mathurin's lap and stood, then slowly approached Marie while his hand pulled the dagger from his boot.

"Why did you call the Countess a spy, Michel?" he asked the tyke, although his icy stare never left Marie's face.

At the sound of Phil's ominous tone, the boy hid behind Francois again, but this time he spoke. "Delphine said the Countess was the *loup garou*. She said she was a spy just before she went to sleep."

At this piece of information, Marie huffed. "The *loup garou*. Are you all mad?"

The stony glare of Phil's eyes and the determination behind them took Francois aback, startling him so that he released his grip on Marie. But it didn't matter. In an instant, Phil took Marie's collar in his hands and shoved her against the post of the ladderway, the blade of his dagger thrust against her jugular.

"What have you done to her?" he shouted.

Marie's eyes grew as wide as walnuts and blood dripped where the tip of the blade met her precious, ivory neck. "Nothing," she insisted. "I did nothing."

"What did you give her?" Phil belted out, a combination of rage and fear echoing in his words.

"Nothing," Marie insisted. "She is ill."

"She's definitely drugged," Charles stated from behind. "Her condition isn't normal."

Phil's anger intensified and he shoved the dagger closer. A small stream of blood poured down the blade. "Tell me," he shouted. "Tell me or I shall drag you behind this ship and let the sharks rip you to pieces. Right after I slit your

CHERIE CLAIRE

208

aristocratic throat."

"Laudanum," Marie finally choked out. "I gave her laudanum."

"Dear God," Francois heard Charles say and a shiver ran through him, but all he could comprehend was Phil and a bloody dagger blade. He gently took hold of his cousin's sleeve and begged him to release her.

"She hurt my Phiney," Phil said in a rage.

"Then lock her up and we'll see her hanged in New Orleans," Francois said. But Phil refused to budge. "Phil," Francois said louder, "killing her won't help Delphine now."

The icy glare in Phil's eyes remained unchanged. "But it will help me," he ground out between his teeth.

"Phil," Mathurin commanded from behind. "Let her go, son. We must tend to Delphine. There is no time to waste."

A profound change occurred in Phil's countenance and he pulled the blade away. Marie choked and held a gloved hand to her neck as if she might be dying.

"Take this traitor to her cabin and see that she and her maid never leave it until we reach Louisiana," Phil told Sebastien.

"Aye, aye, *Capitaine*," Sebastien said quietly, leading a horrified Marie down the ladderway.

Phil returned to Delphine's side and raised her lovingly in his arms. No one spoke as they followed him to his cabin where Delphine was laid upon his bed. He knelt at her side, holding her hand to his lips and whispering her name.

"Bring us blankets," Charles ordered Mathurin, who looked ready to burst into tears. "And water and a spoon."

Francois wanted to ask why a spoon, but there wasn't time for questions. He took Delphine's other hand and gauged her pulse, still barely discernable but alive. He then checked her eyes, but any sparkle of life had disappeared behind her lids.

"Is laudanum lethal?" he asked Charles.

"It's a drug used to help people, but it can be fatal in large doses," Charles answered.

"She was trying to vomit."

The voice was so tiny, Francois almost missed it. How brave his little Michel had become since the start of the voyage, but then Michel had grown quite fond of Delphine.

"Smart girl," Charles said. "Let's hope she expelled enough of the drug."

"What do we do now?" Francois asked. "Must we only sit and wait?"

Mathurin returned to the bedside with an armful of blankets and a pitcher of water. Charles took the pitcher while Francois and Mathurin covered Delphine. During all the time they discussed her condition, Phil never moved, one hand holding his beloved Phiney, the other stroking her tangled hair, while tears poured down his cheeks.

A pain so intense gripped Francois that he thought he might choke from the emotions. Only a few years hence had he stood in Phil's very shoes. So helpless. So despondent. All one could do was wait, while the heartache proved unbearable.

"I'm thinking she's been without food and water these past two days," Charles said, trying to wake Phil from his lethargy. "She might die from lack of water as much as from the drug."

Francois took the pitcher from Charles's hands, then grabbed the spoon. He had to keep his cousin busy and he suddenly knew how to do it.

"She might not be able to swallow," Charles instructed Phil as Francois placed the spoon in his cousin's hand. "But if you could manage to get some nourishment in her, even a teaspoon, it might save her life."

Phil looked up at the two men, his eyes glazed with shock and grief. Somehow in the haze of anguish he understood.

He nodded, then cradled Delphine's limp head in his arms while Francois poured a minute amount of water on to the spoon. Gently, Phil slid the spoon between her lips, but the water was refused entrance.

"Keep trying," Mathurin whispered.

Almost an hour passed before the pitcher was empty, and no one was certain how much of it had trickled inside Delphine's parched lips. She remained still as a corpse, her breathing shallow, and her pulse a distant beat.

Mathurin couldn't take any more of the sight, the tears breaking through his tough seaman exterior at last. He kissed Delphine's forehead while his tears dampened her face, then left the cabin to assist Sebastien and Vincent on deck. Charles decided to leave as well, ushering out the Acadian women who insisted on helping.

"Nothing can help us now," Charles said. "Only time will tell."

Francois decided to stay, if only to keep Phil anchored to family. He sat at the foot of the bed, watching his cousin hold Delphine in his arms.

"It's all my fault," Phil said. "I should have warned her about Marie. I should have told her about the espionage."

Phil had a point, but Francois was done criticizing his cousin. "You had no idea this would happen. You were only trying to do what was best."

Phil closed his eyes as if the gesture caused him great pain. "I failed her," he said with such emotion, Francois had to turn away.

"How will I ever live without her?" Phil whispered after a long pause, gazing to his cousin for answers. When Francois turned back, he knew what Phil was insinuating, that he knew that Francois had watched his own family fade beneath death's grip. But what would Francois tell him now? That life held no meaning for him since the moment he buried his son and wife at sea? That he walked the world a shell of a man?

"Do not dwell on that, my friend," Francois answered. "Think instead of the living. Talk to her, reassure her that you are here, that you care, that you always will care."

"Of course, I do." Phil rested his cheek on Delphine's forehead, most likely as cold as her palms, Francois thought.

He leaned forward and grabbed Phil's forearm. "Speak it out loud, cousin. If she must pass, let your voice be the last thing she hears."

Phil said nothing, but nodded, and Francois knew he would not be comfortable speaking in his presence. Francois rose from the bed, placed a comforting hand on his cousin's shoulder and squeezed. "I'll be right outside if you need me."

With a heavy heart, Francois left the cabin, closing the door slowly in his wake. Delphine was in God's hands now, a God he had defied since losing his beloved family and homeland years before. What God would have allowed such atrocities upon a peace-keeping people, Francois thought. Surely this God had forsaken them in their time of need, as he was forsaking them now.

Yet, if a God indeed existed, would he come to the aid of such a loving, caring woman? Dear Delphine with a heart of gold? Francois had to take the chance. He knelt beside the cabin door and prayed, asking Mary, too, for divine intervention.


The first thing Delphine comprehended as she forced her heavy eyelids open was an intense pounding in her skull and the mounds of cotton someone had stuffed inside her mouth. When her tongue reached up to test her lips, she knew it wasn't cotton, but rather a longing for water that parched her so.

Was someone near who would help her or was she back in the grips of her prison? She vaguely remembered climbing the ladderway, but what had transpired since? Would that dreadful maid be pouring drugs down her throat once she discovered Delphine was awake?

Delphine dared not moved, but somehow the light was different from Marie's cabin, the feel of the space wider and offering a masculine scent. *Mon dieu*, she prayed, let this be Phil's cabin.

She opened her eyes slightly and found a male head of brown hair lying across her lap and her hand held tightly within another's. Lifting her head slightly caused her enormous pain, but the small movement proved it was Phil before her.

Delphine wanted to cry in relief, but she doubted there were tears inside her parched body. Instead, she squeezed his hand and whispered Phil's name.

Phil bolted awake, his hair pulled forward from its tie and cascading about his forehead like a madman's. His bloodshot eyes were wide with alarm and lines of worry etched his face. But he was the dearest sight Delphine had ever seen.

"Water," she whispered, amazed that the sound emerged from her dry throat.

Instead of rushing to her aid, Phil pressed her hand against his lips, kissing her fingers over and over again. Dear God, was he crying?

"I'm fine," she assured him. "Water."

Phil quickly recovered, wiping his face with his sleeve and shouting out Francois's name. His cousin immediately opened the door, making the sign of the cross as he looked upon Delphine's face, then appeared as if he might cry as well. She should have been gladdened by their show of emotion, but Delphine worried she might expire at any moment if she didn't get a drink. She raised her hand and placed an index finger to her lips.

"Water," Phil shouted. "She needs water."

Francois rushed out the door, while Phil attempted to raise Delphine's shoulders. The world tilted as her head left the pillow, carrying Delphine close to unconsciousness. She tried to push him away, but Phil hugged her close, kissing her forehead, her cheeks, her hands again.

"Phil," she whispered. "Please put me down."

"I'm sorry, pet." He placed her head back upon the pillow, but his hands continued to touch her face, her hair, as if they had been apart for years. "I'm so sorry."

Something in his apology gripped Delphine's heart and refused to let go. Was he sorry he left her at Carmelita's to visit Marie, to love that horrid woman after he had made love to her? Was he sorry because now he knew of the Countess's true nature? Amazingly, tears began to burn at the corners of Delphine's eyes.

Francois rushed in and placed a cup of water at Delphine's lips. The nourishment was semi-clear, which made her realize they were only a few days away from Santa Domingo and a fresh water supply, more than likely entering the Gulf of Mexico now. Louisiana was only a week's sail away.

The realization should have given her hope, but when she looked toward Phil, his guilty eyes stilled her heart.

"Can you ever forgive me?" he asked her, still holding on to her hand.

Now that the water renewed her strength, Delphine pulled her fingers from his grip. "No," she stated firmly.

Nothing she could have said would have injured Phil more. The pain that shown back at her was alarming in its intensity. But she couldn't help herself, despite how much he anguished over what had happened to her. He had betrayed her in the worst way. How could she ever forgive him for leaving her bed for another woman's?

Her head demanded that she retreat into slumber, and Delphine closed her eyes in resignation. "I need to sleep. Please leave me."

Phil paused, staring at her for several moments, then she heard the door to the cabin open and close. When Francois placed a hand on her forehead, the tears poured forth. Finally, the sob lodged in her throat broke free and she managed to turn her head slightly into the pillow so Francois wouldn't witness her outburst.

"Don't judge him so harshly," she heard Francois say. "He loves you so."

Deep inside, Delphine knew that to be true, but there were too many contradictions and her head ached from the pain of it all. She sobbed into her pillow before the darkness returned. Then she gladly let sleep overtake her distress.

Days passed and still Delphine found it difficult to rise from her bed. An endless stream of Acadians and crew members entered the cabin to bring her food and water, which renewed her strength somewhat, but still she was unable to shake off the lethargic remnants of the drug.

Fortunately, the headaches were decreasing and the dizzy spells relegated to quick movements. As long as she moved slowly and continued to rest, Delphine saw her health returning. But it was a laggard process.

Phil stopped by the cabin daily to check on her, but he remained distant and silent. Delphine had no wish to speak with him or breach the subject of his infidelity, so his reticence was just as well. Still, her heart ached at the sight of him and she longed to be back in New Orleans in the comforting arms of Jean and Gabrielle. She needed the strong presence of her father and the unbiased opinion of Gabrielle. She needed someone to explain what had happened, to make sense of it all.

Delphine woke that afternoon after a long nap to find the cabin eerily quiet. Not a soul lingered in the room, ready to assist her needs; even the Acadian women were unusually absent. The ship had become silent in its movements as well, slowly sailing upon calm waters with a soft wind from the east. The air, too, had turned thick and humid, bugs flitting in through the portholes while in the distance seabirds called out.

Suddenly, she heard Phil shouting orders and the men hustling above deck to change course. They were tacking against a current, she could feel it beneath the floorboards. If Delphine wasn't mistaken, they were sailing up the Mississippi.

A surge of energy poured through her veins and she fought the desire to rush through her dressing and bolt to deck. Her head still groggy, Delphine pulled on her dress as slowly as she could manage, then remembered to grip the railing of the ladderway as she hurried up to the deck.

Delphine didn't know which felt more liberating, the Delta breeze teasing her curls for the first time in days or the sight of New Orleans appearing in the bend. She felt Charles reach her side and offer his arm for support, but her eyes never left the welcoming sight of her hometown nestled in the crescent of the mighty river.

Charles led her to the hatch by the main mast, and helped her sit down. Then both he and Francois joined her, her two friends flanking her sides as they watched the ship fight the currents toward the docks.

"So, this is the promised land everyone brags about," Francois said.

"It's hardly the promised land," Charles answered with a laugh. "It's hot, humid, and infested with bugs of all kinds, some that are way too large and fly. But it's home."

"Yes, it's home," Delphine reiterated, trying to keep her tears at bay.

Michel peered at them from behind the main mast and Francois pulled the boy into his lap. "Look, Michel," Francois said with emotion, "this will be our new Acadia."

Delphine took each man's hand, grateful for all her friends had given her. They were her heroes, even little Michel.

"Will we see you again, Phiney?" Michel asked shyly.

Delphine tucked a strand of hair behind Michel's ear, then tugged on his earlobe. "Of course, you will. You will be staying at my house as my guest until you receive your land grants."

"Do you want your dagger back now?"

She had completely forgotten about the borrowed dagger. She hardly needed it now. Besides, after all that had transpired, the last thing she wanted at present was another reminder of Phil.

"Keep it," she said to the boy, fighting back more tears. "I won't be needing it any longer."

# CHAPTER SIXTEEN

PHIL DIDN'T THINK IT WAS possible for Delphine to inflict more hurting words than she had in his cabin, but giving away his dagger sliced him to the core. It had been a present on her fifteenth birthday, a day he had taught her to dance.

She wouldn't look at him either, gathering with Francois and Charles at the main mast without so much as a glance to the wheel. Phil tried to brush the painful feelings away, concentrating instead on getting the ship to shore.

"Ahoy," a soldier called out to them.

"*Señor*," Phil answered in Spanish. "I need several soldiers to board my ship. I have two prisoners who must be taken to the Cabildo."

The man nodded and called to nearby soldiers who headed in their direction. The news brought curious stares from many residents on shore and excitement quickly spread to the Acadians on deck, already anxious to touch their feet on Louisiana mud and a freedom from life in exile. If only Phil could feel as hopeful.

"Grab that line," Phil shouted to Vincent.

The bow bumped hard against the makeshift dock, and the crew members rushed to tie *La Belle Amie* in place. The soldiers on shore pulled a gangplank toward the ship, but the first person to test its strength wore no uniform. Phil recognized the boots before the length of Jean came into view. Within seconds, his partner jumped aboard ship and met his daughter halfway to the railing, pulling her tightly into his massive arms.

Phil watched as Jean clutched his daughter's thin form, witnessed his eyes filling with worry. He looked over Delphine's shoulder in his direction for answers.

"I'll explain," Phil said to him with a heavy heart.

It was then Delphine finally regarded Phil, tears staining her pale cheeks. God, how he wanted to right all the misconceptions that had occurred since leaving France, to take her in his arms and kiss away all her sorrows and hurt, but how? She wouldn't even speak to him.

Phil approached Jean and the men shook hands, while Delphine turned away and attempted to compose herself.

"My carriage is here," Jean said. "Let me take Phiney home and warn Gabrielle that we will have several guests for dinner."

"There are twenty-three Acadians." Phil couldn't help himself; he turned toward Delphine and their eyes met briefly. In that instant, his heart ached, wanting to hold her as Jean did. "There is a gentleman here named Charles Armand who could use a place to rest before returning home upriver."

"They are all welcome," Jean said. "If not at my house, then at Coleman's. But, as you might have noticed, New Orleans is not at her best."

"Storm blew in?"

"Hurricane, only a few days ago." Jean pulled his daughter close, kissing her forehead. "Sunk all of Galvez's vessels and destroyed a few homes. I'm thankful you were spared that catastrophe."

Phil nodded, thinking a hurricane would have been welcomed compared to the anguish he suffered during the past week.

"Who is the lady?"

The soldiers marched on to deck, dragging a reluctant

Marie and Josephine behind. Marie still appeared her best, wearing her finest gown, her hair set in the latest coiffure. No one would have been the wiser to her deceptions had it not been for the bandage at her throat. But even it was masked with a necklace of jewels.

"Marie Labarthe, Countess de La Candelier," Phil said as she walked by, her eyes full of hatred at the sight of him.

Delphine turned away into the comfort of her father's shoulder, but Jean stared at him in disbelief. "You're kidding?"

"I wish I was," Phil said, again cursing the day he set eyes on the woman. "She ended up being my contact in France, but not the legitimate one. She's a spy, working for England. We discovered this when an English frigate nearly blew us out of the water."

"*Mon dieu*," Jean said, and Phil wondered if he was astonished at her espionage or that she and Phil had met again. It was the most ironic of circumstances when one considered the story, especially since it was Jean who had fished Phil out of the harbor when Marie betrayed him the first time. If he hadn't ached so, Phil might have laughed.

"What happened to her throat?" Jean asked.

Sebastien called out for instruction and one of the soldiers waited to hear of Marie's crime. Jean patted Phil on the back. "Let us go. I shall return within the hour and we will talk."

Phil nodded and headed toward the grouping of soldiers. Then he remembered Jean's question. "She had a run-in with the tip of my blade," Phil said, as they headed toward the starboard railing. "If not for the ethics of my crew members, that blade would have finished what it started and the Countess de la Candier would be at the bottom of the Gulf of Mexico right now."

Jean smirked as he watched Marie being led into a wagon. "Just as well. Let Galvez deal with her crimes."

Phil looked at his partner and best friend one last time

before they headed to shore. Would Jean feel the same way when he learned that Marie almost murdered his daughter?

"She did what?"

Gabrielle moved from her position at the back of Delphine's bath where she was trying to untangle her mass of curls. Her rich Acadian eyes glistened with worry.

"I'm fine," Delphine said, placing a wet hand on Gabrielle's cheek. "I survived."

Gabrielle grabbed her hand with both hands. "I want to know everything. Does your father know?"

Delphine shook her head. "I told him I was sick, but he doesn't believe me."

"You're never sick, why would he?"

Gabrielle rose and poured them both a large glass of wine. When she handed Delphine the glass, she took a large sip, hoping the wine might ease her suffering. But it only made the tears come.

"I want to hear everything," Gabrielle commanded, wiping her face. "Starting from the moment you landed at St. Malo."

Delphine took one more sip, then placed the glass on the floor. Sinking deeper into the tub, she explained it all, starting with meeting her grandmother in her large, cold house to Phil's guilty apology in the cabin. Gabrielle listened intently to the end of the story, then rose and retrieved a comb. When she returned, she moved to the back of the bath and began smoothing out Delphine's hair.

"He didn't sleep with Marie," she said matter-of-factly. "Phil never would have done such a thing to you. Never."

Delphine assumed as much, but her confused mind had let her think the worst. Suddenly, she felt guilty that she hadn't given Phil a chance to explain.

"Then why did he leave me? Why did he go to her

hotel?"

"If he knew her to be a spy, why not?"

Delphine thought of what Phil had said on deck to Jean. He said he had known of Marie's traitorous activities since the English attack. If that was true, then all his flirtations with the Countess during the voyage had been staged, no doubt to obtain information.

"Pirate's Rule Number Four," Delphine recited to herself. "Know thy enemy." Hadn't she done the same thing to Marie while in France?

"He loves you," Gabrielle said as the comb finally freed the knots in her hair. "He came to us after you sailed. When he heard you had left for France, he didn't even speak to say good-bye, exited the house a defeated man."

Thinking back on their lovemaking and the way Phil had held her as he carried her to the bed, Delphine knew that Gabrielle was right. Then there was that time in her grandmother's study when he had professed his love. Only Delphine had interpreted it as being platonic.

"Delphine," Gabrielle said, hugging her stepdaughter from behind. "Before Phil learned that you were to become a Countess, Jean and I could have sworn he was going to ask for your hand."

Delphine gripped Gabrielle's arms about her and set her tears free. No matter what it took, she would make this right.

Jean took the news well, Phil thought, considering that his daughter had skirted the threshold of death. Phil only wished he could forgive himself as easily.

"It wasn't your fault," Jean said.

Phil grimaced as if a knife slid through his middle. "Of course, it was. I should have told her." He began pacing the main cabin, anything to relieve the agony of it all. "I was worried she would go sneaking around Marie's cabin and look what happened?"

"Delphine is notorious for getting into trouble," Jean said. "You did the right thing."

If only he could believe that. "No, I was wrong. I should have told her. She thought I was still in love with Marie and I let her believe it."

"Are you?"

Phil stared at his partner, wondering if Jean imagined he cared for the Countess all these years. "No," he stated firmly.

Jean accepted this and nodded, not appearing surprised in the least. "You're still not to blame. I know Delphine. She would have loved the thought of having a spy on board, particularly your former lover who caused you ruin."

Phil rubbed his forehead, thinking about the nights he and Delphine had shared in that very cabin, nights when he could have been honest with his feelings. "I should have told her."

"Then she might have been poisoned at the beginning of the voyage."

Phil paused at the end of the bed, gripping the bedpost tightly. No, he was to blame. She was his confidant, always had been. And she had suspected Marie of more than espionage, he was sure. Delphine had been looking for more than a letter from the English governor that night.

"What aren't you telling me?" Jean asked.

Perhaps things like titles and land didn't matter, as Francois had said. Perhaps the only reason to live in this wretched world was for the love of another. Phil had certainly experienced that brutal lesson watching his beloved Phiney slip beneath death's blade.

"I love your daughter," Phil finally said. "I'm sorry, Jean, but I can't live without her."

He glanced at his partner, but Jean's features betrayed nothing. He stood staring at him emotionless.

"I know she will lose everything," Phil said, taking the

opportunity to state his mind, "but we love each other. For so long I have wished the best for her, a stable marriage, a husband of nobility, but that's not what Delphine needs. She needs me and I her. I will make her happy the rest of my days, I swear it. She will never want for a thing as long as I draw breath, you can rest assure of that."

Jean said nothing, but the edges of his lips curled up slightly. "It's about time."

Before Phil could comprehend his words, Jean strolled forward, his hand outstretched. The men shook, then Jean pulled him into a tight embrace. When he finally pulled away, Jean patted him on the shoulder affectionately.

"Couldn't think of a better son-in-law," he said, his eyes glistening.

"Then you're not upset?"

Jean laughed, his dimple deepening. "Do I look upset?"

Phil expelled his breath, then leaned back against the bedpost. "But she loses everything marrying me. I'm a commoner."

The grin on Jean's face lessened only slightly. He pulled a bottle of rum from the bottom desk drawer and poured them both a glass. "I have something to tell you," he said, handing Phil his. "We are not as destitute as you might think." Tipping back his glass and sighing as the rum hit his throat, Jean continued, "We have taken on a partner since you left for France. In fact, this partner hails from St. Malo, most likely a friend of the Delaronde family."

Phil was thoroughly confused, but he let Jean carry on. "He wrote to me from France, saying he had met our beloved Delphine, heard her tales of Louisiana, and was entranced by our mission. He enclosed several thousand *livre tournois* and asked to be a third partner in our operation."

"Who is this man?"

"Someone by the name of Pierre Magon. Sound familiar?"

Phil had to laugh. Magons were as common to St. Malo as corsairs.

"*Tapez dans un buisson, un Magon en sortira,*" Phil recited. "Shake any bush and a Magon will fall out of it."

"Well, whatever bush he fell from, I'm grateful for it."

"And you trust this man?"

Jean laughed as he poured them both another round. "The man sent us a small fortune with no questions asked. If he was careless enough to send two pirates cash, then I'd say he can be trusted." Jean handed Phil the glass, then drank his fill. "Besides, I checked up on the man, sent letters to France and got an affirmative answer."

The glass stilled in Phil's hand on the way to his lips. "How long ago did you receive this money?"

Jean studied the movement in the harbor through the dirty porthole. "This ship needs a massive cleaning."

"Jean?"

Jean waved his hand without looking around. "I meant to tell you, something always came up."

Something wasn't right here, but Phil doubted Jean was being dishonest. "What aren't you telling me now?"

Jean turned and offered his trademark dimple, only his eyes remained cautious. "I spent the money."

Phil relaxed. "I trust your judgment. Surely, you don't think I need to know of everything you do."

Jean's dimple deepened and he placed his empty glass upon the desk. He reached inside his coat pocket and retrieved a parchment, then handed the letter to Phil.

"What's this?" Phil asked, taking the parchment.

"A royal grant. Signed by the king."

What joke was this? His partner was always one to jest, but now seemed such an inappropriate time considering they were discussing her daughter's ruin by marriage to him. Still, Phil unfolded the letter and found King Louis's signature at the bottom. He glanced up at Jean to see what mischief his friend had bestowed, but suddenly Jean was quite serious.

"It's a letters patent," Jean said, refilling their glasses. "They're not that difficult to obtain, really. All it took was a letter from Galvez and a hefty sum and King Louis was all too happy to admit you into the nobility."

His breath stolen from his lungs, Phil glanced quickly down at the paper in his hands, searching through its contents until he recognized his name.

"Now, don't get too excited," Jean said, handing him his glass. "You're merely a nobleman, as am I. But as soon as you marry Delphine, you shall be titled as well."

Phil felt the glass being placed in his hand, but he needed to sit down. It was too much to absorb at once. Could it be possible that all their troubles disappeared with that one piece of parchment.

"If this is true," Phil said with a catch in his throat, "you have saved my life for the second time."

Jean smiled, raising his glass high. "It is true, *mon ami*. To you and Phiney. May you be as happy as Gabrielle and I have been these last ten years."

Phil met his glass, then tossed back the rum. "I don't know what to say."

"Consider it an investment," Jean said, placing a hand on his shoulder. "I expect you two to see this enterprise turn profitable again."

Phil nodded, a sense of bliss overtaking him as he acknowledged that happiness was finally in store for him. "Now that my task is done for Galvez and the Americans, we will return to doing what we do best, smuggling goods and making money."

The smile that lingered on Jean's lips disappeared. "I'm afraid that may have to wait a little bit longer."

Phil should have known, considering that Spain had entered the war against England. If the English were indeed planning on capturing New Orleans, they would do so as soon as they received news of Spain aligning with France.

"Time is of the essence," Jean said. "Galvez believes the English do not know of Spain's entrance into the war. He plans to attack Baton Rouge before the English hear word and attack New Orleans first."

Phil's heart, so quickly infused with joy, deflated at the knowledge. "When do we leave?"

# CHAPTER SEVENTEEN

"Y OUR AIM IS TOO HIGH, Michel. You need to hold the blade in front of your chest, *comme ca.*"

Demonstrating the correct use of the foils, Delphine dashed forward slightly to set Michel into action. For a tiny child, he moved quickly out of harm's way, dogging her blade expertly.

"Good," she said with a grin. "You learn fast."

"I shall be able to defend the city should the English attack," the boy said proudly.

Delphine lowered her blade, reminded of the conflict at Baton Rouge. For a few odd moments she had been spared thinking of the men marching upon the English fort upriver, but now her heart constricted at the image her mind played over and over inside her head. While her thoughts were with Phil and the rest of her family, Michel charged and knocked the blade from her fingers.

"Not bad," she exclaimed.

Michel bowed politely with a smug smile upon his face. "It was excellent, actually. I have unarmed the famous Delphine Delaronde."

My, but the tyke had grown bold in a such a short amount of time. Delphine was glad of it, knowing he would need such bravery and arrogance surviving in the new world. But she had one more lesson to impart.

"The name's Delphine Bouclaire."

Before Michel had time to inquire, Gabrielle and her two sisters entered the courtyard. Every morning they had attended Mass to pray for their men while Delphine watched the children. Teaching fencing in men's breeches was preferable to crying inside the St. Louis Cathedral. "Haven't you two done anything else besides fence today?" Gabrielle asked.

"I bested her," Michel said proudly.

Gabrielle raised an eye.

"He did," Delphine said, placing a hand over her heart dramatically. "I may have to retire now."

"That, my dear, would be very hard to believe." Gabrielle picked up Julian, her youngest, a dark-haired boy who also sported the Bouclaire dimple, and gave him a squeeze.

"I know how you feel," said Emilie, Gabrielle's oldest sister, who also greeted her assemblage of tykes. "If only the children had been older, I would have gone with them."

"Lorenz and the others never would have allowed it," said Rose, the youngest of the Gallant sisters and the mother of two sets of twins, all busy climbing the courtyard's banana trees.

"It didn't stop her before," Gabrielle said with a grin.

When the family first entered Louisiana and began a search for their father, Emilie had followed her best friend, Lorenz Dugas, into the wilderness. The story of the Gallant sisters, who had reunited their parents torn apart by the Acadian exile, had become legend in Louisiana. And Lorenz had become part of the family along with Rose's husband Coleman.

"I detest waiting," Delphine said, kicking a cup that had fallen into the dust. "Why must women always be left behind to wait?"

"If Mama could do it for fourteen years living in exile, then I suppose we can endure a few weeks."

Give it to Rose to make sense of it all, Delphine thought. They all looked upon her petite form and smiled, but her statement did little to relieve their suffering. As she had the morning the men left for battle, Delphine felt as if her heart might shatter into millions of pieces.

Gabrielle placed an arm about Delphine and Emilie took her hand while she placed a protective arm about Rose's shoulders. "We will live through this," Emilie commanded, like the big sister she always would be. "Our names aren't Gallant for nothing." With a side glance to Delphine, she added, "And as for you, Countess Bouclaire-Delaronde, you're a Gallant whether you wish it to be or not."

Thank God for family, Delphine thought, cherishing the comfort of her adopted family. "I am proud to be a Gallant sister. And I cherish the day I met you all."

The foursome put their heads together and laughed, although inside they all still quivered with fear. Suddenly, a soldier appeared at the back end of the courtyard, knocking loudly upon the gate.

"Excuse me *señoritas*," he announced. "I am looking for Mademoiselle Delaronde."

Delphine stepped forward, forgetting she had donned male breeches. "I am she."

The soldier stifled a smile, then bowed politely. "Mademoiselle Delaronde, I am in need of your service."

"Countess Delaronde," Emilie interjected.

The soldier blushed and began to correct his mistake, but Delphine interrupted. "How may I help you, sir?"

"A prisoner was in our care, Countess. She has escaped, stealing one of our carriages and heading north. We thought, perhaps, you might know…"

"Marie Labarthe?"

"The very one," the other soldier said nervously. "She has great skill with her charms. She tricked one of our young comrades with her seductiveness."

Delphine didn't need to think twice. She retrieved her blade from the grass and sheaved it, then turned to her sisters for support. It was no surprise that they had read her mind.

"I will get the gun and your horse," Emilie said and headed for the stables with Rose.

"I will pack you some provisions." Gabrielle hiked her skirts and ran toward the kitchen.

Only the soldiers seemed confused. "Do you know where the Countess De La Candelier is, mademoiselle?"

Delphine pulled on her father's coat, then rolled the sleeves up to find her hands. "Of course, I do. She has gone to inform the English that our forces are moving upriver. If we do not stop her, Galvez will lose the benefit of a surprise attack."

"Where do you think she's heading?" the other soldier asked.

"She's heading for Lake Pontchartrain," Delphine answered. "There's been an English ship patrolling there for the past two years. She wishes to make contact with them."

"How do you know this?" the first soldier asked.

Emilie returned with the flintlock and pistol, which Delphine placed on her shoulder and inside her waistband, while Gabrielle arrived with a satchel of food. Rose's youngest set of twins placed apples inside her pockets and Michel reached her side handing her the beloved dagger.

Delphine glanced around and offered them all a brave smile. For the first time in weeks, she wasn't afraid.

"I know this, *señor*, because I told the Countess about this ship myself."

"But can you be sure?" the other asked.

With the help of her oldest son Richard, Rose led the horse into the courtyard and Delphine mounted the mare. She tucked the extra gunpowder and satchel behind her saddle, then tightened the reins.

"Unfortunately, *señor*, I know the Countess all too well, and I can assure you she is heading toward the lake. To head toward Baton Rouge would mean swamp and our delicate Countess does not have the temperament for such a trip. The British at our backs is the quickest route. Now, if you wish to keep up with me, I'd advise you to mount your horse now."

With a quick kick to the mare's flanks, Delphine charged away in the direction of Lake Pontchartrain, the Spanish soldiers struggling to follow.

It wasn't long before the massive lake became visible, a lone ship sailing in the distance, but the Spanish soldiers remained far behind. When Delphine spied a deserted carriage alongside an abandoned farmhouse, she dismounted her horse and tied her to a secluded cypress.

She silently drew closer to the house, wondering if they had arrived too late. When she heard noises and the sound of a woman cussing coming from inside, Delphine knew luck was on her side that morning. She drew the dagger from her boot and entered the dwelling, moving as soundless as a snake.

Marie stood beside the far wall, her skirt ripped in places and her hair tangled with briars and twigs. She spit out angry words more natural to a sailor while she attempted to smooth out her filthy bodice.

"Those are not very becoming words of a Countess."

Marie wiped around to face her. "What are you doing here?" she said in shock.

When the two women stood boot to muddy slipper, Delphine had to laugh. "Didn't you learn anything from our discussions, Marie? Or did you not think Louisiana was really a swamp?"

Marie raised a hand to strike her, but Delphine was quicker. She intercepted her wrist, then turned her arm behind her back so it was close to breaking. "I wouldn't take a chance with me, Countess," she whispered to Marie from behind. "You're on my soil now."

"Let me go, you whore," Marie yelled out.

Delphine did as she was bid, releasing Marie so suddenly she fell to the floor. The contention caused her pause, but Marie wasn't through fighting.

"He never loved you," she said with a snarl. "I own Philibert body and soul."

Delphine leaned against the side of the kitchen table and examined the blade of her dagger, dusting it off on her sleeve. "Funny, I didn't think men came with mortgages."

Marie narrowed her eyes and tilted her chin from her place on the floor. "He visited my cabin every night of the voyage. We were planning to marry."

Delphine lifted a lazy leg over the edge of the table. "I knew exactly where he was aboard ship, Marie, but then you don't expect me to believe the word of a traitorous bitch such as yourself."

The Countess attempted to rise and strike Delphine again, but she never made it past the table's corner. Delphine placed a quick boot to her shoulder and she fell against the far wall. Delphine stood and gazed down at her nemesis, lying crumpled in a corner. "As I said, Marie, do not take chances with me. You will not win."

Marie felt the wall behind her, then glanced in both directions to study her escape. "You can't hold me here. The English are on their way. I've already signaled their ship. I'll have you arrested and hanged."

"No doubt, Countess. I'm sure you've slept with enough Englishmen to carry quite a weight with the officers."

"At least I can go to my grave knowing that I've been worshipped by many." The Countess let her gaze travel down the length of Delphine. "What will you be known for, Delphine? A snit of a girl with a dagger beneath your skirts? A bastard girl that society laughed at behind her back?"

Delphine should have been irate at the thought of St. Malo snickering at her colonial ways, but it was the word bastard that burned her veins. She knelt upon the floor before Marie, pinning one of Marie's arms with a knee and thrust the notorious dagger beneath her pearly, scared throat.

"Call me that again, Marie," she whispered heatedly. "I dare you to insult my father again."

Marie used her free hand to grab Delphine's arm to pull the dagger free, but the movement only forced Delphine to deepen the blade beneath the skin. "You really should stop antagonizing us swamp rats, Marie. Your lovely neck can't take much more of this."

"Stop," she choked out. "You're still a Countess. What would your grandmother think of you now?"

In truth, her grandmother might have approved. But Delphine had no intention of doing anything but scaring Marie. Not unless the need arose. Somewhere in the dark recesses of Delphine's mind, she hoped it would.

"My grandmother always disliked you. Ever since your wedding, the night you betrayed Phil in front of all those people. Or did you really believe society worshipped you all those years."

"They knew nothing," Marie said proudly. "Not even after I killed my insipid husband and poured his money across the Channel. For years I sent Frenchmen to their graves and still they asked for my company, the men always eager to make my acquaintance, eager to kiss my feet."

Delphine thought of Phil, of a young man so desperately in love that he nearly lost his life. She thought of the Acadian families they had rescued in St. Malo, innocent women and children so close to being brought back to an English prison because of the traitorous actions of one woman. She thought of the way Marie had cowardly drugged her tea, ready to discard her body into the ocean to cover up her deeds.

Twisting the blade ever so slightly, Delphine broke skin where an ugly scare already existed. Marie gasped as a small stream of blood trickled down the front of her bodice. In that instant, Delphine wanted her dead.

"When you meet your maker and he judges you for those you have destroyed, you can tell him that men were always eager to make your acquaintance." She felt the tears burn at the corners of her eyes at the injustice of it all, but rage still dominated her body. "I hope he damns you to hell."

Marie finally relinquished hope, closing her eyes for the moment when the blade would sever her life force. But the door behind them opened and a voice brought Delphine back from the darkness of rage.

"Drop the blade, Delphine."

At the sound of Charles's voice, Delphine withdrew her dagger. Marie grasped her throat to make sure it was intact, then scurried along the wall to put distance between them.

"There are Spanish soldiers coming," she told him. "We chased her here after she escaped the Cabildo." Suddenly, Delphine felt drained of all energy. When Charles offered his hand, she let him help her to her feet. "They should be arriving any minute now to take her back to the city."

"It doesn't matter," Charles said. "We run the lake now. I have plenty of men to do the deed."

Delphine wasn't sure what Charles meant by that, but she was too tired to inquire. She leaned against the table and watched as he and three other armed men escorted Marie out of the house, Charles instructing the men to be diligently wary of the Countess's charms. But when Charles returned, Delphine wanted answers.

"We headed upriver with Galvez's men, ready to conquer the English forts of Manchac and Baton Rouge," Charles explained. "But along the way we met an American privateer by the name of William Pickles who desired to take over the English ship *West Florida* on Lake Pontchartrain. If he accomplished this feat, it would provide a Spanish-American defense behind New Orleans."

Delphine glanced out the window and noticed that the ship she had seen before was docked at the water's edge with several men coming and going. Indeed, the ship carried close to a dozen cannon, an impressive defense at that.

"Being seafaring men, as opposed to militia, we decided to join him."

"We?" Delphine asked, her breath catching in her throat.

"Well, I'm hardly capable of leading an attack at sea."

Before Delphine had time to inquire further, the door swung open wide. Two boots hit the floorboards as a tall shadow fell upon them. When Phil's eyes met hers, her breath ceased completely.

They stared at each other for several minutes before Phil finally spoke, his tone harsh, perhaps condemning. "Leave us alone, please Charles."

Charles nodded, then paused as he passed Phil at the threshold. "Don't be too hard on her, Phil. She did manage to catch our prisoner."

When Charles exited the building, Phil closed the door behind him.

"Marie's out front," Delphine said in her defense. "The soldiers will be taking her back to town so if you want to speak to her, you should do it now."

Phil said nothing, merely stared, which unnerved Delphine to the core.

"The Spanish soldiers came to my house, Phil. They said Marie had escaped and I knew where she was going. She and I had discussed the *West Florida* in France. She had been particularly interested in the English on Lake Pontchartrain."

Still, he said nothing, and Delphine wanted to scream from the silence. At last, he stepped closer, allowing her a chance to study his countenance for anger. As Phil inched toward the light of the window, Delphine detected tension in his jaw.

"I'm sorry I didn't stay at home. I know I shouldn't be

here, but…"

Before she had time to finish her thought, let alone her sentence, Phil's arms pulled her forward, his lips meeting hers. Finally, realization hit and Delphine relaxed beneath his grip, winding her arms about his neck and eagerly deepening the kiss.

They maintained the frenzied hunger for several moments before finally coming up for air. While Delphine sought to control her ragged breathing, Phil nibbled a trail from her lips to her earlobe, then paused at her neck, his breath hot on her ears.

"I love you, Delphine," he whispered, and all the world disappeared.

Delphine turned to meet his lips once more, this time placing her hands on either side of his head to savor every precious moment. Phil reached down and secured his hands behind her back, then lifted her up and around until she broke free with laughter. When he set her back down to earth, he gazed at her lovingly, then his lips sought hers once more, biting, teasing, savoring the feel of her mouth while his hands discovered every aspect of her being.

Through the haze of their lovemaking, Delphine heard the door open, but it took the sound of a throat being cleared to finally break them apart. Phil never let Delphine go, but turned toward the intrusion.

"Sorry to bother you two," Francois said with a wicked grin, "but the men need their orders."

"Send any on with the Countess to New Orleans and make sure she will be bound in chains," Phil said. "Give explicit instructions that they do not give her liberties."

"And the rest of the men?"

"Tell them to remain on deck with Pickles. I believe our good captain wishes to travel to the north side of the lake and claim it in the name of the United States."

Francois nodded, sending a quick smile toward Delphine. "And what might your needs be, *Capitaine*?"

Still holding tightly to Delphine's waist, Phil spoke to his cousin as if she wasn't there. "Bring Father Felician to me. Tell him I need his services."

At this, Delphine pulled away slightly to gauge his expression. "Father Felician?"

Phil grinned smugly. "A priest we picked up in St. Gabriel, an Acadian who insisted he help fight the English."

Whatever smile Francois had bestowed on them before, it increased tenfold. "May I have the honor of standing as your best man?" he asked his cousin.

Now, it was Phil's turn to beam. "I'd be honored and privileged to have family present."

Francois bowed toward them both, then left the house still sporting his mischievous grin. When Delphine turned to ask Phil to explain, he captured her lips again, but this time, she pushed him away. "Father Felician?" she repeated.

Phil immediately dropped to one knee, his sword rattling against the floorboards. He took Delphine's hand and pressed it to his lips. "Mademoiselle Delphine Bouclaire, Countess Delaronde, will you honor me by being my wife?"

Delphine's chin dropped open and she stared at him in a stupor.

"Will you be my partner, share my ship, my voyages, my cabin?" He paused at the last word, his eyes glistening with promise while a smile teased his lips.

"Phil, I…"

"Will you bring me my coffee, help reef my sails, wrestle an alligator if necessary?"

She wanted to slap him for teasing her this way, was about to tell him what a horrid man he was when suddenly his smile disappeared.

"Phiney," he whispered heatedly. "Please end my suffering and grant me happiness the rest of my days. Please say the word that will be my salvation. Tell me you will marry me."

Delphine leaned forward, brushing the wild curls at his forehead. She gazed into the dark eyes that had stolen her heart so many years ago, the eyes that had and would haunt her the rest of her life.

"What took you so long?" she whispered back.

# CHAPTER EIGHTEEN

EVERYTHING HAPPENED SO QUICKLY, IT wasn't until the ceremony concluded that Phil noticed his wife appeared more like a man than a blushing bride. Her hair was in its usual state of disarray and her clothes breathed dust, no doubt from the ride in from New Orleans. Even her boots were laced with the gumbo mud inherent of the lake area.

"I've married a swamp rat," he whispered to her, taking the opportunity to nibble on her ear.

She shivered at the gesture, moving out of his reach since they shared the room with Charles and Francois, not to mention a priest. "Ah, but I clean up nicely," she whispered back. "I am a Countess you know?"

It was then that Phil realized she had married him without thought to her title and had exchanged her land and fortune for his love. He had to tell her, if nothing else but to relieve her mind. "Delphine, we must talk."

She gazed at him, deep in thought, and Phil worried if she regretted her rash decision to marry him. "I told you before it never mattered to me."

Before Phil had time to rebut, Francois was proposing a toast. "To my favorite cousin this side of the Atlantic."

"To your only cousin," Phil interjected.

Francois sent him a mock bow amidst the laughter. "To my only cousin, but one I've grown quite fond of, despite his stubborn nature and sometimes bad judgment and poor decision-making skills."

Phil placed both hands upon his hips, but he had to laugh. Over the past few weeks, as they fought a common enemy as a team, he had become quite fond of Francois as well.

"Let me include poor timing," Charles added. "Phil finally comes to his senses to marry the finest woman in the colony of Louisiana and he chooses a moment when she is in breeches and boots."

Everyone laughed, including Delphine, who performed a curtsy holding the sides of Jean's coat like a skirt.

Francois held his glass up once more, this time seriously. "But here's to an outstanding couple who most definitely belong together. May you both be as happy as I have been in marriage. And may your bonds last you the rest of your days, all of them healthy, peaceful, prosperous ones."

Phil raised his glass to Francois's but the thought of his cousin's loss clouded his happiness. "May you, too, find happiness in your new home."

Francois attempted a smile, but Phil somehow knew he would never marry again. "I found happiness once, *mon ami*, and that was enough." Waving his glass to those around him, Francois added, "For now, I have friends and family and for that, I am eternally grateful."

Delphine rushed forward and kissed Francois's cheek, then thought better of the slight affection and wrapped her arms about his neck. Francois seemed startled at first, then returned the hug. "I'd welcome you to the family, but I'm wondering if I should be offering condolences instead," he said.

Delphine laughed. "My family is no walk in the park either. You would be wise to sail back to France."

Francois placed a hand over his heart. "What? And miss my chance at shooting at the English? Never."

"Speaking of the English," Charles said, grabbing Francois's sleeve. "Perhaps it's time we returned to the ship."

Charles hugged Delphine and shook Phil's hand, while Francois made his good-byes to his cousin. Then they both moved to leave. Only Father Felician seemed surprised at their sudden departure. He was ready to continue with another round until Francois took him by the shoulders and pushed him toward the door.

"What's the hurry?" the priest asked. "The ceremony just ended."

"Newlyweds," Charles said softly. "They should be alone."

Father Felician gazed back in shock. "In the middle of the afternoon? Surely not."

The last image Phil received was Charles and Francois pushing the priest out the door, while Francois returned quickly to nab another bottle of wine. Then the door clicked shut and they were blessedly alone. Now was the time to tell Delphine the news.

"Delphine, we must talk," Phil told her, but he was quickly interrupted with a kiss.

"Later," she whispered, grabbing the front of his shirt. "The bedroom is on the second floor."

Phil didn't have to be given more encouragement. He leaned down to capture Delphine by the back of her knees, then pushed her over his shoulder and carried her up the stairs, her giggles echoing the whole way. The first thing to go at the top of the stairs as soon as her feet reached earth again were her muddy boots, one containing her blessed dagger, then Jean's coat.

She, in turn, eagerly removed Phil's coat, letting it fall upon the floor, then her fingers found his shirt buttons while their lips ravaged each other's. He pulled her shirt free from her waistband, slipping his hands underneath her shift, moaning as he finally touched bare skin. He couldn't be rid of the clothing fast enough, couldn't wait to make unending love to her.

They backed up toward the bed until Phil's feet touched something hard on the floor. When he turned, he realized it wasn't a bedroom at all, but a storeroom quickly cleaned and converted into a place for two people to sleep. In its center were two bunk mattresses placed together and covered with homespun sheets and a blanket. Above, a mosquito netting cascaded down. And surrounding the love nest were rum bottles filled with wildflowers.

"Charles and Francois did this," Delphine said over his shoulder. "While you were speaking to Father Felician, they brought the mattresses and sheets in from the ship."

When Phil met her eyes once more, his brown irises glistening with happiness and strands of his chestnut hair escaping upon his forehead, Delphine knew true bliss was at hand. She may have doubted it earlier, not trusting her ears when he had asked for her hand. But they were married now, standing before their rugged marriage bed, ready to meet the world as one.

Stealthy, Phil took her head in his hands, gently brushing his lips upon hers, then deepening the kiss until their tongues joined in union. As he savored the reaches of her mouth and she his, they both moaned, which brought a round of chuckles.

But, Delphine didn't have time to recover. Still giggling, Phil took the opportunity to raise the shirt over her head, fling it across the room, then lift her up against him and carry her toward the bed.

Delphine wouldn't let him have the upper hand, however. She wrapped her legs around his waist wantonly, pulling her fingers through his coarse hair, freeing it from its tie. Then she tilted her head and bit his right ear.

"You brazen woman," he whispered, placing a hand at the small of her back and pushing her forward, then taking a nipple into his gently teasing teeth. Through the sheer fabric of her shift he suckled and rolled the nub back and forth between his hot, wet lips.

Wild sensations roared through her and Delphine thought the world might explode right there and then. But she didn't have time to let it. Within seconds, Phil had tossed the netting aside and thrown her down upon the makeshift bed, his tall form falling on top with her legs still wrapped around his middle.

They laughed again but the merriment didn't last long. Phil quickly unbuttoned the shift and yanked it from her shoulders. She, in turn, lifted his shirt above his head, savoring the feel of brown curls gracing his tanned chest. Then they fell into an embrace, enjoying the feel of their naked bodies against one another.

Phil kissed her everywhere, beginning with her nape and descending to her belly, the insides of her knees, the dramatic arch of her foot. But he returned to her breasts, savoring the feel of them in the palms of his hands. His tongue danced upon the tips, the most delicious minuet she had ever experienced, and Delphine arched her back in reverence.

He reached a hand around to the small of her back, then pressed them close together and moaned. Delphine felt every inch of his desire, her feminine core ready to burst at the contact.

Phil broke away briefly and stared into her eyes. "It hurts the first time, pet."

Still relishing the heated sensations pouring through her body, Delphine smiled. "Only for women who spend their lives drinking tea and attending balls. Never for swamp rats who are descended from pirates."

Phil paused, his hair still wild about his forehead. Heavens, but the man at his disheveled worst stole her breath away. She placed a hand on his cheek and smiled, trying to relieve his worries. "Make love to me, *Capitaine*," she whispered.

Whatever merriment they had shared before disappeared from his eyes, but Phil obeyed, removing their breeches until nothing came between them. His long, muscular form paralleled hers on the bed, and he spent several minutes absorbing the sight of her, brushing her skin with the tips of his fingertips until they rested at the place where heaven existed.

Delphine rested on her back and gave him entrance, closing her eyes when his fingers entered her and his thumb brushed the spot that generated lightning. She knew what he was doing, preparing her for the union. But she wanted him now.

"Come inside me," she whispered through the pleasure of his touch.

"Patience, my love," he whispered back.

Delphine owned many traits, but patience wasn't one of them. She knew he would deliver her pleasure, as he had done that day in Santa Domingo, but tonight, she wanted more. Tonight, she wanted him.

Delphine pushed his hand aside, then quickly sat up upon the bed. Before Phil had time to consider her movement, she straddled his waist, rising and falling back to earth to take in the whole of him.

He was much larger than she had anticipated, her body stretching furiously to absorb it all. Suddenly, Delphine regretted her haste as her breath left her lungs and her body screamed in protest.

Phil's eyes widened in alarm and he rose to meet her, taking her in his arms while their bodies remained joined. "Dear God, Phiney, what have you done?"

What had she done? She was forever rushing into things without much forethought. But she wasn't giving up now. She wanted this and she would see it through. And she would be damned if she let it hurt.

Delphine inhaled and expelled, feeling the union settle more comfortably around her hips. Now that he was at her side, she slipped her legs around his waist and wrapped her arms about his neck.

"That's much better," she said, suddenly aware that they were joined, that their union filled her like nothing had before.

Still gazing intently into her eyes, Phil took her hips and raised her slightly, then brought them back together. The movement caused more pain, but Delphine focused on his eyes, focused on the wondrous scent of him, the way tiny lines appeared about his eyes when he smiled at her. Only he wasn't smiling now, most likely because she had begun to grit her teeth.

"I love you," he said in his usual brotherly fashion, "but on this trip, I captain the ship."

He immediately tightened his grip of her and moved her on her back. This time, Phil entered her slowly, gently pushing farther and farther inside her with exquisite Bertrand control. This time, it was he who began to grit his teeth as he carefully restrained his movements in care of her comfort.

"It doesn't hurt you, does it?" she asked, watching his jaw tense.

Phil smiled grimly and shook his head, the curls dropping again across his slick forehead, wet from perspiration. "God, no," he whispered so passionately Delphine felt the goosebumps scatter across her skin.

Now, that the initial shock was over and she knew her body offered him exquisite pleasure, Delphine relaxed and began to enjoy the wavelike movement of their passion. The feeling resembled the first time he had made love to her, but a deeper, more satisfying pleasure built within her, rising further and further to the surface as he pulsated back and forth.

Delphine raised her ankles around his thighs to give him better access and Phil plunged deeper. When he took hold of her bottom and pushed farther inside, Delphine's world began to quake. She tilted her head back, dizzy with the rolling sensations, closing her eyes to let the pleasure wash over her.

And it did so with alarming force. She gasped loudly, then cried out as spasms rocked her body, causing tiny white lights to flit above her sight and a wave of intense contentment to overtake her. She heard Phil cry out her name, then hold her tightly, as he, too, joined her in ecstasy.

Within minutes, the amazing voyage was over, but as Delphine sailed down the ebb of the astonishing wave, she felt Phil's kisses upon her face. For the first time in her life, she knew happiness was truly hers.

"Delphine, we have to talk."

She didn't know if it was the subject of Marie or the fact that his naked body was lying next to hers, ready for the taking, but Delphine had no use for speeches. She looped a fingertip around his nipple. "Does this feel as good to you as it does to me?"

A shiver ran through him and Delphine suspected it did, but Phil captured his hand. "There is something I need to tell you."

If it had to do with Marie, she'd rather not know. Or perhaps she would, but not now. Not when they were so blissful together. "How soon can we do it again?"

At this, Phil smiled. "I'd be happy never to leave this bed, but I think you need a rest."

Delphine rose slightly and leaned her head on an elbow, looking down on his face with a frown as some of her curls brushed against his chest. "Rest?"

Phil laughed as he took one of her strands and tugged at it playfully. "Should have figured you would never need rest." Then his gaze turned solemn. "But we really must talk, pet. There are things you must know."

Delphine sighed and fell on her back, staring at the intricate lace of the mosquito netting. "Agreed. But only if I may start first."

She felt his hand in her hair, stroking it gently, reverently. When she gazed back at him, so much love poured forth she was filled with shame for once believing he had betrayed her.

"What do you want to tell me?" he asked softly.

She nestled closer, wondering how he would take the news. Only her grandmother had known, and they had never spoken of it since the day they had initiated their mission. Delphine swallowed, then forged ahead. "You asked me to be your partner," she said softly. "Well, I already am."

Now it was Phil's turn to raise himself on an elbow. "What do you mean?"

"In actuality, I have lost my position as partner, since now we are married, but I was until an hour ago."

The lines around Phil's eyes appeared as he sent her something between a frown and a smile. "Delphine, what are you talking about?"

Delphine exhaled, wondering how he would accept the news, but it had to be told. "I know about the business, about *La Belle Amie*. I know you and Papa have been having financial trouble."

His frown intensified but she continued. "I knew Papa would never accept my help so I sent him money under the name of another. I asked to be made a third partner and Papa agreed."

"Pierre Magon"

Delphine's chest constricted realizing Phil knew of the pact, and the fact that he wasn't smiling made her wonder if he was angry. She suddenly felt defensive. "I only wanted to help, Phil. I'll never forgive you two for not telling me. If it hadn't been for a comment Gabrielle made and me searching through the books…"

Phil sat up, crossing his arms about him. "You looked through our books?"

Delphine rose and met his eyes boldly, pulling a sheet up to cover herself. "Of course, I did. How else would I have known about our business?"

Phil attempted to lean forward and state that it was his and Jean's business, not *theirs*, but that was as far from the truth as Phil was from the nobility. Delphine had always been a part of their operation, as natural to *La Belle Amie* as salt water under her keel. In hindsight, they should have told her, should have shared the bad times with her along with the good. And considering that he almost let her die once, he should have told her a lot of things.

Suddenly, the absurdity of the situation struck him and he began to laugh. It was her turn to cross her arms about her chest. "What's so funny?"

"Your money," he finally said. "Do you know what your father spent it on?"

She raised her chin, pretending to know more than she did. "He spent it on keeping the business going."

Phil slipped his fingers through the hair at her cheeks, relishing the sight of his brave, beautiful wife. God, but he loved her, risking her life for her family, handing over her fortune to her father to save his ship and relinquishing her title for the sake of his love. No woman would ever hold a candle to Delphine Bouclaire Bertrand, Countess Delaronde.

"He spent it on me," Phil said softly, letting his thumb caress her cheek. "He bought me a letters patent."

It took several moments for the knowledge to sink in, but awareness dawned in Delphine's eyes when she realized the scope of that statement. "You're noble, now?"

"Well, I always considered myself noble, but now it's official."

A smile spread across her lips, but not for the reason Phil suspected. "Philibert Bertrand," she said with a giggle. "Count Delaronde."

Phil grabbed her shoulders and pinned her down on the bed. "Captain Bertrand."

Delphine laughed. "Too late. You've already married me."

Phil slid a leg over hers and playfully held her arms above her head. "Call me that again and I'll have to leave this bed."

Delphine knew better. She rubbed against him, making his desire all the more potent. "Count Delaronde," she whispered with a wicked grin.

All of Phil's resolve disappeared, so he kissed her soundly, wondering if they would ever rise from that bed. When he pulled away and gazed into his wife's face, so full of adventure, he knew titles were for other people, in another part of the world. "Do you think we could just be Bertrand?"

Delphine pulled her hands free and wound them about Phil's neck, bringing him so close their two bodies melded together. "Do you think I can still be your partner?"

Phil leaned his head back and laughed, a profound joy filling him, then he kissed Delphine's face again and again. "You have always been my partner. I would never expect anything less in a life married to you."

Delphine tilted her head back to allow him more room to work his magic. Her hands navigated down his back and it was everything Phil could do not to ravage her on the spot. "I make a good partner. I have a fortune to contribute."

It took Phil a while to comprehend her words, but when he did, he paused in his lovemaking. "I thought that was what you sent to your father."

Now, it was Delphine's turn to laugh. "That was nothing. I have much more than that. Surely, you didn't think a few thousand *livres* was all I inherited."

A few thousand *livres* was the largest fortune Phil could imagine. He stared at her as if she were the queen of France.

"Phil." Delphine sat up and took his face in her hands. "You are a very rich man."

Yes, he was, Phil thought proudly, but it had nothing to do with money. Still, the thought of being free from financial constraints made his brain whirl. They could resume transporting Acadians into Louisiana, could run guns to the Americans if they desired. Charles had insinuated on returning to St. Malo.

Leaning back upon the bed, Delphine grinned as if she read his mind. "You *are* a patriot, aren't you?"

Phil thought back on the reason he began his long adventure to help Galvez and the Americans. In the beginning, he had only wanted to protect his angel, yet he knew, now, that it was more than that. Perhaps the cause of liberty did burn in his veins, the idea of independence not such an unattainable vision. But Phil no longer wished to insulate Delphine. He wanted her there by his side, fighting with him all the way.

Soon, they would be back aboard *La Belle Amie*, heading upriver toward possible battle. He would savor their moments together, make love for one last time. But now, he had some explaining to do about a certain traitorous Countess and the reason he had lied to Delphine that night in his cabin so long ago, when a vision in yellow had bestowed a kiss.

"Delphine," he said again. "We need to talk."

# CHAPTER NINETEEN

"THE BRITISH HAVE EIGHTEEN CANNON, we only ten," Galvez said as he paced the length of the tent. "Their seasoned troops number more than four hundred, ours not nearly as much and then there is the rest of our group — peasants, Indians and Negroes, without discipline or subordination."

Jean felt the hairs on the back of his neck rise. With a quick glance to his Acadian brother-in-law, Lorenz, he realized he wasn't alone in his thoughts. Emilie's husband may be a peasant, but he was quite capable with a gun and more than willing to meet the British, the people responsible for his parents' deaths and his family fleeing their Nova Scotian homes two decades before.

"Peasants, Indians and Negroes might be the ones to tame this oppressive beast." Lorenz pulled his rifle on to his shoulder appearing as if he may bolt, but Galvez lifted his hand in appeasement.

"I'm worried the English are superior to our forces," the governor stated. "However, we have captured Manchac, intercepted their forces from Pensacola and cut them off from Natchez."

"We could wait them out," suggested one of his officers. "The Baton Rouge fort is now isolated. The English will have to surrender eventually."

Jean didn't approve of waiting. It had been almost a fortnight marching up the Mississippi to take the first English fort at Manchac, a journey that had decimated their ranks with sickness, then almost another two weeks to Baton Rouge. He longed to be rid of his filthy clothing and in the arms of his wife and children.

"We have too many who have fallen ill," Coleman Thorp added from the back of the tent. The husband of Rose, Coleman was raised an Englishman at Natchez but considered himself distinctly American. For the past two weeks he had suffered from numerous bouts of fever. Jean knew he shared their feelings. It was time to meet this enemy and return home.

The men all turned their attention to Galvez, who stood lost in grievous thought. Several minutes passed before the governor spoke.

"I am mindful that many of you are heads of family," he finally said. "And that a costly victory would fill the whole Province with grief and mourning. But we must attack immediately before my small force melts away."

Jean didn't know what the governor expected, but the morale of the men inside the tent increased tenfold. They were all more than ready to take shots at the English.

"The first problem we must address is getting the artillery in place," Galvez said. "Their fort is quite impregnable."

Jean nodded to his brothers-in-law, men he had spent the night and most of the day discussing this very problem with. Coleman and Lorenz nodded back, urging him forward.

"If you please, governor," Jean began. "We may have a solution to your problem."


Jean elbowed his way to the front of the grove of trees, the muddy earth cold and dank beneath him. The spot offered the strategic position for he and his men.

"I can reach them from here," Lorenz said, pulling his

rifle forward. "We should be able to keep them busy well into the night."

Coleman soon joined them, placing a stash of gunpowder by their sides. "Are the men ready?"

Jean turned and signaled to his detachment, a miniature group of the men Galvez had described. They immediately began chopping down trees and constructing earthworks.

"Time for fun," Lorenz said, as he took a shot at the fort, breezing a hat from an English soldier's head.

Realizing Galvez's army was building a position against them, the English rallied and began volleying shots in their direction. They were well fortified, a hastily but solidly build fort surrounded by an eighteen-foot-wide ditch with an earthen wall on one side. But their brisk shots bounced off trees, sending nothing but shards of wood about Lorenz's head.

"Is that all you can do?" Lorenz shouted, firing off another shot that sent three men running from their post.

"How long till daybreak?" Coleman asked, using a cannon's gunpowder as a target.

Jean patted him on the back, knowing the man still suffered from the fever. "Six, seven hours. If you want to bow out, Coleman, no one will think you a lesser man."

Coleman began reloading his musket like a seasoned soldier, sliding the ramrod down the barrel to pack the gunpowder and ball. "I appreciate the concern, Jean. But I would never miss out on this. Tomorrow, we shall see history being made."

Jean smiled at his comrade, a man he once disliked simply because he was English, but now loved like a brother. Years ago, when he, Coleman and Lorenz had helped the Gallant family find their father, Coleman had spoken of creating a new nation where ideas like liberty and freedom from invasion by English forces would become a reality. Perhaps he had been right. Perhaps freedoms like they had never known would soon come to pass.

Only time would tell now. If their plan worked, tomorrow would indeed be an historic day.

The early morning sunlight turned the cypress trees a distinct orange and still the English focused their attention on the grove. Suddenly, a group of men started shouting from the fort and Jean knew their secret had been discovered.

"Here, we go," Jean shouted, before the blast of cannon fire rocked the walls of the fort.

While Jean and the others pretended to be establishing a position for their artillery, Galvez was installing his cannons in a garden on the opposite side of the fort. The English had spent the night playing target practice with Lorenz and Coleman while Galvez had quietly rolled his artillery into position.

The English immediately turned their cannons toward the Spanish and Louisiana residents and the battle began, but Galvez had managed an advantage of the first shot. It wasn't long before he blasted several holes into the fort's sides.

The battle raged for several hours, but by mid-afternoon the English appeared defeated. At half-past three, the fort broken and tattered, two English officers emerged to surrender.

"This battle signified many things," Coleman said, as he watched the officers patrol by. "One, that the English should trouble us no more on the Mississippi and we can live in this territory free from tyranny."

"Let us hope," Jean added.

"Two, that our time on this march is at an end and we can finally toast our success and go home." The three men laughed, then marched off to join the celebration around a massive campfire, where men sang happily and hoisted their cups in triumph and others ran about filling vessels with wine. Jean grabbed one of the young boys and captured his bottle.

"Where did you find this?" Jean turned the bottle between his fingers, studying the glass. "This looks familiar."

"Of course, it's familiar," his partner's voice rang out. "We smuggled that shipment in from Barbados last summer."

Jean felt Phil's hand land squarely on his shoulder as he made the connection. "Glad to see you're still alive," Phil said.

"Glad to see you brought the wine," Jean retorted. "Although your timing is perfect. The English have surrendered."

Phil laughed as he handed a bottle to Lorenz and Coleman. "I know several women who are going to be pleased to see you all intact and healthy."

"What happened with Pickles?" Coleman asked. "The last time I saw you, you were headed toward Lake Pontchartrain."

"The lake is ours," Charles said proudly, as he placed a box of wine at their feet and Francois pulled the top off the box and several men grabbed bottles. "Pickles remains captive aboard the ship, which is now being used to patrol the lake behind New Orleans, but we decided to sail up the river with provisions."

Lorenz took a long swig from the bottle and smiled in contentment. "Very glad you did, boys. So very glad you did."

"Is there food aboard that ship?" Coleman asked, nodding toward the masts peeping above the treetops. "We could use a decent meal as well."

Phil grinned slyly and leaned toward them all. "Heaven awaits aboard that ship, my friends. All the sustenance a man could want."

"What is taking your husband so long?" Emilie said, twisting her skirt into knots. "I knew I should have gone with him."

"Phil wanted us to stay out of danger and that's what we should do," Rose said, although Delphine knew her petite relative was ready to bolt across the gangplank.

Only Gabrielle remained quiet, watching the shore like a hawk while the hoard of children ran about at her feet. Even Michel appeared worried, clutching Delphine's skirts as he, too, studied the shoreline for signs of Francois.

"They're fine," Delphine said, as much to soothe her own ragged feelings as to comfort the others.

Certainly the gunshots didn't help, ragged gunfire echoing over the Mississippi. But the shots were half-hazard, sounding more like a celebration than a battle, making Delphine wonder if the worst had already happened.

"That's it," Emilie announced, "I'm going."

Before anyone could intervene and stop her, Phil's head appeared above the ridge, followed by Jean, Coleman and Lorenz. At the sight of their husbands, all three sisters ran across the gangplank, nearly colliding with each other and laughing at the image. Almost instantaneously, all fell into their husband's arms, kissing and hugging them to both savor the feel of their bodies once again and to check for injuries.

Phil left the three couples and boarded the ship, tousling Michel's head before taking Delphine's hand. She held it tightly, gazing at her father and sending a prayer up that Jean stood before her.

"You didn't think any harm would come to a Bouclaire, did you?"

Delphine met Phil's smiling eyes, but she knew he had been just as worried. "I'm assuming we won."

"Of course, we won." Phil pulled her against him, as he had done so many times in the past week, his eyes slowly examining her face and his nose gracing her hair, as if he

were savoring the sight and smell of her. "The English surrendered in a matter of hours."

Delphine pulled back slightly to take in this news, but
she didn't have time to acquire further. Phil captured her
lips with a forceful kiss. He tasted of wine and smelled like
gunpowder, and she felt as she had the first time they kissed
in his cabin a lifetime ago, that the world had disappeared,
replaced by an overwhelming sense of contentment.

When they broke apart, their bliss disappeared. Her
father stood on deck, gazing at them as if they had lost
their minds.

"Uh, Papa," Delphine began, feeling like she had when
she was eight and Jean had caught her stowing away on *La
Belle Amie* on a trip to Mexico. "I'd like you to meet Count
Delaronde."

Phil screwed up his features at the sound of his title, as if
he had bitten into a lemon. "I thought we were going to
dispense with titles."

Jean turned to Gabrielle, who shrugged. "They couldn't
wait. They did promise to let us throw them a large party
when we return to New Orleans."

"What?" Jean bellowed. "No wedding?"

Delphine had to laugh. Her father and Gabrielle had wed
aboard the ship on a hasty trip to New Orleans in search of
Gabrielle's father. Jean must have been thinking the same
thing, for his features softened and a dimple appeared, then
he grabbed his daughter so tight she stopped breathing.

"May you be as happy as I have been," he whispered to
her.

When Jean released her, he sent his partner a disapproving look, but Phil knew better. "Don't let him fool you,
Delphine. He's the one who set this in motion."

Jean offered his hand and the two men shook. "Nonsense.
If you hadn't appeared in my house that night looking like
a lovesick puppy, I wouldn't have gotten the idea."

"You mean, *I* wouldn't have gotten the idea," Gabrielle

interjected.

Phil cleared his throat and turned his eyes toward the distant bank. "When was this?" Delphine inquired.

"Never you mind," Phil said, picking up a box and heading back to shore. If Delphine wasn't mistaken, his face had turned a deep blush.

"Some things were meant to be," Gabrielle said with a wide smile, sliding her body into Jean's embrace. "And some people were meant to be together."

How true that was, Delphine thought as she watched Phil order provisions to shore. When he turned and caught her eye, a knowing glance and smile passed between them.

Regardless of Galvez's victory, the women and crew members worked into the night unloading provisions for the army and helping sick and injured soldiers aboard ship. Close to midnight, they set sail for New Orleans, the decks crowded with the infirm who sported cheerful morals despite their ill health.

Somewhere in the middle of the night, after Delphine finished dispensing food and whisking the children off to bed, a blessed silence descended upon the ship, save for the sails flapping in the breeze as they tacked back and forth in the bends of the mighty river.

"So much easier heading downstream, isn't it?"

Delphine sat upon the quarterdeck, grateful for the chance to rest her feet next to a human over ten years of age. Francois appeared equally tired, Michel's petit head resting in his lap.

"We won't be heading upriver again," Phil said to his cousin from his place at the wheel. "That's Jean territory. More than likely, we will be traveling back to France soon."

"More guns?" Francois asked.

"Of course, more guns," Charles said from beneath his hat. For the past half-hour, the patriot had stretched out by the railing, appearing to be asleep. He tilted his hat up with his forefinger, glancing in their direction. "We may have won a battle, but the war rages on in the colonies."

Delphine's gaze shifted across the deck, studying her father's face, wondering what his role in the continuing conflicts would be. When he caught her staring, he smiled. "I'm sticking with Galvez," he answered her unspoken question. "I'll continue to run guns up the Mississippi but I'll remain close to home. With two children under foot and another on the way..."

With a gasp, Delphine turned toward Gabrielle, who waved off her protestations as if babies occurred every day.

"You," she said, pointing to Delphine, "must take your father's place at sea, especially if you're a partner now."

They hadn't spoken of her role in the enterprise, and she had yet to explain her deception but it appeared she didn't need to. Jean and Gabrielle rose from their place on deck, kissed her, then headed for the ladderway and their cabin, each sporting enormous grins.

"*Bonsoir*," was the last thing her father said before disappearing below deck.

Delphine glanced at Phil, who appeared equally surprised. "I think we underestimated him. God knows I did."

"So, when do we leave for France?" Charles asked with a grin.

"As soon as I can convince Francois to come with me," Phil said.

Francois looked up, amazed they were speaking of him.

"You don't really want to be a farmer, do you?" Phil asked. "Running around chasing animals, digging in the dirt. Rain washing all your hard work away. Besides, Alain will never forgive me if I come back to France without you."

Delphine watched as the Acadian considered the possibility of sailing away with them again, his eyes lighting up at the prospect, but when he glanced down at Michel, the light disappeared.

"Francois," Delphine said, touching his knee. "Michel has already made his wishes known to us, ever since the day he bested me at the foils. He has his heart set on becoming a pirate now. He would hate to leave you behind, but if he must sail without you…"

At this, Francois laughed. "Well, then, I can hardly leave my adopted son with such rapscallions as yourselves." Turning toward Phil, he added, "Are you sure you want me around?"

"Hell, no, I'm not sure," Phil said. "You're a royal pain in the ass."

Delphine rose and kissed Francois on the cheek. "That means he can't imagine sailing without you."

"Where are you going?" Phil called out to her as she headed toward the ladderway.

Delphine said nothing, simply sent him a sly look. In that instant, Phil moved so fast, even Delphine was amazed. He called Mathurin over to take the wheel, ordered Vincent to tighten the mainsail and was at her side in an instant, Charles and Francois laughing at their backs.

"My, my," Delphine said with a chuckle, then rushed down the ladderway, Phil close at her heels. She flew inside his cabin, but wasn't fast enough to shut the door. Phil slipped in behind her, grabbed her waist and pulled her tightly against him, closing the door behind him with his foot as they both giggled.

"Don't you have a river to navigate?" she asked, sliding her hands inside his waistcoat and enjoying the feel of his tall, muscular body.

"There's only one thing that would ever deter me from my ship," he said so seductively, Delphine felt tiny shivers scatter across her skin.

"And what's that, *mon capitaine?*"

They were standing in the same place the night Delphine had professed her love, their lips a breath apart, their bodies melded together. A cooling river breeze floated in through the porthole, teasing the perspiration collecting on her neck. Phil wasted no time ridding Delphine of her clothes, while she, too, assisted in removing his waistcoat. When her hand reached down to the sash at his waist, his hand stilled her actions with a grip on her wrist.

"How many times have I told you to stop touching my sword," he said in between kisses.

Delphine leaned back to meet his eyes, a teasing smile upon her lips. "Are you sure that's what you want?"

His black eyes glistened in the moonlight, while he removed his hand and placed it in the small of her back and pressed her closer, the feel of him fulfilling her like nothing else. "I have everything now that I have ever wanted."

He kissed her then, and Delphine knew with sudden clarity that she, too, had become complete, that she had fulfilled her pledge to her grandmother. That happiness wasn't a dream in fairytales, but in the arms of a pirate and a ship heading for distant shores.

# AUTHOR'S NOTE

*"We have it in our power to begin the world anew."*
—Thomas Paine

*"Humanity has won its battle. Liberty now has a country."*
—The Marquis de Lafayette

THE AMERICAN REVOLUTION WOULDN'T HAVE ended in victory had it not been for the colonists' good friends and allies. France began aiding the Americans in 1776, eager to take shots at Britain after losing the Seven Years War. In 1777, France officially recognized the colonists as an independent, sovereign nation, but they made it official with a treaty of allegiance in February 1778, due to the charming personality of Ambassador Benjamin Franklin who won the hearts of Paris.

Spain joined the fight in 1779, creating a true American hero in Louisiana Governor Bernardo de Galvez. Not only did Galvez capture the British forts at Manchac and Baton Rouge, taking more than 1,000 prisoners in Louisiana, he went on to capture Mobile and Pensacola in 1780 and 1781. At the time of Galvez's campaigns, Britain was struggling to fight the colonists in the South. England's ongoing battles with Galvez helped to lessen their troops against the Americans.

Galvez also aided Oliver Pollock, an Irish-born American who spent his fortune financing the shipping of guns and ammunition up the Mississippi River into the American interior. Through his work, Pollock is credited with allowing George Rogers Clark to help conquer the

Northwest Territory.

Between Spain and France, millions of dollars were contributed to the American cause. Most of the gunpowder and firearms used in the American Revolution came from France, plus many ships for the cause, including the one helmed by John Paul Jones. A French fleet was crucial to the victory of Yorktown, where the English surrendered in 1781, and much of its costs were met by Spanish funds and Spanish assistance (Spain guarded French territories in the Caribbean, allowing the French fleet to travel to the American colonies).

John Paul Jones did indeed utter the words, "I have not yet begun to fight" while in the midst of battle, but at a slightly later date. In mid-August 1779, at the time of Phil's sailing, the Scotsman was conducting raids around the coast of Britain in his French ship named for Benjamin Franklin's famous publication, *Poor Richard's Almanac*. On Sept. 23, 1779, the *Bonhomme Richard* became embroiled in a fight with a British frigate, the Serapis. Both ships fought dangerously close, blasting each other from point blank range. As the *Bonhomme Richard* appeared ready to sink, the English captain asked if Jones would surrender, thus inciting his famous reply. In the end, the *Bonhomme Richard* did sink, but Jones managed to take over the *Serapis* causing the English to surrender. A Revolutionary War hero, Jones is known as being the father of the American Navy.

There were many Acadians repatriated back to France after being exiled from their homeland in Nova Scotia and Prince Edward Island by the English beginning in 1755. Like Francois Bertrand, the exiles lived in poverty in port towns such as St. Malo and Nantes, at the mercy of their mother country who didn't know what to do with the displaced colonists.

"Distrustful of their leaders, unable to subsist on the government dole, and unable to find arable land or a niche in France's feudalistic society, most exiles resolved

to leave the mother country – surreptitiously if necessary," writes Carl Brasseaux in *The Founding of New Acadia*.
In 1777, twenty-two Acadians left the west coast of France
for Louisiana through the intercession of the Spanish
government. But, several years later, a Frenchman named
Henry Peyroux de la Coudreniere, married to an Acadian,
and an Acadian cobbler named Olivier Terrio, laid the
groundwork for the majority of exiles to immigrate to
Louisiana. Through the assistance of Galvez, now back in
Spain as a hero and claiming the ear of King Carlos, Spain
backed the emigration plan and funded the transportation
of the largest group of Acadians to enter Louisiana beginning in 1784.

Most of the exiles from France settled in southwestern
Louisiana, where today a memorial stands on their behalf
in the town of St. Martinville. Now called Cajuns, their
culture and language continues.

On a different note, Delphine's formal title of Delaronde
is not entirely correct, although I have chosen it for sim-
plicity sakes. As a member of the titled nobility, she would
have spelled her name de la Ronde.

# ABOUT THE AUTHOR

CHERIE CLAIRE IS THE AUTHOR of *The Cajun Series* of historical romances, including *Emilie, Rose, Gabrielle, Delphine, A Cajun Dream* and *The Letter*. She lives in South Louisiana where she works as a travel and food writer when not indulging in Cajun culture.

Visit her web site *www.cherieclaire.net* and write to her at *CajunRomances@gmail.com*.

# ALSO BY CHERIE CLAIRE

**The Cajun Series**
Emilie
Rose
Gabrielle
Delphine
A Cajun Dream
The Letter

**The Cajun Embassy**
A Ticket to Paradise
Damn Yankees
Gone Pecan

**The Viola Valentine Mysteries**
A Ghost of a Chance
Ghost Town
Trace of a Ghost

Read more about Cherie Claire at
*www.cherieclaire.net.*

# NEXT IN THE
# CAJUN SERIES...

**a new generation finds love in the state called
Louisiana**

# A Cajun Dream

❧

*Franklin, Louisiana, Lower Bayou Teche, 1848*

IT WAS THE HOTTEST SUMMER to date, a humid blast of heat that sucked the life from South Louisiana residents, wilted even the hardiest of plants, and sent animals into the dark recesses of buildings and earth. The air was still and thick and a silence reigned as if the insects were even too scared to breathe.

Amanda Rose Richardson gripped her gardening basket and searched Main Street, absentmindedly tugging down on her bonnet to keep the noonday sun from scorching her forehead. The slight mid-morning breeze from the Gulf that had offered a hint of respite had dissipated, leaving the harsh Louisiana sun alone with its victim.

Had she mistaken the time? Perhaps it was later than she realized. It was close to lunchtime and still he hadn't come.

She dared not wait much longer. Another few minutes and her clothes would become pasted to her skin, outlining her figure for all who walked the busy streets of Franklin.

What would her father say to that? she wondered, the familiar anxiety taking hold of her usually calm demeanor. She could see him now, criticizing her actions in his dark, heavily paneled study. Likening her to her mother.

Glancing back at the stately house she had called home for the past ten years, Amanda knew what she had to do. It wasn't her fault she was born a female, or that her mother had run away with the French Opera Company when she was less than twelve years old. Today was her birthday, a landmark date, and she would cross into adulthood an experienced woman.

She knew it was doubtful her father would finally agree that some man in the great state of Louisiana was well bred enough to marry his only child. Suitors Amanda had liked were quickly discarded as incompetent loafers, even the ones from the finest families in Franklin. Rich men from important families Amanda had met in surrounding cities such as New Iberia and St. Martinville — on the rare occasions Amanda had been allowed to accompany her father on business — were rejected on everything from "poor breeding" to "bad judgment in obtaining wealth." By the time Amanda had reached nineteen, she became convinced she would live her life as an old maid.

Today she turned twenty-one, and there was little hope of her marrying. When once her dance cards were filled with names, now Amanda sat out between numbers, watching as one by one her friends entered into matrimony. Only Sally Baldwin remained, but she was scheduled to marry in the fall, just before sugar cane harvest.

It was Sally who suggested Amanda consider Henry Tanner. Her father's plantation overseer was notorious for romancing the ladies, Sally had insisted. Henry Tanner had blatantly kissed Katherine Blanchard, who everyone knew was engaged to Bernard Mann, on a buggy ride home from a dance. According to Sally, Katherine had been outraged at the dapper man's actions, but cherished them all the same, bragging about his feathery kisses along her neckline and the way he had held her hand and the romantic sonnets he recited to her in the moonlight.

If he could offer Katy Blanchard, who was promised to someone else, a quick glimpse of romance, surely he would be willing to give Amanda, a single woman of social standing and wealth, something to remember when her youth faded into spinsterhood.

With Sally's help, Tanner had agreed to secretly escort Amanda to the public ball that evening at the Franklin Exchange. Amanda's father would be gone on business and he sternly forbade her to leave the house in his absence, even though Amanda would be surrounded by her closest friends merely blocks from her home. Amanda never defied her father before but, situations being what they were, she had to do something drastic. She couldn't spend her whole life not knowing the romantic advances of a man.

A droplet of perspiration trickled down her back. Her friend wasn't coming, Amanda thought, or he had arrived too early and she had missed him. Another five minutes and she would appear as if someone had thrown her into the Bayou Teche.

Amanda knelt and gathered up her gardening tools, placing them neatly into her hand basket along with the rows of cut flowers. She would try again tomorrow.

"Good morning, Miss Richardson," came the familiar accented voice from above her head.

Gazing up and over her white picket fence stood

René Comeaux, his chestnut eyes peering down at her intently from beneath a wide-brimmed planter's hat, its crest accented by a bright scarlet sash. He lingered at the fence's gate as he had every morning the past month, his tall, imposing figure casting a welcoming shadow over Amanda's smiling face, one boot resting amiably against the lower fence post.

For not the first time during the past few weeks, Amanda felt the butterflies taking flight inside her stomach.

René Comeaux had spent the morning convincing himself not to walk down Main Street past the Richardson house. It was useless, a waste of time. Yet here he was staring down at the flushed, smiling face of an angel. Amanda Rose Richardson possessed the most impressive sparkling blue eyes framed by curls of the brightest, blondest hair he had ever seen. Her heart-born smile literally radiated warmth throughout her face, and its heat poured over him like a wild prairie brush fire common to southwestern Louisiana.

She contained all the grace, elegance, and warmth he imagined the perfect woman would have. She was charming, intelligent, friendly and kind. And from their first meeting in her front yard, when she unhesitatingly offered her hand in greeting after he tipped his hat to her from the street, he'd been hopelessly in love with her.

Yet, she was an American. Not from a working class American family who had moved into the new state hoping to carve out a place for themselves as Réne's family had when they were exiled from Canada by the English. Amanda Rose Richardson was from one of the finest American families in Virginia, descendants of American revolutionaries. In Louisiana, her father had made a name for himself as an intermediary between New Orleans' French population and its newly formed American government after the Louisiana Purchase. For some reason René had not understood, the Richardsons had chosen to move from New Orleans to the small, yet booming southwestern Louisiana town of Franklin where James Richardson served as the parish judge. Through a series of successful sugar cane ventures, in addition to his political career, James Richardson had become one of Franklin's richest and most influential citizens.

None of this mattered to René. He had seen his share of the rich, be they French, English, Spanish, or American. Like most Acadians, he vowed allegiance only to his family and his land. Political authorities were not to be trusted or admired. His people had realized that during a century of oppression when almost every government they had encountered had treated the Acadians with disdain or neglect.

Still, Amanda Rose Richardson was not an impossible dream. Among his people, René Comeaux was a rich and influential man as well. He would make a fine husband, able to care for Amanda in the way she was accustomed. Or close to it. He was formally educated — the first in his family to do so, — was successful in his father's cattle business and his own ventures, and he spoke English fluently.

But James Richardson had refused to even allow him to call on the girl.

"No child of mine will ever be married to a Frenchman," the elder Richardson had bellowed in his suffocating study. "My Amanda Rose would never even consider an offer from an Acadian, no matter how much money you make. You can take your immigrant concerns elsewhere."

Frenchman indeed, René thought, feeling the anger burn at his temple. The fool man didn't know the difference between René's people and those who had arrived directly from France. He might speak the mother tongue and be descended from the French, but René was an Acadian, now and forever.

And an immigrant! The man surely was confusing René with *les Americains*. Amanda was native born to Louisiana, but her father certainly wasn't. René was the third generation of the Comeaux family born in the Louisiana Territory.

Looking down into the deep, blue depths of the eyes of the woman who had cast such a spell upon his unawakened heart, René wondered what he was doing there. Despite all of her father's threats, he couldn't stay away.

Yet, he couldn't remain either.

"I see you're visiting town late today," Amanda said, breaking the silence that had lingered uncomfortably between them. "I was about to go inside, to escape this sweltering heat."

Why was she smiling? Why was she consistently friendly to a man her father had said she despised? If it were true that she would never accept an Acadian man to call on her, why was she always so agreeable when they met on the street every morning?

"Mr. Comeaux?" She gazed up at him with those eyes the color of robin's eggs. God, she was beautiful. He felt perspiration trickling down his back.

Perhaps she had been mocking him all these weeks, greeting him with pleasure at her fence, then denouncing him to her friends when he was out of earshot, using that awful pronunciation of his nationality: "Did I tell you about that *Cajun* man who thinks I am good enough for him, that actually asked my father if he could call on me? He actually had the gall to think I would consider marrying him!"

"Is something wrong?" Amanda's smile had been replaced with a frown.

René had endured enough torture for one morning. At any moment now he expected her father to step out of the house, further humiliating him by publicly sending him away. One last look and he would move on.

"Good day to you, Miss Richardson," he said proudly, tipping his hat. "I will not let an immigrant impose on your time any longer."